Joanna Bolouri worked in sales before she began writing professionally at the age of thirty. Winning a BBC comedy script competition allowed her to work and write with stand-up comedians, comedy scriptwriters and actors from across the UK. She's had articles and reviews published in *The Skinny*, the Scottish *Sun*, the *Huffington Post* and *Heckler-Spray*. She lives in Glasgow with her daughter.

Also by Joanna Bolouri

The List
I Followed the Rules
The Most Wonderful Time of the Year
Relight My Fire

All I Want for Christmas

JOANNA BOLOURI

Quercus

First published in Great Britain in 2020 by

Quercus Editions Ltd
Carmelite House
50 Victoria Embankment
London EC4Y 0DZ

An Hachette UK company

A CIP catalogue record for this book is available
from the British Library

PB ISBN 978 1 52940 690 0
EB ISBN 978 1 52940 691 7

10 9 8 7 6 5 4

Typeset by CC Book Production
Printed and bound in Great Britain by Clays Ltd, Elcograf S.p.A.

For my lovely family.

PROLOGUE

'You've already got quite the queue forming, Nick. Can we get a move on, please; kids can get rowdy. I'm not paying you to preen. Let's go!'

It's only my first shift at Southview Shopping Centre and I already dislike my supervisor Geraldine, whose sullen head has snaked around the door and appears to be propping it open with the weight of her own self-importance. She can't be any older than forty, yet has the dead-eyed glare of someone who has been forced to reincarnate as the same retail manager for centuries. The longer she stands there, the more I'm aware of the faint buzz from the shopping mall which creeps past her and invades the once quiet staffroom. It sounds as busy as she implies.

'Be right there!' I reply, trying to sound chipper, when in reality, I'd happily welcome the sweet release of death right now.

Anything but this.

Geraldine retains her scowl and slowly retreats, the

click of her heels gradually disappearing as she makes her way through the double doors at the end of the corridor.

As I step into my oversized black boots and tighten my belt, I feel a tiny bead of sweat slowly trickle down the side of my face and absorb into my beard. Jesus, it's hot. Why do shopping centres always have their temperature set to *Sahara*? I'm going to be a human puddle by 5pm, if the utter humiliation doesn't kill me first.

I mop my brow with my sleeve and adjust my hat, taking one last look in the staffroom mirror. I hardly recognise myself, which I guess is the point, and I'm grateful. Being recognised is not something my currently fragile ego could handle. I sigh loudly as I smooth my jacket over my oversized belly.

Welcome to the lowest point in your life, loser. Just be thankful Christmas only comes once a year.

Taking a deep breath, I reluctantly trudge out of the staffroom and towards the same double doors that Geraldine's cloven hooves passed through a few minutes earlier. Emerging into the brightly lit shopping floor, what feels like the entire city of London stops to stare at me. I cannot believe I agreed to do this. As my cheeks begin to turn bright red, my transformation is complete.

'MUMMY! LOOK! IT'S SANTA! IT'S SANTA CLAUS!'

Oh, fucking hell. Here we go.

CHAPTER ONE

Four weeks earlier

'Oh, come on! You've got to be kidding me. That can't be right.'

I stare at my phone, hoping the digits shown on my online banking account will magically rearrange themselves into an amount that doesn't make my stomach catapult into my throat. I click on my recent transactions, hoping that I've become the victim of identity theft and a stranger is the reason I am almost completely broke.

As I skim down my purchases, my stomach leaves my throat and plummets to my feet. There's no mistake. This was all me: same places, same amounts, same days of the week. Not only am I skint, I'm predictable. I'm not sure what's worse.

I glance at the corner of the living room where my most recent Amazon purchase sits untouched, mocking me for being stupid enough to waste money on an unused gym membership while simultaneously ordering kettlebells online to work out at home. God, I'm an idiot. A skinny-armed idiot. I should return them and get my forty quid back, although I'm not sure it's going to touch the sides of the hole that I'm going to have to dig myself out of. Still, it would be a start.

I close my phone, tossing it on to the couch with a groan while I pace the floor of the large flat I soon won't be able to pay rent on.

It's just a blip, I reassure myself. *You'll get back on your feet. Maybe just cut back . . . Set a budget!*

Budget. God, I hate that word. Yes, admittedly, as someone who is technically unemployed, I perhaps should be a bit more frugal, but I'm certain Angela isn't down for staying in with her penny-pinching boyfriend seven nights a week. She's a girl who likes to be seen. It was touch-and-go when she found out I'd been fired.

'But you were taking me to Marbs, babe,' she'd reminded me, like I hadn't already surreptitiously tried to get the deposit back. I watched her scroll through Instagram, never lifting her head to look at me. 'What about Marbs?'

'I know, honey, it's just that—'

'What about Marbs, babe?' she repeated, almost singing the words at me. 'I didn't get non-surgical lipo and a ker-atin treatment just to hang around London . . .'

'I appreciate that, but Marbella might have to—'

'WHAT. ABOUT. MARBS?'

It's funny, when you're dating a former reality-TV star, reality is the last thing that they're concerned about. Angela is beautiful, independent, sexy and probably the most career-focused person I've ever met (and I once worked with a guy who missed his son's birth to have dinner with a client). I have always worked hard for what I want, and Angela is no exception. Three grand and a sunburned nipple later, I still had a girlfriend and she had two pictures of her tanned derriere in the *Sun*.

Naïvely I didn't think I'd be unemployed long enough to miss the money, but in the four months since I was fired from Kensington Fox LLP, I've had twenty-three interviews, followed by twenty-three identically worded rejection letters.

'Thank you for your interest. We wish you every success in your future career.'

I'm not even sure I have a future career. It's clear that doors are closing just as fast as word is spreading about my dismissal. How the hell did I get everything so wrong?

Angela believes I'm too handsome to be unemployed, which is sweet of her to say, but she also believes ponies are baby horses, so I'm not relying solely on her judgement for the time being.

I give myself a shake and begin productively clearing away the old pizza boxes and beer bottles from the coffee table. They're all mine, of course, no one else around here is using Domino's to self-medicate. As the money has dwindled, my need to lie around the flat feeling sorry for myself has increased. My flatmate and former colleague, Matt, tries his best to be supportive, but even I know it must be difficult to rally someone who has discovered a fondness for Stella Artois at 8am.

'You need to snap out of this, Nick,' he'd demanded last week. 'Get yourself back on track. You made one mistake—'

'Two!' I corrected quickly. 'I made two.'

From the comfort of the couch I had observed Matt messing with his dirty blond hair in the hall mirror, not oblivious to the subtle eye roll directed at my response. He strode through the living room and into the kitchen, his sticky pomade fingers grabbing his wallet from the worktop.

'OK, fine, you made *two* mistakes but—'

'Actually, three, but they didn't find out about the third one, so it doesn't count. Does anywhere do breakfast kebabs? Is that even a thing?'

Matt sighed. 'Look, all I'm saying is it's not the end of the world, mate. You'll find something. I'd knock the morning drinking on the head, though.'

'Technically, I started drinking last night so it's still part of my drunking evening . . . evening drinking. Bah, you know what I mean.'

'All I'm saying is, it's a slippery slope . . .'

'Your hair's a slippery slope,' I mumbled, but Matt wasn't listening. He was too busy being employed.

'Mm-hmm,' Matt replied, as he marched towards the front door. 'I'm off. Get a shower, pal.'

I would be lying if I said I wasn't more than a little envious of Matt. Despite his overuse of hair product, Matt Buckley is a shrewd man with a healthy bank balance, an investment plan and a couple of wealthy parents to fall back on. Mostly I'm envious that Matt still works at Kensington Fox. As much as I miss the money, I miss the work more. I loved that job: the buzz of the office, the meetings, the after-work drinks, the networking, the camaraderie, but now I'm on the outside, desperately trying to get back in, somewhere, anywhere, and failing miserably.

I've blown through most of my savings, as well as the hundred quid Matt keeps in the emergency tin on top of the fridge. I feel that right now, life itself is an emergency. Being skint isn't exactly unfamiliar territory. Growing up on a housing estate in Tottenham with a single parent wasn't the most affluent start, but it meant that I quickly learned how to graft. I started working part-time when I was at school to help Mum out, using every spare minute in between school and shifts to study, which led to a scholarship at university, where I worked evening shifts at the twenty-four-hour Asda, while my friends got shit-faced at whatever foam party or theme night was being held at the students' union.

My main concern isn't that I've been fired for missing a crucial filing deadline (which wasn't entirely my fault) or that I accidentally threw up over an important client's wife the same evening, it's that I've worked my arse off to get here and I'm about to lose it all.

CHAPTER TWO

Three weeks into an extremely chilly October and there isn't anyone in London who doesn't have a copy of my CV. Even Ahmet who runs the Kebab House is keeping me in mind for any future vacancies. I could do deliveries or become an Uber driver, but even that requires a car and I don't have the cash, even for a shitty one.

Apparently, I'm too qualified for McDonald's, but not qualified enough for Debbie's Dog Grooming, because seemingly *law school doesn't mean shit when you're faced with an anxious dog who doesn't want his nails trimmed, Nick.* While I feel Debbie was rather harsh, it does make me realise how few real skills I actually possess. Yes, I can organise mergers and negotiate multimillion-pound contracts, but I have no idea how to operate a till, mix a cocktail or make a coffee appear from one of those giant, frothing machines. I'm almost out of options. Hopefully today will be better; God, please let it be better.

Quickening my step, I pull my flimsy jacket around

me as I make my way through Covent Garden towards GL Recruitment, owned by Greta Lang, a woman who dumped me five years ago. We'd dated for three months and I'd spent that time trying to remember how she took her tea, while she had spent the same time determining that there was zero future for us and had written me off. Looking back, she had a point; I could never truly commit to someone who drinks decaf. Regardless of *'not being the one for her'*, we've remained good friends and as I press the buzzer at the entrance, I'm hoping she'll be the one to pull me out of my current sinkhole of despair.

Greta's office is small, elegant and extremely vibrant, which perfectly reflects her as a person.

'Take a seat, Nick, can I get you anything?' She brushes down the front of her shirt, scattering tiny baguette crumbs at her feet. I've obviously caught her at lunch.

I yank out the chair at the front of her desk and shake my head. 'Apart from a job? Nah, I'm good.'

She smiles and sits behind her desk, moving her glasses from her face to the top of her head. She missed one crumb which now nestles in her brown hair. When we dated, Greta was a blonde, like Angela, but I much prefer her as a brunette. It makes her green eyes pop. Shit, I don't think I ever noticed she had green eyes; she was absolutely right to dump me.

Greta taps a few keys on her laptop and clears her throat. I recognise that sound. It's the same sound she made before she broke up with me, before she explained very tactfully that we were finished. That is the sound you make when you're about to give bad news.

'I'll be honest, Nick; it isn't great news.'

I knew it.

'We just don't have many corporate law vacancies at this time of year. It's all temp Christmas positions, which were snapped up by students months ago. After the festive period, you're more likely to—'

'Still be unemployable?'

Having a friend who works for a recruitment agency is only useful if companies are actually hiring. The longer I remain unemployed, the worse it looks on my CV. Greta's pity smile is not what I need to see right now, but she offers it anyway.

'Lawyers get fired and hired all the time,' she responds, with a look on her face which says otherwise. 'I'll find you something. You might just have to lower your expectations in the meantime.'

'I have no expectations. Did you know that you have to be qualified, trained and have a portfolio to wash a dog?'

'What? I hadn't thought . . . wait, you don't even like dogs.'

'I know but—'

She starts rummaging through some paperwork. 'How do you feel about rabbits? I might have something with rabbits here . . .'

'I was thinking more like temporary clerical work, perhaps?' I interject. 'Data entry, maybe?'

My stomach churns at the thought of tapping mindlessly on a keyboard or filing for eight hours a day, but it's better than nothing.

'If I had it, I'd be putting you forward for it, Nick. I'm sorry. I am trying. But I've pretty much exhausted every avenue I have. I've looked into retail and call centres, as well as data entry . . . it's just a tricky time of the year.'

'I know,' I say, rubbing my forehead. I can feel a headache brewing. 'Right now, I'll do just about anything.'

'I'm sure something will turn up,' she replies, sounding less than optimistic. The crumb from her hair finally falls on to her desk. 'Positions come in all the time.'

I nod and do my best to look reassured, but I don't think she's buying it.

'Chin up, Nick,' she says softly, determined to finish our meeting on a positive note. 'Will I see you at the party tomorrow night? Might be just what you need, you know . . . take your mind off things? Though I'm not sure we got your RSVP . . .'

'Yup, looking forward to it!' I lie, forcing the corners of my mouth upwards. 'I gave the RSVP to Matt; he must have forgotten to post it. You know what he's like!'

Another lie. I had completely forgotten about the party. The silver and white monochrome engagement party invitation is currently on my coffee table being used as a coaster.

'Excellent, we'll see you tomorrow then! Matt too!' Greta beams like a woman who has just solved all my problems. She is also beaming like a woman who is expecting a gift. Did she provide a gift list? If I can't afford actual coasters, how the hell am I supposed to afford an engagement present?

Determined to add my name to whatever Matt has purchased for the happy couple, I thank Greta and swiftly leave her office, mumbling something about catching the bank before they close. As I step back out into the chilly air, I stop and take a deep breath which catches the growing lump in the back of my throat. How is this my life? I have no money, no job prospects, an inappropriate jacket for the weather and tomorrow I'll have to endure a room full of successful people who have their shit together nodding politely while I say that I'm taking a break from Kensington Fox and exploring new avenues, like my life-long dream of grooming dogs . . . or rabbits, if Greta has anything to do with it.

I take out my phone and text Angela, asking if she fancies going to this party, then Matt, letting him know that he's responsible for my missing RSVP, before heading into Charing Cross station to catch my train back to London Bridge. Matt responds first:

No probs. Glad you're leaving the couch.

Shortly followed by Angela:

Sorry bbz, have plans. Call u later xoxo

I reply with *No worries*, but in truth, I'm slightly perturbed. Angela never misses a party, so she must be attending something equally entertaining. Something better. Something she didn't invite me to. She always invites me. Is she embarrassed to be seen with me now? My paranoia begins to kick in and continues booting the hell out of me all the way home.

Matt arrives back at the flat just after 7pm to the sight of me tossing clothes from my wardrobe on to my bed. My normally tidy room now looks like a jumble sale.

'Lost something?' he asks, looking mildly amused.

'I can't find my Paul Smith shirt,' I reply. 'I wanted to wear it tomorrow.'

'Jesus, you're such a woman. Just wear something else.'

'But I like that one. It shows off my tits.' I grin and pretend to flick my hair back.

Matt laughs and begins to help me look. 'Is it the denim one? Pretty sure you spilled curry on that.'

'No, it's the yellow one.'

Matt pauses. 'You mean the one your girlfriend hates?'

'Yes! I haven't seen it since we—' I stop rummaging and look over at Matt, who raises his eyebrows.

'She wouldn't . . . would she?'

He shrugs. 'Well, she did make her feelings on that shirt known to everyone in the bar that night . . .'

It's not yellow, Nick, it's mustard. Vomit-coloured mustard and it's not your colour. It's not anyone's colour! What were you thinking?

I shake my head, unwilling to believe that she would just throw away a Paul Smith shirt, but deep down, I'm less than certain. She once binned a full-size bottle of Jo Malone perfume that I bought for her birthday because she didn't like the limited-edition bottle as much as the normal bottle.

'Ask her,' Matt suggests. 'I'm pretty certain she'll admit it if she did. She's ballsy like that.'

Matt doesn't like Angela. He's never said it outright, but I can tell by the way he tenses up every time she's around. He's wary of her and I've never understood why, considering some of the women he's brought round to the flat. Jesus, he once briefly dated an American woman who called him *Daddy* in a baby voice, regardless of who was in earshot. Angela might be a tad shallow sometimes, but she has a good heart.

'I'm not going to ask my girlfriend if she threw away my shirt,' I insist. 'I'll look like a psycho.'

He laughs. 'True, and if she admits it, you'll have to deal with the fact you're dating a *psycho*. Which is worse?'

'I'll buy a new bloody shirt,' I mumble, as I begin picking up clothes from my bedroom floor. 'I'm pretty sure I have store credit from John Lewis.'

'You could buy a bottle of champagne for Greta and Will while you're at it,' Matt suggests as he walks into the living room. 'I'm not doing a joint present, like we're a couple, mate. That's just creepy.'

'No problem, *Daddy*.'

'Fuck off, Billy-No-Shirt.'

I grab the rest of my clothes and fling them back into my wardrobe, vowing to sort them out later. Right now, I have to figure out how to buy a shirt and a decent bottle of champagne with fifty pounds.

CHAPTER THREE

'Boys! So glad you could make it!'

At least I think that's what Greta says as we walk into Bar Black, but the place is so noisy, it's hard to be sure. She hugs me – wrinkling my new blue shirt, which might be a little on the tight side since one of the buttons pinged off on the way here, but was seventy per cent off – before thanking me for the gift I'm carrying. I really hope she likes 2018 sparkling rosé. Matt hands her a box containing two Swarovski crystal-embellished champagne flutes and I hate him.

'We're all in the VIP area,' she yells, gesturing towards the stairs at the back of the pub. 'Will is up there, go grab a drink! I won't be long.'

We push through the crowds and head up the stairs to the function 'room', a cordoned-off area which overlooks the main bar. Until now, I've never noticed how pretentious it's become. When we first started coming here, Bar Black was called Libertines and was far less polished and sterile. Then again, so were we. Part of me misses the comfy patchwork couches and retro jukebox, which have now been replaced with shitty club anthems and slippery bar stools. There are plenty of other bars in London, but this one just feels like ours, even with a strangely designed bar perch lodged up my arse.

It's busy for a Tuesday, with most of the clientele arranged in after-work drink cliques, all smelling like a mixture of stress and Tom Ford. It's the same faces week in and week out. These are my eighty-hour working week, ladder-climbing, self-starting, content-creating, upwardly mobile contemporaries and right now, I'm struggling to feel like I belong. I'm starting to see my world very differently.

'This must be a bit strange for you,' Matt says, dragging my gaze away from a woman who's trying to furtively vape into her handbag. He gestures towards Greta's fiancé Will, who's chatting with our mutual friend Harriet. 'I mean, you used to date Greta and now she's marrying this guy.'

This guy is Dr William Howard, the forty-three-year-old, Ferrari-driving surgeon that Greta began dating after me. I've met him at least ten times, yet I'm not even sure he knows my name.

'Why would it be weird?' I reply. 'I mean, yes, we dated, but I'm very happy she found someone. I'm not secretly pining for Greta, mate.'

'No, I know. I just mean because, well . . .'

'What? Because he owns a house in Notting Hill, has a private clinic on Harley Street, a hairline which refuses to recede and I'm just a jobless prick with a girlfriend who might possibly be kidnapping my clothes?'

'Pretty much.' Matt nudges me, playfully. 'You'll be alright, bud. Just try and have a good night.'

'Oh, I will,' I reply, taking a glass of champagne from the table. 'I'm delighted for Greta, you know that. She deserves to be happy.'

'To be honest, I'd marry him for a shot at his car,' Matt states, waving to Will. 'No offence, mate, but you have to admit, our Greta did well here.'

Matt's right, of course, but I didn't need reminding what a fucking loser I am in comparison. I'm very aware. Besides, Matt was the one who introduced me to Greta, so really, this is all his fault. I down my glass of champagne and grab another, while Will makes his way over to us.

'Alright, guys, nice to see you!' Will exclaims, shaking our hands vigorously. 'Just popping to the little boy's room, back in a sec.'

Little boy's room? Who says that? I start to feel three per cent better about myself.

We sit down in a small booth beside Harriet, a pale, delicate woman who was in halls with Matt and Greta. She studied English Lit and now writes bestselling crime novels. I ventured into their little circle second term of my law undergrad and never left. She's here with her husband

Noel, a man who looks like he keeps ancient secrets in his tremendous beard. They're good people.

'You remember Brian Wilson?' Harriet asks Matt as he slips off his coat.

He frowns. 'From The Beach Boys?'

She laughs. 'No, he used to live in the flat above us in Brixton. Skinny guy. Had that cat with the funny ear. You'll remember him, Nick.'

I nod. 'Wasn't his cat called Phil Wilson?'

'Yes! So, I was telling Greta, I met him in Costa last week! He was back visiting relatives. He lives in France now. Four kids. Makes his own wine or something. He's done so well!'

France, eh? Maybe I should move to France? I think to myself, knocking back my third glass of champagne. *Surely my reputation hasn't reached across the Channel. I'd need to learn French though.*

'Are you driving?' Matt asks Harriet, motioning to the bottle of sparkling water in front of her. It's a reasonable question considering Harriet is notorious for being the first one smashed, but the last one standing. Harriet nods before pushing back her chair to reveal the reason why.

'Twelve weeks,' she proclaims in her loud Welsh accent, rubbing her non-existent bump. 'We've only just started telling people. No booze, no fags, no sushi, no mayo. I'm also sick as a dog. It's all very inconvenient.'

Noel sits there and beams proudly. 'But it's come at a

good time. I've just been promoted, so we can actually afford to move somewhere bigger.'

'Head of digital marketing,' Harriet boasts on Noel's behalf. 'It's been a hectic few weeks all round.'

As we congratulate them, I do my best to ignore the little voice in my head, but it's determined to scold me.

SEE! This is what grown-ups do, arsehole. Get your life in order.

Forty minutes and a shot of tequila later, I watch Greta and Dr Better-Than-Me make a short thank-you speech to the crowded room. I see a few familiar faces, but a lot seem to be 'couple' friends who will have to pick a side after the divorce. One thing I'm certain of is that no one here has ever stepped foot in an Aldi, whereas I'm on a first-name basis with Greg the cashier.

'We're so happy you came!' Greta enthuses. 'It means so much to us.'

Will nods and slips his arm around Greta's waist. 'Four years ago, this beautiful woman agreed to have dinner with me and four weeks ago she agreed to be my wife. I'm the luckiest man alive. She is magical.'

Jesus, even women in the bar downstairs are awwing. I mean, Greta's great and all, but magical? Does she go all Penn & Teller on his ass when they're alone?

'Anyway, the wedding will be mid-March, you'll all receive your invites shortly. Now, please eat, drink and be as happy as we are! Cheers!'

As we all raise our glasses and wish them well, I try

very hard to be positive, but being surrounded by impressive people celebrating engagements, babies, promotions and wine-making neighbours from Brixton past is giving me anxiety. I'm trying very hard not to take everyone's success as a personal affront, but it turns out I'm fairly self-obsessed. I excuse myself and head to the bathroom. Knowing my luck, I'll end up pissing beside a fucking Nobel Prize winner.

Thankfully, I'm alone, apart from one cubicle which seems to be occupied by someone with a suspicious sniffing disorder. As I wash my hands, I stare at myself in the mirror, hoping that little voice in my head will provide a rallying pep talk ... perhaps affirm my worth in the world. Tell me I'm destined for great things!

Your hair looks crap.

Bollocks. Defeated, I retreat back out into the hallway, ready to get unnecessarily drunk, but I'm stopped by Greta and an older woman, who's dressed like she's running for office.

'Nick! Just the man I was looking for! This is Alice, I thought you two should meet!'

Why, is she a complete prick too?

'Terrific,' I respond, shaking Alice's hand. 'Nice to meet you. Excellent party, Greta, I'm having the best time.'

Greta grins at me excitedly, while Alice doesn't say a word. Who is this woman? Christ, is Greta trying to set me up? I know Angela isn't here, but I still have a girlfriend.

Besides Alice is clearly not my type because Alice is hitting sixty. I'm not adverse to older women, but twice my age is pushing it just a bit.

'So how do you know each other?' I ask.

'Alice is my neighbour, *but* also manages Southview Shopping Centre, you know, the mall near your flat?'

'Um, sure – funnily enough, I just bought this shirt there. John Lewis do a decent sale,' I reply, pointing to my shirt-covered torso and wondering why the hell I just said that when a simple 'yes' would have sufficed. Now Alice is looking at my torso and I want to leave.

'Oh wonderful,' Greta continues, 'because Alice was literally just telling me about a position she has available. It's fate!'

Job talk! Thank God. I unclench. Alice is free to look wherever she likes.

'It's seasonal work but would be ideal for you.'

'OK, perfect, what—'

'No travel expenses, no stress, you've already had background checks done—'

'Background checks? Why—'

'And of course, you're very personable. Kids love you!'

'Greta, what on earth are you talking about? What's the position?'

'Santa,' she replies, grinning at me. 'I think you'd make a perfect Santa.'

CHAPTER FOUR

Present Day

Santa's grotto at Southview Shopping Centre is less of a cosy, festive cavern filled with gifts, and more of an open-plan, penned-off Christmas area with an impressive, surprisingly tastefully decorated tree, some fake snow and, of course, a huge throne for Santa to sit on. A red carpet covers the floor from throne to entrance, where the queue is already winding around the nearby juice bar.

You can do this, Nick, I reassure myself, waving to the eager children. *You're employed and spreading Christmas cheer, what's not to like?*

'Vamos! You're late!'

Startled, I whip around to see a woman in her thirties, no taller than five foot, dressed like an elf and obviously as enthusiastic to be here as I am.

'You are Nick?'

'Yes.'

'Izzy.'

'Nice to meet—'

'Look, I wear this costume, but I not your servant, OK?' she informs me. 'Don't ask me to help. Last year I have this one crying and that one crying and that's no my job, OK?'

I wish she was as charming as her Spanish accent.

'Um, sure. OK.'

'You deal with *los niños*, I have the money, OK?'

She waves her little point-of-sale credit card machine at my face, while I nod in agreement. I feel like I'm involved in some sort of heist.

I sit on my ridiculous throne as Izzy allows the first child and her mother through, nervously telling myself that this will be a piece of cake.

You've been in a boardroom with Deborah Meaden, for Christ's sake. They're just kids. Get it together.

I smile and wave to the approaching child. She takes a step back and clings to her mum's leg. Excellent start, Nick.

'Keep it under a minute for each child,' Geraldine had advised at my induction, 'Name, age, what they want, let the parents take a picture, give them a gift from the sack, then on to the next. I need you smiling and swift. Any questions?'

'Are there boy-gifts and girl-gifts?'

'No,' she'd snapped back. 'Gender neutral. New guidelines. Also, lap-sitting is entirely at the parent's discretion, but the younger kids enjoy it.'

The small child currently trying to flee from my knee makes me believe otherwise.

'Polly, it's OK, darling, just look over here! Smile for Mummy!'

Polly is having none of this shit. I look down at the screaming, wriggling toddler in the furry blue hat and empathise. She holds on tightly to a half-eaten Milky Way. She wants to be here less than I do.

Her mum pleads with me through thick-rimmed glasses, telepathically impressing the need to make this situation better, but I have no idea how. Polly is the first child I've seen today and by the look on my supervisor's face, she might be the last.

'Oh, now *now*!' I say, in a voice which startles even me. It's like Santa meets Ed Kemper. I try again in a slightly less serial-killer-esque tone. 'No need to cry, little one. Tell Santa what you would like for Christ—'

'MUuuuUUmmm!'

This is horrible. An undoubtedly blurry photo is taken as I hand Polly a wrapped selection box, before she's placed back into her stroller by her flustered, apologetic mother now promising ice cream to appease her. The last thing that kid needs is more sugar.

I barely have time to take a breath before the next little darling has hurled himself on to my lap. At least this kid is enthusiastic.

'What's your name?' I ask him, staring at the snot

bubble which has formed in his left nostril. God, this is grim. I see Geraldine skulking off towards the food court and immediately relax a little.

'David,' he replies, eyeing up my scratchy, nylon beard. It's already driving me nuts, given that underneath is three days' worth of itchy stubble regrowth.

'And how old are you, David?'

'Six!' He replies with such a gusto, I can't help but smile. Most adults say their age like it's shameful secret, but David's got the ageing thing nailed.

'And what would you like for Christmas?'

'A trampoline! Like Robbie's. One with a net so we can do giant flips and tumbles and bounce and bounce and bounce!'

I glance at his waiting parents who are frantically shaking their heads behind their physically boinging child, letting me know that large, costly outdoor trampolines aren't happening anytime soon. His dad mimes being on a bike and I nod.

'Hmm, the elves had a problem with the trampolines this year,' I reply. David stops springing, the excitement on his face quickly draining.

'But they've made some amazing bikes! Haven't you, Izzy?'

Izzy's head spins around independently from her body and glares into my soul, indicating that she will kill me if I try and get her involved with los niños. I turn back to David.

'So how about a nice new bike? Wouldn't that be fun? Fancy new helmet too?'

David doesn't say a word. He moves off my lap and folds his arms, glaring first at his parents and then at me. This is horrendous. How many children am I going to have to disappoint today? I need to convince him that bikes are better than trampolines.

'They're so cool, David! Honestly! Coolest bikes you've ever—'

'NO! IWANTATRAMPOLINNNNEEEEEE.'

The screaming sound piercing my eardrum is almost enough to distract me from the sharp pain in my shin, but not quite. I yelp as David and his small yet powerful right foot are scooped up by his dad before he can inflict any further damage.

'Fucking hell, kid! No need for—'

I hear the smallest gasp from a girl in the front of the queue and the sound of at least ten jaws hitting the floor, as David is carted off by his embarrassed parents.

'Mummy! Santa said the F-word.'

Oh God.

'Outrageous!' one silver-haired granny yells, pulling her mildly amused child away by the arm. 'Come on, Rosie, we're not staying here.'

'I'm s-sorry,' I stammer as several of the parents and kids disperse, scolding me for being the worst Santa ever.

The back of the queue doesn't seem to realise anything is wrong, but I have no doubt that someone is already asking to speak to a manager. Once Geraldine finds out, I am so fired.

The rest of my day doesn't run any more smoothly. I've never seen so many spoiled brats in light-up trainers demanding iPads, PlayStations and something called Ricky the Trick-Lovin' Pup, which is apparently a toy dog but sounds like a toy pimp.

At 5pm I see Izzy pull across the rope behind the last child, letting everyone know that Santa is closed. After today, I'm starting to understand why Izzy seems so annoyed. Working with children is clearly a calling rather than a seasonal vocation.

'And what's your name?' I ask the rosy-faced blonde girl who is already trying to grab for my beard. I'm so glad she's the last one.

'Jennifer,' she replies. 'I am three!'

'And what would you like for Christmas?'

'A Barbie house with the . . . ACHOOOO!'

Something slimy flies from her nose and lands squarely on my hand, making me gag. Horrified, I try and flick it off while her dad just laughs like it's adorable. It's not adorable, it's fucking green.

'Barbie house, gotcha,' I reply, handing her a gift. 'Merry Christmas.'

I don't even smile as her dad takes a photo. I've had

enough. I'm hot, sweating, bruised, covered in mucus, and I'm leaving. Geraldine can shove this job up her arse.

Shaking my head, I stand from my throne, ready to rip this stupid beard from my face. Even though the grotto is closed, there's still a crowd admiring the Christmas display so unveiling my face right now would be a terrible idea. All I want to do is get home, shower and enjoy a cosy night in with Angela to celebrate my new job.

As I prepare to leave, I see a boy who looks around five sneak under the rope.

'Little boy, we are closed,' Izzy informs him, but he swerves around her and dashes straight for me.

'Santa, I—'

'Come back tomorrow,' I say. 'Santa is going home.'

'But I won't be here tomorrow,' he replies, frantically. 'And I haven't told you what I want for Christmas!'

'Sorry, little man.'

I reach into my sack and pull out a selection box. 'Take this. Free chocolate is better than nothing.'

As he takes the gift, his huge brown eyes start to fill up with tears. 'But if I don't tell you my Christmas wish, it won't come true! Please, Santa.'

'I'm sorry but—'

'Santa!' Izzy snaps. 'You can do one more, yes.'

I nod. Partly because Izzy scares the shit out of me, but also because I cannot be responsible for one more crying child today. Besides, I think he's melted Izzy's heart a little. That should be rewarded.

'What's your name, little boy?'

'Alfie,' he replies, following me back to my throne. I take a seat while he stands beside me. 'Alfie O'Brien.'

'Alfie. That's a great name. And how old are you?'

'I'm four.'

'And what would you like for Christmas?'

Alfie takes a deep breath and quietly says, 'I want my mum to be happy again.'

Yikes. I feel uncomfortable. I'm even less equipped to deal with selfless children than spoiled, selfish ones. The look of sincerity on his face is killing me.

'I'm sure she's very happy!' I reply, cheerfully. 'She has you, right?'

He looks at his feet. 'She pretends to be, but she's been sad since my dad died. I hear her crying sometimes.'

'Oh, I'm sorry, mate.'

He shrugs. 'Please make her happy, Santa. That's all I want for Christmas.'

Now my eyes are welling up. This sweet little boy thinks I can take away his mum's grief and I have no idea how to respond.

'Um . . . well, you see—'

'ALFIE! Oh, thank God you're here, I've been looking everywhere!'

I turn to see a woman racing towards us, wearing

one of the bright blue aprons from the café opposite the grotto.

No, thank God you're here, I think to myself, *I was totally out of my depth there.*

'That's my mum,' Alfie whispers, waving to her.

She sweeps up Alfie and kisses him repeatedly on the cheek.

'I nearly had a heart attack!' she tells him. 'You cannot just run off like that! I was going to call the police . . . and the Avengers . . . and Spiderman . . .'

'Spiderman is in the Avengers,' Alfie replies, giggling. 'Sorry, Mum, I just had to see Santa.'

As Alfie's mum looks at me apologetically, I suddenly feel my chest tighten and a little tingle shoots all the way down my spine. Oh God, she's lovely. I see where Alfie gets his big eyes from. They're like two dark pools of . . . *Jesus, this isn't appropriate, Nick, you idiot, she's a grieving widow. Get a hold of yourself, man.*

'I'm so sorry,' she blurts out. 'One minute he was with me, the next—'

'It's fine!' I reply, now more aware than ever of how stupid my Santa voice sounds. I clear my throat. 'Very nice boy.'

Fucking hell, now I sound Russian.

She smiles and ruffles Alfie's mop of brown hair as I look anywhere that isn't directly at her. Damn, she smells good.

'We're going to miss the bus; let's go, Alfie. Say bye to

Santa.' She takes Alfie by the hand and begins to lead him towards the exit.

'But Santa didn't say he'd get me what I want for Christmas!' he exclaims, looking back at me. 'He needs to say it!'

Oh God, what do I do? People are staring!

'Santa, PLEASE!'

'OK, OK, you got it!' I reply, even throwing in a thumbs up for good measure. His little face lights up and he returns the gesture. Seconds later Alfie and his mum are gone.

'Imbecile!' I hear Izzy snarl at me. 'You just lie to him and now you ruin Christmas for the child.'

'What was I supposed to do? Tell him no? You saw how cute and desperate he was.'

'Well, now he will hate Santa.'

'Well, you hate Santa too, so maybe you can form a club together?'

She rolls her eyes and flounces off with the credit card machine while I make my way back to the staffroom, feeling like shit. Have I just ruined that kid's Christmas? Eager to get the hell out of there, I grab my clothes from the locker, shoving them into my backpack, and start walking home – belly, beard and all. I need a drink.

Twenty minutes later, I arrive home to see Angela standing outside my building.

'Hey, sweetie! You're early!'

I pull the door and hold it open for her. Angela looks at

me bewildered until it finally clicks. She steps tentatively towards me.

'Nick? Is that you?'

'Yup!' I laugh as she roughly unhooks my beard from my ears. 'Careful with that, my boss will make me replace it if I damage it.'

'Your boss? You got a job?'

'Yes . . . this is my new job! What do you think?'

Without a word, Angela walks around me and up the two flights of stairs until we reach my front door. I enter first with her following quickly behind me, loudly slamming the door.

'Whoa, leave the door on the hinges, sweeth—'

'NICK, WHAT THE FUCK IS GOING ON?'

I'm beginning to think that Angela is less than impressed with my new job.

CHAPTER FIVE

As I open my fifth beer, I realise that I don't think I've ever seen Angela quite so enraged as she was earlier. I also think that *less than impressed with my new job* was an understatement.

'I cannot believe this . . . you're Santa,' she'd repeated, over and over. 'Santa! My boyfriend is Santa.'

'Christ, Ange, I'm not the real Santa. I didn't just vanish down a chimney. Relax.'

She stood up from the couch dramatically, like she was objecting in court.

'This is no time for jokes, Nicholas.'

Sometimes, when Angela is mad, she'll sternly call people by their full name, like a parent expressing their disapproval. The main problem with this is that I was christened Nick. I've never been a Nicholas. She knows this, but it doesn't suit her narrative right now.

'Why are you getting so upset?' I asked. 'It's a job. I needed a job, desperately, and now I have one!'

'Because, you can do better,' she'd snapped. 'Jesus, Nick, my friends shop there. *I shop there!* God, this is so embarrassing.'

'It's six weeks' work, Angela. You're overreacting. Yes, it's not ideal, but it's also not a big deal either.'

'Wait, is this like a charity Santa?' she enquired, almost hopefully. 'Like raising money for a good cause – sick kids or dogs or something? I can work with that.'

'Nope,' I reply. 'Normal kids. Paying gig.'

'Ugh, for God's sake. I cannot deal.'

As I watched her pout petulantly, hands on hips, I realised that it wasn't me that she felt could do better. It was her. I'd be lying if I said I hadn't felt slightly mortified that this was my last resort, but I honestly thought she'd find it funny. Matt did. He laughed so hard I thought his brain might short-circuit.

'You can stop now,' I'd requested, watching him hold his sides. 'At least I can pay rent this month.'

'Saint Nick!' he exclaimed, his shoulders shaking. 'It's perfect! Oh God, can I sit on your knee? Will there be elves? Please let there be elves.'

'Fuck off.'

He'd continued to laugh even as my couch cushion hit him squarely in the face, but unlike Angela, he was happy for me. His mate being Santa wasn't an embarrassment, it was a source of great amusement.

Angela finally sat down again, but by the way she

fumbled with her handbag at her feet, I could tell she had no intention of staying.

'I think we need a break, Nick. We're on very different paths right now. Maybe some time apart will—'

'Oh, come on! This is just a temporary—'

'Sorry, babes, I need some space.' I watched speechless as she put her bag on the crook of her arm and stormed out.

That was three hours ago. I'm now spending what's left of my Friday night bingeing on Chinese food and terrible Christmas movies.

Around 1am, I hear the familiar click of the front door closing, followed by an unfamiliar giggle.

'Matt, buddy,' I yell. 'Is that you?'

The living room door opens and Matt strides in with a tall blonde woman carrying her shoes in her left hand. She gives a little yelp when she sees Santa sitting in the dark, balancing a plate of Singapore noodles on his belly.

'Oh Christ, Nick,' Matt says, turning on the living room light. 'This place looks like a bomb went off.'

'It did,' I reply, wincing at the harsh light now drilling into my eyeballs. 'A big Angela-shaped one. She's embarrassed by me; can you believe it? She's quite mean. Why didn't you tell me she was mean?'

I see Matt scan the untidy room, the table covered in open takeaway containers and empty beer cans stacked in a tower. He turns to the woman beside him, who has the same puzzled yet disgusted look that Angela had earlier.

'Leanne, babe, my room's second on the left. Give me a minute, yeah?'

She nods and retreats into the hall, while Matt takes a seat beside me. He smells like fresh air and lager.

'Are you supposed to take that Santa outfit home?' he asks softly, picking a noodle from the furry trim. I shrug.

'Fuck knows. To be honest, I forgot I had it on. There's a beard kicking around here somewhere if you want a shot?'

'Should I ask how your day was? Are you watching . . . *Home Alone*?'

'Yup. Christmas marathon on the movie channel. No idea where the remote is. My day was fucking awful; honestly, you have no idea. I've been sneezed on, shouted at by a Spanish elf, kicked, screamed at and Angela's dumped me.'

Matt makes a yikes face. 'Jeez, sorry, Nick.'

'Annnd,' I continue, 'I lied to a little boy. This sweet little dude with a dead dad and a sad mum and I've ruined his Christmas.'

I glance at the television in time to see Kevin being reunited with his idiot parents. I hurl a spring roll at the screen. Sure, Kevin is a brat, but he deserves better.

'It's all bullshit!' I yell. 'In real life, social services would have been called. Alfie's hot mum will never have a happy reunion. There are no happy endings!'

'Who the hell is Alfie?'

I lift my last spring roll, but Matt intercepts it and

takes the polystyrene container away from me before I can throw anything else.

'I'm sorry you're having a hard time, fella,' he says, nudging me. 'Get some shut-eye and we'll talk in the morning.'

He walks over to the door and switches off the light again.

'I'm here for you, buddy, but you need to get a grip. Remote's on top of the telly.'

Matt closes the door and joins his date while I continue swigging on my beer. I smile as I see *Scrooged* is on next. At last, a film I can relate to.

CHAPTER SIX

'Ugh. How can anyone live like that? He still has food stuck to his face!'

As I slowly open my eyes, I hear a mumbled reply from Matt about me having a hard time, followed by the sound of the door slamming shut. God, what time is it? I feel rough.

'She seems nice,' I say as Matt joins me in the living room. 'I love the smell of contempt in the morning.'

'I've made you a coffee,' he replies. 'Budge up.'

Matt plonks down beside me, placing a strong, almost tarry-looking coffee on the table. I must have fallen asleep with the television on, as *Miracle on 34th Street* is almost at the end.

Matt remains quiet as I come to, undoubtedly wanting to kick me up the arse for scaring off his date, but knowing that at this moment, it's pointless. I'm a mess; my life is a mess. As I watch the little girl wax lyrical about the magic of Christmas, I think about Alfie and his mum. I shouldn't have given the kid false hope. What am I supposed to do? Snap my fingers and bring his dad back? Magic up a new Prince Charming?

'I believe . . . I believe . . . it's silly, but I believe . . .'

I sit bolt upright on the couch as the little girl on screen makes her Christmas affirmations. Maybe there is something I can do.

'Matt, you've put it about a bit, yeah?'

He stops sipping his coffee and narrows his eyes.

'I have no idea what you mean.'

'I mean you've pretty much slept with every over-entitled blonde under fifty in London, right?'

'How dare you!' he replies, pouting slightly. 'But yeah, that's fair.'

'So how about going on a date with someone with a bit of substance? A real woman. Someone who doesn't draw on her eyebrows and—'

'Nick, what the hell are you talking about?'

I excitedly move round on the couch to face him. 'I met this woman yesterday. Total ten. And she's nice. Like super nice. Caring and funny . . . makes Avengers jokes.'

Maybe I'm overselling Alfie's mum here, given that our interaction yesterday was only a few seconds long, but her son is adorable so she's very unlikely to be Aileen Wuornos.

Matt thinks for a moment then narrows his eyes.

'If she's so great, why don't you ask her out? You're single now, apparently.'

I shake my head. 'Ange said she wanted some space; it'll blow over. Besides, look at me. This woman deserves someone who isn't a complete frickin' disaster.'

'I dunno, mate . . . maybe. What's her name?'

'No idea.'

'How can you not know her—'

'Listen, I can't explain but I have a very good feeling about this. Just say yes and I'll do the rest. I'll get you a name and a number and everything. Please. Look at me. I need this.'

Matt laughs and puts down his mug.

'OK, fine. I don't think Leanne will be back anyway, after seeing the state of you last night. It didn't seem to go down well when I handed her the bra off the floor either, given that she was already wearing hers.'

'So, you'll do it?'

'Yes, but I'm doing this for you, you weird, weird man.'

'Yaass!' I exclaim, punching the air. 'You won't regret it . . . one thing, though. Don't be your usual shagger self . . . you know what I mean. Respect her.'

'Yeah, alright, Oprah.'

'Amazing! Right, I have to head into work. This is going to be so good.'

'You might want to shower and Febreze the shit out of that Santa costume, mate. No offence, but you smell rank.'

He's right, of course, I stink, but I'm not offended. What

I am is a genius. An honest-to-God, Christmas-miracle-performing genius.

I arrive into work half an hour early, cleaned up and carrying my Santa suit which now smells 'April Meadows Fresh'. I'm hoping Alfie's mum is working today and if not, I'll at least get her name from one of the other staff. I'll grab another coffee too. Matt can't make a decent coffee for shit.

I walk into Belle Blend and head to the counter, trying to be as casual as possible.

'Americano with cold milk, please,' I request, scanning the room.

'Sit in or takeaway?'

'Takeaway, thanks.'

I spot her. Third table near the back. She's wearing her hair back today, but it's definitely her. I shift from foot to foot, willing the barista to hurry up, but it looks like there're a couple of orders before mine.

Act natural, Nick. You might be about to change this woman's life, but don't be creepy about it. You were cool once. Channel your twenties.

She begins wiping down the table to my left, but catches me staring. Dammit. I'm bad at this.

'Can I help you with something?' she asks, raising an eyebrow.

'I thought it was you!' I reply, breezily. 'Alfie not giving you the runaround today?'

She smiles politely. 'Do I know you?'

'Christ, sorry, yes! I looked a little different yesterday,' I reply, gesturing towards the grotto. 'White beard. Eight reindeers. Dangerously overweight.'

She laughs loudly. 'Of course! Sorry, the voice threw me off. Your Santa voice is much deeper and, well, slightly questionable.'

'Yeah, I'm still trying to figure that out,' I reply, my face flushing. 'Is it really that bad?'

'It reminded me of that film where the murderer asks the babysitter if she's checked on the children. I much prefer this one.'

'Noted.'

Americano with milk!'

'Oh, that's me, two secs.'

I grab my coffee and return to her table, pretending like it's not burning my hand off. I want to save the rainforest and the baby monkeys too, but I really wish they hadn't gotten rid of those cup-holder things.

'Anyway, thanks so much for yesterday,' she continues. 'You must think I'm mother of the fucking year. My sitter dropped him off here and he was supposed to just sit quietly for two minutes but . . .'

'Don't be silly, I'm sure it happens all the time. I'm Nick, by the way.'

She wipes her hands on her apron and holds one out. 'Sarah. Honestly, thanks again. He was so happy on the way home, couldn't stop talking about you! You made his day!'

My initial rush of pride is soon diminished by a pang of guilt. She'd be horrified if she knew I'd just promised her kid something that might be impossible.

'It was nothing,' I reply. 'Part of the job description.'

'I hope he asked for a Nintendo Switch,' she says, gesturing over to another member of staff who's trying to get her attention. 'I've been busting my ass doing extra shifts to afford that thing.'

'Yup,' I lie. 'That's exactly what it was.'

Fucking hell, Nick, stop lying to this family, you moron.

She picks up some empty cups and a half-eaten pastry. 'Sorry, Nick, I need to go. Morning rush is crazy. Nice to see you again though!'

Shit. I've been so busy chatting, I forgot why I came in here and my shift starts in five minutes.

'A date!' I blurt out. 'How would you feel about going on a date?'

She stops for a second and starts to blush. Good God, she's pretty.

'A date? Like, a *date*-date? I'm not sure I—'

'Just dinner, maybe some drinks. I swear you'll have a great time! Say yes!'

'Um . . . OK. Yes. Why not. I could use a night off.'

'Amazing!' I reply delightedly, pulling out my phone. 'Let me get your number.'

Grinning, she begins typing her number into my phone. I'm so happy right now I could kiss her. I want to call Alfie and tell him that phase one of the plan is now underway.

'So just send me a text or—'

'I'll get Matt to call you!' I reply. 'You won't regret it!'

'Wait . . . Matt? Who is—'

'Shit, I need to run . . .' I give her a slightly (very) awkward hug, bolting for the exit before she can change her mind. I'm already halfway to the grotto, practically skipping through the mall towards the staffroom when I hear:

'You are late again.'

I hold up my coffee cup at Izzy in response, mouthing the word 'sorry' and ignoring her loud tut as she passes me in full elf costume. Being a few minutes late is worth it. Everything is going to plan and for the first time in months, I'm starting to like myself again. As I remove my jumper, I can faintly smell Sarah's perfume on the neckband and smile. Matt's a lucky man.

CHAPTER SEVEN

'Jesus, mate ... smile much? I take it things went well then?'

Matt has been home from his date with Sarah for approximately seven minutes and that smug grin hasn't left his face for one second. I watch him grab some leftover chicken from the fridge before joining me on the couch. I feel like his mum, waiting up on a Saturday night to see how his first date went. At least he didn't drunkenly bring Sarah home with him. I'm very proud.

'Yeah ... it was good,' he replies, inspecting a very dry-looking chicken wing. 'I took her for tapas though so I'm still starving. How long have these been in the fridge?'

'No idea,' I reply indifferently, trying to keep him on topic. 'So, it was just *good*? Really? Not fantastic? Your face says it was at least great.'

He bashfully rubs the back of his neck. 'It was pretty fantastic actually, really good fun. To be honest, she was not at all what I was expecting.'

Now I'm smug. I *knew* he'd like her. How could he not? She's delightful. 'Do you honestly think I'd set you up with a troll? Oh, ye of little faith.'

He raises an eyebrow. 'Bethany Andrews?'

'Apart from her . . . and everyone pees in the shower.'

'Yeah, but usually the shower is on.'

'Point taken.'

He kicks off his shoes and stretches his legs. For someone six foot three, his legs look surprisingly short. I sit up a little straighter as I try to judge if he has an abnormally long torso. 'It's weird. I just didn't expect Sarah to be so . . .'

'Lovely?'

'Exactly,' he responds, finally braving the chicken wing. 'She's stunning. She's really grounded as well . . . and smart and funny. Offered to pay half the bill . . . it's been a while since anyone I've dated offered to pay for anything.'

'You just haven't been dating the right women,' I reply, quickly realising the parallel between our lives as Matt continues filling me in on the date. I'm no better at relationships than he is. The only thing Angela ever paid for in our relationship was her Uber ride home after she ended it. Sarah sounds like she is one of those women who don't rely on anyone to take care of them. My mum was like that . . . maybe it's a single-parent thing.

He nods. 'You were right about me dating someone different. I've never met anyone like her. I might be getting ahead of myself, but I think she could be ... well, you know ...'

'Worthy of a second date?'

'Quite possibly, mate,' he announces, throwing the chicken bone on the plate. 'I know it sounds crazy but there's just something about her. Her smile, maybe ... Do we have any hot sauce? This chicken is bland as fuck.'

As he traipses back to the kitchen in search of condiments, my mind flashes back to Sarah smiling at me in the grotto and I feel a slight pang in my chest. It's so strange – I hardly know the woman, but somehow, it's now become my mission in life to make her happy. Matt's a great guy; she could be happy with him. I'm doing a good thing here.

I might only be a lowly shopping-centre Santa, but I, Saint Nick, am well on the way to changing two and a half lives. Maybe I should be focusing on my own, given that it is such a mess, but I'm channelling my inner Santa and the Christmas Spirit and all that shit. Who knows, Alfie's Christmas wish might just come true.

Tuesday in the grotto is thankfully much quieter than the outrageously busy weekend Izzy and I were subjected to. On Saturday alone we had three vomit incidents, nineteen criers and countless tantrums from both parents and children alike. I've never heard an elf threaten to murder someone in Spanish, but as it turns out, it's rather endearing. Over the past few days we've developed a much more harmonious working relationship which involves me bringing her doughnuts and her not setting fire to my beard.

I beckon for the next child and watch him run to me, followed by a teenager covered in piercings.

'Hello. Merry Christmas!' I say, helping him up on to my knee. 'What's your name?'

'Ryan,' he says, bashfully. He's cute; no Alfie, but cute all the same.

'And what would you like Santa to bring you for Christmas?'

'Scalextric! With the rally cars.'

'Good choice!' I say. 'I'll let the elves know.'

I hear the surly teenager exhale loudly as if life itself is boring him to death, rather than him just being expected to tolerate the slight inconvenience of having to take his brother to see Santa.

'He said you weren't real,' Ryan announces, crossly. 'That only babies believe in Santa.'

Surly snorts behind his brother and goes back to his phone.

'You know something,' I say, doing my best not to throat-punch this pincushion. 'I remember when your brother was about your age.'

He gasps. 'Gary?'

Bewildered, Gary stops clicking his tongue piercing against his teeth.

'Mm-hmm,' I confirm. 'I remember Gary asked me for a little brother who would love him and look up to him. A brother just like you.'

'Me?'

I nod. 'Yes, you.'

As Ryan smiles at his brother in delight, I see Gary's cheeks begin to burn, before he slowly realises that he's been a bit of a prick.

'Um, yeah,' Gary responds, sheepishly. 'Must have forgotten. Thanks, Santa.'

'Excellent,' I say, reaching down to get the gifts. 'I think you both deserve something.'

I hand Ryan his gift first. He thanks me and climbs down from my knee, enthusiastically picking at the wrapping paper.

'I take it even edgelords like chocolate?' I ask, holding out a box to Gary. He looks embarrassed but thanks me, scurrying off to lick his wounds. I see Izzy briefly clap in approval before letting the next child through.

At 4.45pm, Geraldine appears, jangling a bunch of keys like a Shawshank prison guard. I see Izzy immediately tense up. She's not a fan of Geraldine either.

'Quick word, Santa,' she insists, moving past the last sour-faced kid who wanted a MacBook. Even I don't have a MacBook; he can fuck off.

'Everything OK?'

She nods. 'I've dealt with the day-one complaints. I

think you're on track now. I did, however, notice that there have been more gifts given than tickets sold. Any reason for this?'

I shake my head, trying not to glance at Izzy, my partner in selection-box thievery. Apart from giving out extras, we've also been dipping into Santa's sack regularly. Neither of us will have to buy chocolate again for a year.

'Sorry, Geraldine,' I reply. 'We put them in the staffroom after yesterday's shift. Maybe the night staff?'

She narrows her eyes and makes an unconvinced 'hmm' sound before turning on her heel and jangling away towards customer service. She absolutely knows it's us but the likelihood of us confessing is the same as her being able to hire another non-alcoholic, DBS-checked Santa this close to Christmas.

'I don't like her,' Izzy states, propping up the tiny penguin which has fallen over for the fifteenth time today. 'Never trust a woman with the bob hair, you remember this.'

I'm not even sure what that means, but I agree anyway. With no one else in line, I take a seat for the last two minutes of my shift to man the grotto, while Izzy starts moving the penguins and polar bears into the staffroom.

'Do people from the North Pole drink gingerbread lattes?'

I turn to see Sarah standing to my left, holding a grey takeaway cup. She can't tell I'm smiling under my beard, but I am.

'All the time,' I reply, climbing down from my throne. 'Though the reindeers make fun of us.'

'Reindeers are assholes.'

'Agreed. How are you?'

'I'm good. Great, in fact. I just wanted to say thanks for introducing me to Matt,' she says, handing me my drink. 'I had a terrific time; we're going out again soon. He's very sweet. And very tall.'

'Yeah, I heard it went well,' I reply, suddenly self-conscious about being a mere five foot eleven. 'He was like a Disney princess when he got home.'

She laughs. 'Excellent. I'll be sure to bring him a glass slipper next time then. By the way, you've made quite the impression on Alfie. He still hasn't shut up about you.'

'I have that effect on people. Children and elves especially.'

We look over to Izzy who's about to lose her shit with a family trying to buy grotto tickets after closing. Her head whips around like she'd somehow heard me mention elves.

'Well, most of them.'

Sarah grins. 'I should get back to work; I'm on 'til eight tonight. Enjoy the coffee!'

'No worries,' I reply. 'I'll tell the reindeers you said hi.'

She bites her lip and grins, slowly backing away towards the coffee shop, while I take a swig of my first ever gingerbread latte. Jesus Christ, people actually drink this shit?

As we close the grotto, Izzy takes off her hat and runs her hands through her hair. I find myself fascinated by the sheer volume of curls she has. How the hell does she hide all that under her hat?

'Your girlfriend over there,' she snaps. 'She knows you stare at other women, yes? What is wrong with you?'

My gaze breaks and I can't help but blush in surprise. 'What? No, I've just never seen your hair down before! It looks nice, that's all.'

She pauses and shrugs. 'OK, I accept that.'

'And she's not my girlfriend.'

'Well, she looks at you like she is,' Izzy replies, continuing to mess with her mop. She stops suddenly, a smile creeping over her face. 'And I think you do too.'

'What . . . that's ridiculous. You need your eyes checked.'

'She has the little boy, yes? You be kind to her.'

Izzy waves her hand dismissively and heads off with the credit card machine and a small selection box hidden inside her hat. That bloody hat is magical.

CHAPTER EIGHT

'You should go out tonight, Nick. Honestly, I know you're not flush yet, but I'll slip you a few quid. Crap, I'm out of aftershave, can I borrow some?'

Matt's seriously making the effort for his third date. He even trimmed his nose hair. I nod and gesture towards my room. 'Knock yourself out . . . and thanks for the offer but I've faced those kids with a hangover once already. Never again.'

'You don't have to get pissed. Just blow off some steam – or better yet, let some hot woman blow the steam off for you.'

'Your puns are terrible, mate.'

Before he can protest, his phone starts ringing in his bedroom and I unmute the television again. He's probably right, I haven't had sex since I lost my job months ago – according to Angela, unemployment just wasn't sexy – but they're showing a *Die Hard* marathon on Sky later and I have a Domino's voucher.

A few moments later, Matt returns to the living room and flicks on the main lights.

'Change of plan, dude. Get this place tidied.'

'What? Why?'

'Sarah's sitter has cancelled last minute, so she's coming here with the wee man,' he replies, frantically moving all of our shit from one side of the room to the other. 'We'll just order pizza.'

I reluctantly start helping. 'So, what? A romantic dinner, just the three of you? That's kind of intense . . .'

'It is,' he replies, pulling his wet socks off the radiator. 'That's why you're also having dinner with us.'

'Um, I'm not sure that—'

'Please, Nick, for me? I really like this girl, but I have no idea how to act around Alfie. You've met the kid, he knows you!'

'As Santa! He doesn't know *me* from Adam!'

'Well, Sarah knows you and it was her idea that you join us. We'll work it out. She'll be here in half an hour. I'd change if I were you – those jogging trousers smell like baked beans.'

I retreat to my room and throw on a T-shirt and jeans while Matt switches on the Roomba and throws dishes into the sink. I can't remember the last time he had a sober woman back here, let alone one with a child. He must be keen.

'Nick! Make sure that bathroom isn't filthy, will you? Women notice that shit.'

'You're not my real mum!'

'Please, mate?'

I sigh and trudge through to the bathroom, cursing Matt under my breath. He gets a girl and I get put on maid duty? Why on earth did I agree to this?

Sarah arrives at 7pm, armed with a bottle of wine and some Ribena for Alfie. Matt ushers them in, kissing Sarah on the cheek and awkwardly ruffling Alfie's hair like it's the first time he's even been near a human child. I wave from the living room.

'Nice to see you again, come on through!'

Alfie is first to charge ahead, obviously unfazed by any of this.

'Are we having pizza?' he asks, immediately plonking himself down on the couch. 'I like pizza.'

'Alfie, this is Matt's friend Nick. Say hello.'

'Wow, your telly is massive,' he replies, giving no fucks who any of us are. 'Is that a PS4? Mum, they have a PS4!'

'Your flat is really great,' Sarah remarks as Matt takes her coat. 'Thanks so much for having us over, I really hope we're not interrupting your evening, Nick.'

Matt laughs with a touch too much scorn. 'He can watch *Die Hard* anytime. The pizza was happening anyway.'

Sarah grins. 'Ah, my favourite Christmas movie.'

'Your date has taste,' I inform Matt. 'Why don't you give

Sarah the tour? Maybe start with the bathroom . . . Alfie and I have pizza to order.'

Impressed with my smooth transition into giving Matt and Sarah a moment together, while simultaneously entertaining her son, I join Alfie on the couch and open the Domino's app on my phone.

'What shall we order?' I ask, entering my postcode. 'I get the feeling you're a pepperoni kind of guy . . .'

'Mum called her friend Meghan to tell her where we are in case we go missing.'

I stop looking at pizzas.

'Oh really?'

He nods. 'I heard her. She was talking about Santa being a cereal or something. Why would Santa be a cereal?'

I do my best not to laugh. 'No idea, buddy, but it's good someone knows where you are. Your mum is obviously very smart.'

He nods. 'Pineapple.'

'Sorry?'

'On my pizza. I like pineapple.'

'Hmm, I won't hold that against you.'

Pizzas ordered, I turn on the PS4 for Alfie and load up Sonic, much to his delight. Matt and Sarah are now back in the kitchen, pouring wine. They make a handsome couple. Matt is right, I need to move on from Ange now that our break seems to have become a break-up. It's only been a couple of weeks since she 'needed some space', but my texts have gone unanswered and her Instagram story would suggest that she is really enjoying her second date with Pete from *Love Island*.

When dinner arrives, we all crowd around the small kitchen table, fighting over garlic bread and wishing we'd ordered more dips. The only weird aspect of this situation is how normal it all feels. It's all so easy. It feels like Sarah and Alfie have been a part of our lives for years instead of weeks.

'Alfie, why don't you take those cookies into the living room and beat Nick on the PS4 while me and your mum wash up?'

I see Sarah's eyes darting towards Alfie and then to me, as if she's waiting for approval. I wink and then grab the cookies.

'Last one to the couch is a hairy banana!'

Alfie giggles and propels himself from the table, quickly followed by me, while Sarah and Matt start clearing up.

Our open-plan living area makes it easy to see the kitchen from where I'm perched on the couch and, hard as I try, I can't help glancing every now and again to see what's transpiring. Alfie isn't oblivious to them either.

'They're going to kiss, aren't they?'

I nod and shoot at his car, which is way ahead of mine. 'Probably. Disgusting, right?'

He laughs and fires back while from the corner of my eye, I see Matt leaning in and Sarah rising on to her tiptoes.

I turn away and continue letting Alfie kick my ass at Sonic racing.

An hour later, Alfie is yawning his head off while Matt retrieves their coats from his bedroom.

'Fun night!' Sarah proclaims. 'You certainly have a way with Alfie, Nick. Thanks for keeping him entertained.'

'Don't mention it,' I respond. 'Helps that he's such an awesome kid. Matt hates the PlayStation; it's been nice to have someone around to beat me in such a humiliating fashion.'

'Can I come back and play Sonic again, Mum?' Alfie asks, sleepily. 'Pleeaassee??'

Sarah smiles. 'Sweetheart, I think Nick probably has—'

'Absolutely nothing better to do,' I interject. 'Listen, seriously. You need a sitter again, I'm here.' I lean in and whisper, 'It'll only cost you an Americano. Unless you still think I'm a serial killer?'

'He heard me, huh?'

'Yup. And now we have no secrets.'

Matt strolls back in as we laugh. 'What did I miss?' he asks, helping Sarah with her coat.

'Nick offered to babysit Alfie,' she responds. 'I might just take him up on that before he changes his mind.' She smiles at me before crouching down to Alfie's level. 'Come and get your coat on, love, our taxi is here.'

'See you soon,' I say as Alfie hugs me goodbye. 'Next time you can teach me Fortnite.'

'Bye, Alfie,' Matt says, leaning in to clumsily hug him. He is a sweet guy, but it is awkward as fuck. 'Thanks for coming.'

'Thanks for the pizza,' he replies politely and hugs him back, before pausing for a moment.

'You smell like Santa.'

'Do I?'

Sarah laughs and takes him by the hand while Matt and I look puzzled, until it clicks that he's wearing my aftershave.

'Babysitting, huh?' Matt says, closing the door behind Sarah. 'What on earth were you thinking?'

'Just helping you out, bro,' I reply. 'Taking one for the team. It means you can see her more often if she doesn't have to worry about childcare.'

He slaps me on the back and laughs. 'I appreciate the gesture, though I'm not sure what you've just let yourself in for.'

By the time I get to bed, I find myself thinking about Matt and Sarah. I'm almost envious. I'm not a jealous person but it makes me miss being in a relationship. I like being with someone, even if that someone just dumped me for dressing like a mythical Christmas character. I reach down and pick up my phone.

Ange, can we talk? I miss you xx

CHAPTER NINE

Either all children are starting to look the same or I'm getting return customers at the grotto hoping to bag some extra Christmas gifts. There's a tiny girl with red curly hair who just sits and stares at me, saying nothing at all. A boy who claims to be nine, but has more facial hair than Matt, who asks for anime figures, and a pair of twins who seem more captivated by Izzy than me. I also recognise the European nannies, making an almost daily trip to the grotto to keep their kids happy while they meet up and have coffee.

However, one kid in particular has visited at least three times, each time asking for an upgrade to his last request. First was an Xbox One, then he added in a games pack. Today he's back with new demands.

'Daniel, isn't it?'

'I want an Xbox One with Lego Star Wars.'

'OK, well, I think the elves have already—'

'And a new headset. A good one.'

'Gotcha. Anything else? A Tesla? Trip to Mars? The Hope Diamond?'

'My selection box.'

I look to his mum to see if she has anything to add but she's too busy on her phone to care. I retrieve a gift from the sack and hand it to him, telling him to be a good boy or Izzy the head elf will pay him a visit. The look of alarm on his face tells me this might be his last trip to the grotto.

I see Sarah arrive for her shift at lunchtime, waving to me as she hurries past. She works so close to the grotto, but I wonder if I'd ever have met her had Alfie not decided to come and find me. Probably not.

Geraldine is still appearing from nowhere and surprising the shit out of me whenever possible. I swear, if I see her head emerge round something one more time, I will lose my mind.

'Quick word, Nick. I've had complaints that *someone* has been using an aerosol deodorant in the staffroom, despite the signs clearly stating that it is prohibited due to setting off our smoke alarms. Know anything about this?'

'Um, no. Maybe the female staff—'

'Lynx. Africa.'

'Sorry?'

'The aerosol was Lynx Africa. After investigation it was found in the bin. We can therefore rule out any female members of staff.'

I desperately want to ask her if she sealed off the room

and dusted for fingerprints, but I also want to keep my job.

'Lynx Africa? Um, I think you're looking for a far younger culprit,' I reply. 'Maybe try the food court staff?'

As she leans in a little, I notice her nostrils quickly flare in and out. She's sniffing me. She's actually sniffing me!

'Wow, it's not me, Geraldine. I use a roll-on.'

'Good to know,' she says, still suspiciously eyeing me up. 'Not accusing ... only asking. Anyway, my daughter Carrie is coming here after school. I can't leave her alone in my office, so she'll be helping you out for an hour while I'm in a meeting.'

'Helping with what?'

'Around four ... as you were.'

She skulks off and I just sit there, wondering if my day can get any more surreal. I had no idea Geraldine even had a daughter, never mind one named after a horror movie. What the hell is she going to do with me for an hour?

'I'm not wearing a bloody hat. I'll just sit on that bench over there, on my phone or something. This is such bullshit.'

Carrie is a fifteen-year-old nightmare. A moody, Geraldine-resembling, grumpy-faced nightmare. At fifteen, logic dictates that she probably could have moseyed around the mall for an hour on her own, but I'm starting to appreciate why her mum wants an eye kept on her.

'Your mum says otherwise, I'm afraid,' I respond. 'And

she's my boss, so take a hat and just make sure no one steals the stuffed toys or something.'

'Why can't she do it?' Carrie asks, pointing to Izzy. 'She's just standing around anyway.'

'Because *she* already has a role and *she* would probably bite your head clean off if you so much as look at her. Trust me.'

'I don't care what my mum says, I AM NOT DOING IT. She's your boss – not mine.'

'You sure about that?'

Carrie's eyes nervously dart around, checking to see if anyone overheard her.

'Look, don't give me any hassle and there's a fiver in it for you. How does that sound?'

'Twenty.'

'Five.'

'Fifteen and I don't wear the hat.'

'Ten . . . you wear the hat and you tell your mum how great I am. Otherwise it's zero and you need to deal with the wrath of Geraldine all night.'

'Deal.'

Carrie snatches the hat from my hand and trudges over to the front of the grotto, while I resume smiling for the marginally more grateful children. Can't believe I just bought a review from someone wearing Uggs.

As it approaches closing time at the grotto, Geraldine retrieves a now ten-pound richer Carrie, and I decide to go and grab a coffee before I trudge back to the flat. I'm also keen to get my phone from my locker and see if Angela has responded yet. I know it's only been a couple of days since I texted her but surely she must miss me, even just a little. I have to believe that our relationship meant more to her than just my employment status.

Izzy and I finish up, congratulating each other on making it through another shift. Once in the staffroom, I quickly check my phone, desperate to see Angela's xoxo or an annoying emoji.

Nothing. Not even a shitty GIF. She used to love sending me GIFs.

I'm tempted to text her again but catching sight of myself in the mirror reminds me of why she isn't likely to respond anytime soon. Part of me is outraged that she's being this superficial, but a bigger part understands that I'm hardly a catch right now. This is London, not some remote island with one man to every six women – although if it was, they probably still wouldn't shag Santa.

I change clothes and nip into the coffee shop, yearning to see a friendly face. I see Sarah behind the counter, arranging the pre-packed sandwiches.

She looks up from behind the glass and smiles.

'Nick! Nice to see you. You finished for the day?'

'Yup, my Christmas cheer has been successfully spread. How are you?'

She closes over the little glass panel. 'I'm well, thanks.

Alfie's a sheep in the nursery nativity though, so I was up all night sticking cotton balls on to his jumper. Latte?'

'The reindeers asked me to buy something more manly. They felt that the gingerbread was a bit girly.'

'Well, sir, what masculine beverage can I prepare for you?'

I grin. 'Just an Americano with milk.'

'Would you like to try our new Peruvian blend for an extra 50p?'

'Would I?'

'I have targets. You would.'

She grabs a cup, fills it with hot water and begins grinding the beans.

'What's the difference between your regular blend and this new one?' I ask, as Sarah starts pressing buttons and pulling levers on the coffee machine. 'What exactly do I get for my extra 50p?'

'Basically, the beans are more expensive. Single-origin. Taste-wise, it's slightly more intense.'

'Hmm,' I reply. 'Sounds plausible, but to be fair you could tell me anything. You could say the beans had been individually licked by kittens and I'd believe you.'

She laughs. 'True. In fact, there is a coffee bean which is plucked from cat poo. I could have said that, but a) it's gross and b) we don't serve it here.'

'I hate that I'm going to have to google that. I'll end up on a watch list.'

Sarah glances at her watch. 'Actually, I was hoping to have a quick word. I'm due a break, if you have time?'

I'm in no hurry to get home. Matt is working late and I'm still a little bit agitated that Angela hasn't texted me back.

'Sure, why not.'

'Great. Let me just make a tea and I'll be over.'

Sarah eventually joins me, bringing two slices of carrot cake with her. 'Perks of being the assistant manager,' she informs me. 'The official line is that these cakes were dropped and are therefore wastage.'

'Wastage cake is the best cake,' I reply. 'I won't hear a word against it.'

She hands me a fork and we begin to eat.

'I hear you and Matt are going out again?' I say, taking a corner of the cake. 'That's a good sign.'

She smiles. 'It's a little out of my comfort zone. Don't get me wrong, Matt's super nice, but it's been a while since I dated anyone ... it's been hard finding time, with Alfie being so young. I feel completely out of the loop these days. Not sure I'd fare well on a dating site anyway, so this has been a much gentler introduction.'

'Oh, it's easy,' I reply. 'All you need is an Instagram filter and an inspirational quote. Men will swipe for less.'

'Talking from experience? Matt mentioned you've just broken up with someone.'

I squirm. 'Did he now? What else did he say?'

'Nothing! Sorry, it's none of my—'

'Don't worry,' I say. 'She broke up with me, but I'm not quite ready to *Live Laugh Love* with someone else just yet.'

Now she's cringing. 'God, I hate all that shit. Pointless platitudes make my brain hurt.'

I nod enthusiastically. 'My ex, Angela, loves them, though she once posted one on Instagram not realising it was from Attila the Hun.'

Sarah almost chokes on her tea. 'Oh God, I'm sorry for laughing; I'm sure she's lovely but . . .'

'It's fine. You're pretty much having the same reaction I did.'

I share a few dating-app horror stories, which I've collected from friends – and by friends, I mean myself pre-Angela – and Sarah laughs loudly, snorting unexpectedly, which sets her off again. It's rather sweet.

'Sooo, Nick,' she begins, pausing briefly to attack her cake with her fork while she calms down. 'I'm glad you came in today. I've been thinking about what you said the other night.'

'You might need to narrow it down. I say a lot of dumb shit.'

'About the babysitting . . .'

'Ah, yes!'

'Well, my sitter can't do many nights over Christmas

and Matt's asked me to go to that new Italian place tomorrow and—'

'Of course, I'll watch Alfie! Matt can just drop me at yours when he picks you up.'

She scrunches up her face. 'Well . . . you were great with Alfie the other night, but have you ever babysat anyone before? Nieces, nephews?'

'Well, I'm an only child . . . and so was my mum, but I'm really good with kids! Actually, I've literally *just* looked after my boss's teenage demon for the past hour, and she survived, so I'm practically an expert.'

'It's just a lot to ask of someone,' she says.

'No problem, the offer is there if you need it. I'll let you get back to work; I should probably head home anyway. Thanks for the cake!'

'Pleasure,' she replies, with a smile. 'Have a good night, Nick.'

I wish her the same and begin my walk home, hoping that she doesn't see me as some creepy bastard whose main purpose in life is to hang around kids. Sarah has every right to decide who looks after her son, but *Jesus, lady, I'm trying to fulfil your child's Christmas wish here. Give me a chance!*

CHAPTER TEN

'Coffee and tea in the cupboard above the cooker. Help yourself to whatever you can find.'

'No problem,' I answer, while I finish setting up my PS4. 'Just go and have fun. Everything's under control here.'

Sarah asks Alfie to run and get his slippers from his room, while Matt hovers around with his hands in his pockets. I can tell he's both excited and still a little nervous. The only time Matt ever gets nervous is when he's invested in something going well.

'Bedtime is eight at the latest and he needs supervision with his teeth, or he'll just wet the toothbrush and pretend he's done them,' she says, pulling on her coat. She's wearing a black dress with cut-out bits on the shoulders. I have no idea what you'd call it, other than hot. I'm almost relieved she's put her coat on.

'Matt does the same, don't worry.'

'And my neighbour Mrs Grainger is in the flat above.

Number seventy-six. She's old, but sharp as a tack, so if you run into any emergencies . . .'

'Gotcha.'

She smiles before looking up the hall to make sure Alfie is out of earshot.

'If he's not happy for whatever reason, call me and I'll come right home. Doesn't matter what it is. I mean, he should be fine, but—'

Alfie runs back in wearing his Spiderman slippers and bounces on to the couch.

'Don't worry,' I reply, softly. 'I'll take good care of him. I promise.'

'OK. Great,' she replies, exhaling. 'I really am grateful you're doing this. Give Mum a kiss, Alfie, and be good for Nick!'

'I will, Mum,' he assures her. 'We're going to play Just Dance! Nick downloaded it for me!'

She kisses him on the head and with one last hesitant glance around the flat, she leaves for dinner with Matt.

'You ready to show me your best dance moves?' I ask.

'Ready, steady, goooooo!' he replies, leaping off the couch. I press play and the first dance battle begins.

By 8pm I'm fucking exhausted, and Alfie has been crowned Dance Champion of the Entire World. His words, not mine. I sit on the side of the bath and watch him brush his teeth while he stands on a little stool so he can see the mirror. Sarah's bathroom is colourful and cosy, with baby blue walls and boat-shaped bath stencils. It's far more fun than our bathroom at home. You can tell she's decorated her house with Alfie in mind and it makes me smile. I also noticed a picture in the living room of her and her husband, holding baby Alfie. She looked unbelievably happy. I can see why Alfie would want that back.

'Time for bed, mate,' I say, as he dries his mouth.

'Do I have to?'

I nod. 'I'm afraid so. Besides, you wouldn't want your mum to get angry at me, would you? She'll never let me babysit you again! And I need a chance to steal back the dance trophy from you.'

He chuckles. 'OK . . . but can I have a story?'

'You bet,' I reply. 'That's the most important part of bedtime.'

I follow Alfie to his room, which is exactly how I imagined it. Compact and comfortable, with matching Marvel curtains and bedspread. Scattered around are various Pokémon cards, toys and a giant stuffed dog perched at the end of his bed.

'Wow, who is this?' I ask, picking it up. 'I've never seen such a big dog.'

'Max,' he replies, climbing into bed. 'Mum says that one day we can get a real dog, but we're not allowed pets here.'

'Sounds like a plan,' I reply. 'So . . . which book are we reading tonight?'

Alfie leans over and picks up a book from his little

bedside table. 'This one. It's my favourite. Mum always does funny voices.'

I sit beside him as he snuggles down and hands me the book. *'Mud Cake and Magic,'* I read aloud. 'I like it already.'

> *Early one morning, with eyes all bloodshot*
> *A witch stared into her empty black pot.*

I gasp. 'A witch? Alfie, is this story going to give me nightmares? I don't have a Max at home to protect me – only Matt and he's even scared of spiders.'

He laughs. 'No, silly, she's not a bad witch, you'll see.'

> *'Frog's coming to tea, I'll make a surprise*
> *But what does a frog eat, other than flies?'*
> *Scabby the cat looked up from his bed*
> *And with one eye open, he grumpily said:*
> *'You cannot cook, and your baking is tragic*
> *If I were you, I'd try and use magic.'*

'This cat is a bit of a grouch.' I laugh. 'I think I like him.'

As I continue reading, Alfie gets very involved, knowing every word by heart and laughing at my attempts to sound like a witch, a cat and eventually a frog. I'm quite proud of myself: for someone who's never babysat before, I'm killing it.

So next time a witch asks you to tea
It's probably best to say 'thank you' and 'please'.
It's never advised to make the mistake
Of being unkind while eating her cake.

'Wow, that frog wasn't very . . .'

I look down and see that Alfie has fallen fast asleep, his little face smooshed into his pillow. I close his book and place it on his table before positioning Max back at the end of his bed to watch over him. I envy his ability to fall asleep so quickly.

Sarah arrives back at 10.30pm, while Matt waits for me outside in the taxi.

'How was he?' she asks, peeking her head around his door. 'Any problems?'

'He was brilliant,' I reply. 'We played, we read about a frog's birthday party, he showed me where you hide the good biscuits – I think it was a roaring success.'

Her face lights up. 'God, I'm so pleased! I can't thank you enough. I usually pay Bianca ten pounds an hour if that's—'

'Jesus, don't pay me,' I respond. 'It'll cheapen the whole experience. Besides, I probably ate my wages in Kit Kats anyway.'

'Are you sure?'

'Pretty sure; you had an entire tin of Kit Kats before I arrived. I didn't even know they came in tins . . .'

'No, stupid. About the money.'

I nod, making my way to the front door. 'Totally. It was either this or sitting alone watching *Real Housewives*, and there are only so many episodes I can watch before I start resenting that I have to work for a living, when really, I'm much prettier than Heather. Anyway, I'd better shoot if the taxi is waiting. I don't want Matt to start talking about politics and annoy the driver.'

Part of me wants to stay. I feel at home here surrounded by Sarah's quirky artwork and interesting little knick-knacks. I just want to chill out, drink wine and chat shit. She has that effect on me.

'Night, Sarah,' I say, lifting my PlayStation bag.

'Night, Nick, and thanks again.'

I zip up my hoodie and rush down to the taxi, where I see Matt in the back, his face illuminated by his phone.

'Alright,' he says as I climb in, 'you survived then?'

'Piece of piss,' I reply. 'He's no bother . . . and you?'

He smiles and shows me a selfie they took together at the restaurant.

'Yeah, we had fun. And you didn't burn her house down or anything, so I've probably earned bonus points.'

'I'm glad it's working out, man.'

He puts his phone away and glances up at her window as we drive off. 'Me too, and it's really nice taking it slow for a change. Normally, I'd be inviting her back to ours already. Not that I haven't thought about it but—'

'Can you stop off at this petrol station, please?' I yell at the driver, cutting Matt off. I don't need to hear that when I haven't had sex in five months. It feels like a lifetime; I can barely walk past the underwear window displays in Marks and Spencer without getting a semi. I nip into the garage and buy some crisps and a sandwich I don't really want before returning to the taxi. I'll save them for lunch tomorrow.

I finally crawl into bed at midnight and as usual, my mind is racing. However, among the typical bullshit, there's one image that, no matter how hard I try, I can't seem to shake – and it's Sarah in that black dress.

CHAPTER ELEVEN

'Ice skating is romantic, right?'

I wipe the Guinness froth from my lip and furrow my brow. We're at the local pub – our weekly Sunday afternoon ritual. It started with rugby season at uni, but we never really stopped, even after we moved to London. When we both worked at Kensington Fox, we didn't see much of each other in the evenings, so our Sundays were pretty sacred. Granted, Matt now has to buy both rounds, and I have to sprint to the grotto for our 2pm opening, but it's still the highlight of my week.

Our pub conversations have gotten decidedly more Mills & Boon since Matt started dating Sarah. Gone are the days of who shagged who at the union karaoke night or complaining about Harriet using a fork to chip off whatever monstrosity she had accidentally fused to one of Matt's decent non-stick frying pans.

'Ice skating? Yeah,' I reply. 'Well, unless you're Tonya Harding.'

'I mean for a date. It's romantic, isn't it? Classy.'

'Yep. Totally. Nothing screams romance quite like public humiliation and a bruised arse.'

He frowns. 'But you see it all the time in movies. Couples holding hands while they skate, kids playing, catching the other person, snow falling and all that shit—'

'Matt, if you want to take me ice skating, just ask. This is getting embarrassing.'

'Shut up. I just don't want to suggest it to Sarah if it's a lame idea. I suggested bowling last week and she wasn't particularly keen.'

I smirk. 'Probably because she's not twelve.'

'I just wanted to find something that Alfie could do with us—'

'Look, I'm sure she'll like this idea, and unlike me, you can actually skate, so there's that . . . just don't do all that fancy speed skating crap. It's very unnerving.'

'Noted,' he replies, pulling out his phone. 'Though my parents will be very disappointed that all those summers in ice hockey camp are going to waste. I'll see what she says.'

I sit quietly while he texts Sarah, briefly imagining a life where your parents could afford to send you to summer camp. My mum could barely afford to send me to swimming lessons.

Once finished, he puts his phone on the table and takes a sip of his drink. 'Sarah says hi.'

'Nice. Is she up for frozen water and sharp blades whizzing past her small child?'

'She is indeed,' he replies, happily. 'We're going Saturday night. And you're coming with us.'

'No chance.' I laugh. 'You can flutter those lashes at me all you like, the answer is no.'

'Oh, come on! It'll be fun,' he persists. 'After all the help I've given you this year, chucking on some skates is the least you can do.'

'Actually, the least I could do is Amazon Prime and a calzone.'

'I'm taking that as a yes, then.'

'Fine,' I concede as his increasingly annoying little face grins back at me. 'You know, I've never seen you put this much effort in with any other woman.'

'She's not just any other woman though.' He takes a sip of his pint. 'I haven't felt this way about anyone since . . . well, you know . . . and it's all down to you.'

'It is, isn't it? I'm like the hero you never knew you needed.'

'Well, I wouldn't go that—'

'Your knight in shining loafers.'

He rolls his eyes. 'I'm trying to say thank you here! You're a good friend, Nick. Though technically you're my knight in scuffed Nikes. You definitely can't pull off loafers.'

I laugh and hold my hands up. 'Alright! Seriously though, I'm really happy it's working out with Sarah.'

'Cheers, mate.'

'But if for some reason it doesn't stick, I think I should choose all your future girlfriends. I obviously have a knack for this shit.'

He nods but the look on his face tells me that my services might not be required for a very long time, if ever again.

'This is a horrible idea,' I tell Matt for the third time as we reach Hyde Park. 'Couldn't you have just taken her to the cinema like a normal, unimaginative boyfriend? Or sit in and watch TV?'

'It'll be fun. We'll grab a hot dog, do some skating—'

'You know I'm shit at skating. My balance is questionable on dry land at the best of times. I'm going to look like fucking Bambi.'

'You'll be fine; stop being such a pussy. It's ice skating, not tightrope walking, no one cares what you look like. There's Sarah and Alfie, hurry up.'

I curse him under my breath as we approach them, plastering on a smile so that Alfie doesn't see just how unhappy I am with this entire situation. The last time I went ice skating was on a school trip in 1999 and I fell so often I was forced to go around the rink holding the teacher's hand. That's enough ice-based humiliation to last a lifetime.

Alfie waves enthusiastically, obviously having the best

time before we've even begun. I smile as I notice that both Sarah and Alfie are wearing matching monkey hats; it's rather charming.

'That was good timing,' Sarah says, leaning in to kiss Matt. 'We've just arrived. I think half of London is here already. Doesn't it look amazing though?'

She's right. The park is brightly lit as far as the eye can see, and buzzing with fairground rides, markets, food stalls and, of course, the ice rink. Just hundreds of people with weapons for shoes, sliding dangerously close to each other. Fricking magical. My stomach drops at the thought of it. I'd rather bungee jump off the side of the big wheel.

'Have you been skating before, Alfie?' Matt asks as we stroll through the fairy light walkway.

'Yes,' he replies, swinging his mum's hand. 'We went to Buckingham Palace. Mum fell a lot.'

'*Alexandra* Palace,' Sarah corrects. 'But the other part is entirely true. I was frequently horizontal. Thankfully, his friend's mum was there to take over while I stuck to the side.'

'Looks like you and Nick will have something in common then,' Matt replies, laughing. God, he's such a dick sometimes.

Sarah turns around to face me. 'You can't skate either?'

I shake my head. 'Like a newborn calf,' I inform her. 'Luckily, Matt is proficient in both skating and taking the piss out of me.'

'Oh, thank God,' she replies. 'I thought I was going to be the only one looking like a halfwit. We can clamber around together, while this pair show us how it's done. Give Alfie one of those little penguin Zimmer frame things and he's off like a shot.'

Knowing that I might not be the only loser out there, I suddenly start to feel better. If Sarah is willing to make a tit of herself, then so am I.

As the speakers blast out some obscure disco track from the eighties, we place our shoes in a locker before strapping ourselves into our boots and attempting to stand upright. It's been over twenty years since I last put a pair of these on, but I haven't forgotten how awkward they make me feel. Sarah wobbles beside Matt before grabbing his arm. He may not be twirling her around in the air exactly, but it's pretty romantic all the same.

Alfie, unsteady and swaying, stomps towards the edge of the rink, desperate to get on the ice, while Sarah yells for him to slow down and wait. He's a hundred times more fearless than me, which is rather embarrassing. I need to get a grip here. Literally.

I finally hobble out on to the ice and immediately grab the side to steady myself. Under the twinkling canopy, 'Dancing Queen' blasts from the sound system, almost drowned out by the skaters who are having a whale of a time. I spot my first faller. Then another, and finally another who takes her mate down with her. They both sit on the ice, laughing too much to successfully get up.

Alfie has nabbed a penguin and is skating happily beside Matt, while Sarah props up the barrier beside me.

'Matt's really good, isn't he?' she remarks as he skates backwards, helping a rosy-faced Alfie along.

'Yeah, he's been skating for years,' I reply as her eyes follow them around the rink. 'Listen, don't feel you have to stay here with me. Go and join them.'

She nods. 'I will in a minute. Once my feet start moving in the same direction.'

I tentatively let go for a moment but regret it instantly. I start to laugh from frustration and/or paralysing fear.

'GAH! This is ridiculous,' I exclaim. 'I abseiled down a fucking building at uni! Why is this so daunting?'

Sarah starts to laugh too. 'I have no idea. It's like, I know what falling feels like, I've done it before . . . there's no big mystery here . . . look, that guy just tumbled and he's about five years away from a nursing home. God, I'm such a wuss.'

Matt and Alfie disappear into the crowd, leaving us to battle our fears alone. Sarah is the first one to break.

'Right. Let's just go for it.'

I grimace. 'What? Like just go? Skate? Out there?'

'Yep. Balls to the wall. Arse to the floor. What's the worst that can happen?'

'People point and laugh at us and then we end up on YouTube where more people will point and—'

'Jesus, you're overthinking this way too much. We're doing it.'

I hesitate but she holds out her gloved hand.

'We're going to look ridiculous; you realise that?' I say, giving the rink one last cursory glance.

She nods. 'Yep . . . but I will if you will?'

I take her hand and let go of the side, feeling an immediate burst of embarrassment as we try to glide as gracefully as possible. I put my left hand out to the side for balance, my arse clenching itself for dear life.

'Left . . . right . . . left . . . right . . .' I hear Sarah say quietly to herself, ignoring the more experienced skaters zipping around us. 'Um, Nick, you actually have to move your legs, I can't just drag you.'

'You're the only reason I'm upright, let's not ruin the moment.'

Staying close to the side, we continue around the rink, giggling manically at every close call or surprise yelp which escapes from my mouth.

'Mum! Look at me!'

Sarah removes her hand from mine as Alfie pulls up alongside us, showing off his penguin skills.

'Wow, you're doing it!' Matt says, skating haphazardly beside me. 'Good job, mate, *face those fears* . . .'

'Get away from me, Jayne Torvill, you're making me nervous.'

He playfully kisses Sarah before whizzing behind me. 'Just bend your knees a bit more and no ... you need to ... Nick—'

I'm going down. Arms like windmills as I veer right and smack into the barrier, my legs desperately trying to regain traction on the ice, but failing miserably.

'Timber!' yells some douchebag in a striped scarf, while Matt tries to help me up.

'One fall down,' I say, brushing my jeans off, 'sixty-five to go.'

'If you feel like you're going to fall, lean forward and put your hands out to the front,' a voice says from behind me. 'Try and relax into it.'

I turn to see a redheaded woman wearing a blue bobble hat standing at the barrier beside me. She smiles, zipping up her jacket. 'Sorry, I didn't mean to intrude, I'm actually one of the guides and—'

'Nick,' Matt says on my behalf, pushing me forward slightly. 'This is Nick.'

'Juliette.'

'Hey,' I reply, still latched on to the barrier. 'Thanks for the tip, I'm sure it will come in useful in about ... oh, three minutes.'

She laughs. 'First time skating?'

'Pretty much,' I reply as Matt slowly creeps away to

be with Sarah and Alfie. 'Definitely my last. You do this torture for a living?'

'I do. Just finished a lesson. Newbies are my speciality.'

Without warning, I wobble again, and she laughs. 'There's no way I can leave you like this. We need to march.'

Within minutes, Juliette has me marching on the ice to improve my balance, teaching me how to get up when I fall and even getting down on the ice with me when I hit the deck. Finally, I manage to glide for more than ten seconds and she audibly cheers.

'Yes! Go on, your bad self!'

'Don't jinx it,' I say, grinning. 'But this is amazing, thank you.'

'My pleasure,' she replies, leading me back towards the barrier. 'You might be a little sore tomorrow, but you did so well! You're a quick learner.'

'You're a damn champion,' I say bashfully. 'You have my undying gratitude. You didn't have to waste your time with me.'

She smiles coyly. 'Actually, I saw you when you came in. I was just picking my moment to say hello . . .'

'I wish it had been a cooler moment.'

She laughs. 'The sessions are only fifty minutes. I had to work quick.'

I like her laugh. It's almost melodic.

'Anyway, I need to shoot off,' she tells me, 'but I could

give you my number . . . you know, in case you have any skating questions or . . .'

'I will absolutely have skating questions,' I reply, my phone practically leaping from my pocket into my hand. She takes it and dials herself.

'And now I have yours. Nice to meet you, Nick. Hopefully speak to you soon.'

I watch her perfectly pert arse skate off before taking a breather off the rink, feeling rather chuffed with myself. Tonight has been far more entertaining than I expected. I decide to change back into my shoes before I can be dragged back on to the ice, but Matt has the locker key.

Scanning the crowd, I soon spot Sarah near the bandstand, holding on to Alfie's penguin while Matt shows off, making both of them laugh. As Alfie commandeers his penguin again, Matt swoops in and kisses Sarah. This is what Matt was talking about – movie romance. I always thought the soppy stuff we were sold in films was bullshit, yet here it is, playing out right in front of me. It's bloody magical; Matt and Sarah alone standing perfectly still, as everyone around them races forward, blurry figures squealing and laughing.

Watching the two of them together makes my heart ache just a little. The feeling catches me off-guard; I should be happy for them. Hell, I should be bloody triumphant – this is exactly what I wanted. Sarah is happy, Alfie's Christmas wish has been granted. So why do I feel so fucking melancholy? Sure, it stings a little to be around such a happy couple after being dumped but, even when we were at our happiest, I never looked at Ange the way Matt and Sarah are looking at each other right now. Jesus, I need to cheer the fuck up and stop being a self-obsessed twat.

As a bell announces the end of the session, I slap a smile on my face and wave them over, more than ready to get these skates off my feet.

'Where's your teacher friend?' Sarah asks, looking around. 'I was going to get her number for Alfie.'

'She had to go,' I reply. 'Though I can give you her number . . .'

'Outstanding work, sir,' Matt says, grinning. 'Top marks.'

Alfie tugs on my sleeve. 'Nick, Mum fell on her bum and swore.'

Sarah smiles and throws Alfie a *stop snitching on your mother* look. 'I could use a drink. Shall we?'

We all agree and make our way back to the changing area before heading into the main section of Winter Wonderland. Alfie drags Matt straight towards the popcorn stand, while Sarah and I grab some drinks and get a table.

'She seemed nice,' Sarah mentions, sipping her lager. 'Really pretty. Good for you.'

'I wouldn't get overly excited,' I reply. 'Number one, she has no idea what I do for a living yet, and number two: see number one.'

Sarah rolls her eyes. 'Not every woman is as shallow as your ex. She'd be lucky to date you.'

I thank Sarah for the compliment, but as I text Juliette the following day, it's still playing on my mind. While it might not bother Sarah, who is decidedly good-natured and non-judgemental, I still fear that the majority of women aren't as generous as she is. I decide the best course of action is to be upfront and save everyone time.

I text her:

Would love to take you for a drink soon but you should know that I'm an out-of-work lawyer, currently employed as Santa in a local shopping centre. This is obviously not a long-term position and I intend to be employed again in the corporate sector as soon as possible.

Then quickly delete it. But instead opt for:

I currently work as this guy 🎅 in a shopping mall. It's not cool or well-paid, but if you're still up for it, would love to take you for a drink.

She replies twenty minutes later:

Would love to. Just leave the sleigh at home.

CHAPTER TWELVE

Three nights later, I meet up with Juliette again at a new Portuguese place in Shoreditch that Matt recommended. It's cosy and rustically pretentious, with wooden-beamed ceilings and specials boards scribbled in a secret language even the waiters have trouble reading. She's a little late, so I grab myself a beer to calm my nerves.

Jesus, Nick, it's a date not a police interview. You're literally just having some food and a chat with another human being. Behave yourself.

I never used to get nervous on dates but the repeated battering my confidence has sustained recently seems to have taken a toll.

Juliette finally arrives, ten minutes late but looking just as pretty as I remembered, only this time her red hair is down; it's extremely wavy when it's not hidden under a bobble hat.

'Glad you could make it,' I say, rising to meet her. 'You look nice.'

'Thanks, you too. Sorry I'm a bit late.'

She sits at the table and takes off her coat, while the waiter asks what she'd like to drink.

'White wine spritzer,' she replies, 'cucumber, not orange, thanks.'

She takes out her phone and quickly checks her mascara on her camera.

'God, that rain is coming down in buckets,' she says. 'Thought I'd look like a panda by now.'

'Don't worry, you look great. How's your day been?'

'Good,' she replies, still flicking her lashes against her finger. 'Busy time of the year, so it's hectic most days.'

I grin. 'I feel you. I must have seen over a hundred kids today.'

'So, you're really Santa? I wasn't sure whether you were messing with me or not!' She picks up the menu and starts browsing. 'I thought those jobs were exclusively for retired grandpas with too much time on their hands!'

'Yeah, I thought so too,' I reply, my stomach growling over the menu. I'm starving. I haven't eaten anything since my last selection box of the day. 'But here I am. I probably wasn't their first choice . . . I think I'll get the chicken. Do you want to get a sharing platter to start?'

'I don't really have a huge appetite,' she says. 'I'll just have the gnocchi, but get what you want!'

I want the sharing platter.

'No, I'm good with just a main,' I respond, deciding that watching me pig out on a first date might not be the best look.

'So, was that your friend's little boy at the ice rink?' she asks, diving into the breadbasket. 'He was cute.'

I nod. 'Yeah, that was Alfie, Sarah's kid. He's great.'

She smiles. 'Do you have any kids?'

I dip my bread into some herby-looking oil. 'Not that I know of! You?'

'Me! God no,' she replies, wide-eyed, like I've just asked her if she supports Trump. 'Heaven forbid. I mean, I like them ... I teach them ... my sister has them ... but I have no intention of making them. I think I'm too selfish, you know.'

'Right ... yeah, it's not for every ...' My words trail off as I watch her lift her knife and check her teeth for food. That's a new one.

'Life's just complicated enough, you know what I mean,' she continues, holding her knife at a better angle to see her incisors. 'I still have so much I want to do.'

Maybe my first date etiquette is a little rusty but I'm almost certain this is a conversation better placed for date three or four ... Christ, after we have eaten, at least. She sees the look of uncertainty on my face.

'God, here I go again,' she says, wincing. 'My friend Clodagh advised me to reel it in a little on dates. She's all, "*Jules, I love you, but you need to lighten the fuck up! It's not a fact-finding expedition, it's just dinner"*, and here I am asking about kids right off the bat.'

I laugh. 'Sometimes it's good to lay your cards on the table. I mean, some things are just deal-breakers, right?'

She smiles. 'Like what? What's a big no-no for you?'

As the waiter places our food on the table, I consider my reply. Do I have any deal-breakers? There must be something . . .

'I dunno . . . the usual: racism, bigotry, not having a starter . . .'

She laughs. 'Dammit.'

'I'm willing to forgive a lot for the right person. Well, except the racism part, obviously.'

She stabs her fork into her gnocchi. 'You seem far easier going than I am. This is probably why I'm single.'

I smirk. 'Is this your way of telling me how high-mainte-nance you are? OK – go on. What's non-negotiable for you?'

By the end of our first and only course, I learn that *not only* does Juliette not want kids, she also doesn't want: marriage, Brexit, a traditional funeral, a shared bathroom, a postman who delivers her mail after 9 am or black pepper on her gnocchi. I think she also mentioned some-thing about dry fasting, but the crunching sounds from my breadstick inadvertently drowned her out.

'I admire your honesty,' I tell her. 'I have to admit, if I'm being serious, the marriage and kids part – I think that's my deal-breaker . . .'

Until recently I hadn't really given it a huge amount of thought; I think I just assumed it would happen further down the line. But now my friends all seem to be settling down: Greta is getting married, Harriet is pregnant, and seeing Matt with Sarah and Alfie at the ice rink, it's hard not to want that for myself. I'd be lying if I said I didn't.

She nods. 'See. Better to get it out of the way. Now we can just have sex and not worry about where this is going.'

I cough into my beer and she laughs.

'I'm kidding. Just trying to lighten the mood.'

'Shame,' I reply. 'Mutual promiscuity is definitely not a deal breaker for me.'

Briefly, as she smiles at me, I wonder if maybe marriage and kids isn't really all it's cracked up to be.

'Dessert?'

'I thought you weren't that hungry,' I respond, our eyes now firmly fixed on each other.

'I'm not . . .'

I signal to the waiter for the bill.

After a mini pub crawl featuring three of the many bars between the tube station and home, I do my best to sneak Juliette into the flat as quietly as possible. This isn't the time for small talk; I don't want to risk Matt thinking one of his terrible dad jokes will make this more fun for everyone. The first night I brought Angela home, he threw open the living room door, yelling 'WHAT TIME DO YOU CALL THIS?' and almost gave her a heart attack.

The flat is dark and for a moment I think Matt might still be out with Sarah until I spot her long black boots in the hall and a chink of soft light from underneath his bedroom door. I relax a little. If she's here, he shouldn't be appearing anytime soon.

The moment my bedroom door closes behind me, Juliette pins me up against it, launching a blitz attack on my face. Stunned for a second, I let this happen before my brain kicks into action and reminds me that this is the part where we remove clothes as quickly as possible, before someone says something stupid and ruins it all. She wriggles out of her trousers while my hands begin twisting open the buttons on her shirt.

We move from the door, our faces still locked together as she leans back on to the bed, pulling me down on top of her. My hand slides up her thigh, while she starts undoing my belt.

'Fuck,' I breathe. 'You sure you want to—'

'Definitely,' she replies, tugging at the waistband on my jeans. 'Take them off.'

Within seconds her knickers are on the floor and her hand is inside my boxers, making me groan a little louder than I planned to.

'You like that?' she asks, my underwear now firmly round my ankles. 'What if I do this?'

I nod as her left hand joins in. I swear if her mouth gets involved it might be game over before it's even begun.

Fuck's sake, Nick. Five months without sex does not mean this has to be over in five seconds. Pace yourself.

Thankfully, she's more than happy to let me concentrate on her for a while, but she completely ruins my plan to quietly go about this. By the time we finish, Matt and Sarah are definitely aware she's here, as is half of London. I shouldn't complain though; she made me sound like a damn rock star.

'I could use some water,' she says as we lie there afterwards, panting like dogs.

I grin and reach down for my boxers. 'Be right back.'

I creep through the living room and into the kitchen, feeling extremely pleased with myself, before almost jumping out of my skin.

'Fucking-fuck! You scared the shit out of me.'

Sarah's eyes widen as she briefly scans my half-naked body. I feel myself blush deep crimson.

'Sorry! Just getting a drink.' She closes the cupboard quietly, holding a glass in front of her.

She's wearing Matt's T-shirt. It looks better on her. It looks freaking incredible on her.

I gulp and attempt to speak normally, as though we aren't both standing half-naked in front of one another.

'Same. Can you grab me another couple of glasses?' I manage weakly.

She nods and turns to the cupboard, while I run the cold tap. As she reaches on tiptoes for the glasses, the T-shirt starts to creep higher. *Oh dear God.* I look away quickly and carefully study the ceiling until she turns to hand me the tumblers, the T-shirt a safe length once again.

'Skating instructor?' she mouths.

I nod, awkwardly rubbing the back of my neck as I fill the glasses. She takes one and smiles. 'I'll leave you to it.'

I give her a second to get into Matt's room before returning to my own. Juliette is already dressed.

'Wow. OK,' I say, watching her zip up her boots. 'You're welcome to stay, you know.'

She takes a glass and downs the water in one. 'I don't do sleepovers,' she replies, handing me the glass back. 'Besides, I have an early start.'

Lifting her jacket from the floor, she kisses me. 'It's been fun, Nick. I'll see myself out.'

As the front door slams behind her, I finish my water before slipping back into bed. A few minutes later, the silence is broken by Sarah and Matt laughing in his room and I can't help feeling a little deflated, lying in my empty bed. I want someone to wear my damn T-shirt.

CHAPTER THIRTEEN

The closer it gets to Christmas, the busier the grotto becomes, with Geraldine employing another elf to help Izzy out. Laura is a pretty, yet annoyingly upbeat PhD student who, unlike Izzy and I, finds this whole experience a hoot. Her desire to be as silly as possible is enchanting for the children but utterly irritating for everyone else. However, I do feel slightly relieved that Izzy's animosity is now almost entirely directed at her instead of me.

'They don't have penguins in the North Pole, do they?' Laura questions, lifting the one stuffed toy which refuses to stay upright. 'Like, it's just polar bears, I think.'

'It's make-believe,' Izzy snarls. 'Why you care? Just keep doing the squeaky elf voice and we get along, OK?'

As she stomps to the front of the grotto, I hear Laura mumble, 'That's my real voice.'

I tell her just to ignore Izzy and she laughs. 'Oh, she doesn't bother me,' she squeaks. 'Not really. I'm just here for the extra cash. I'm two years from finishing my postgrad in criminology; she's good practice for the socio-paths I'm bound to encounter after I graduate.'

While the thought of her squeaking at hardened crimi-nals amuses me, I suddenly feel quite old and useless. She's just at the start of her career and I'm most certainly at the end of mine, playing Santa for rent money instead of using the degree I slaved for. Seeing my student loan taken out of my Santa pay cheques every week might be the most depressing thing I've ever seen. I defeatedly take my place on my throne as Izzy ushers in the first of many kids.

The growing number of visitors also means that the grotto now opens two hours earlier. Thankfully, to com-pensate, I've been given a lunch break, complete with a twenty per cent food court employee discount. I am officially part of the Southview Shopping Centre family. Yay, me.

'Please don't wear your uniform during lunch,' Geral-dine insisted, handing me my swipe card. 'Santa doesn't stop off for Big Macs or Wagamama while he's working. You don't want to be besieged by children while you eat, and I don't want to be hearing complaints from parents about food stains on your costume. It's happened before.'

I agree and go into the staffroom to change into my own clothes before I meet a smiling Sarah, who's waiting for me by the calendar stand. She picks up one and scans the back cover carefully.

'It's December. You're welcome.'

'Photoshopped photos of cows drinking beer,' she says, her nose wrinkled with loathing. 'What a time to be alive. Puts me in the mood for burgers though. You ready to eat?'

Hanging out with Sarah at work has now become a regular occurrence. First it was the odd coffee between shifts but now we've progressed to lunch, although I'm pretty sure my employee discount was a deciding factor. She's not employed directly by Southview so has to pay normal prices like everyone else.

Yesterday we ate noodles at the slightly grubby Thai place and today it seems we're getting burgers. It's nice to be able to hold a decent conversation with the woman Matt is seeing for once. His usual types are sullen, snooty and unlikely to laugh at my jokes, but Sarah is really easy-going. Our lunches make my days here a little more bearable.

'You didn't have to do the dishes at mine the other night,' she said, shaking a little packet of salt for her fries. 'I appreciate it but you're not the hired help.'

'Don't be daft. Alfie fell asleep pretty early and I was washing my mug anyway.' This time Sarah and Matt went to the new cocktail and steak place at Piccadilly. Between dating Matt and my food court discount, Sarah's food bill must be a fraction of what it was when we first met.

'It makes me just a little uncomfortable.' She laughs. 'Like you think I'm not keeping a clean house for Alfie or something.'

Her face looks just a little strained as she says this, and I can tell she isn't really joking. It's as if she's worried that I think she's a crappy parent. Nothing could be further from the truth.

'My mum raised me by herself,' I say, nicking one of her chips. 'She also hated accepting help. It was like she refused to rely on anyone because she knew they'd inevitably let her down.'

'Ah, so you're a mummy's boy, huh?'

'Yeah, guilty as charged,' I reply quickly with a smile, not wanting to get into a discussion about my mum over a lukewarm Burger King. 'All I'm saying is, I did her dishes too. Sometimes it's just nice to have a hand.'

Sarah smiles and pinches the pickle I've removed from my burger. 'You're a good guy, Nick. I can see why Matt thinks so highly of you. You know, I'm so glad we met.'

'I'm glad you guys met too,' I reply, my phone vibrating on the table beside me. I swipe it open to see a new message. 'I knew that you two would—'

'No, *you*, silly!' She swats my arm. 'I'm so glad I met *you*.'

As I look up from my phone, our eyes lock and just for a moment, neither of us look away, her smile slowly fading to something more confusing.

'Matt,' I say, holding up my phone. 'It's Matt.'

As she breaks my gaze, the world begins moving around us again. That was weird.

'Right, yes,' she says, clearing her throat. 'Do you need to call him or . . .'

'Nah, it's just dad stuff. I used the last of the milk apparently and should therefore replace it. And he wants me to use my discount to pick up a few dozen six-packs of beer. How he sees me getting on to the bus with that, I don't know . . .'

'Ah, for the big birthday bash, right?' she asks. 'He mentioned it the other day.'

'Yup. One every year. Can you make it to the party?'

She scrunches up her face. 'I mean, I can but . . .'

'What?'

'The thought of meeting all his friends at once is a bit . . . you know . . . yikes.'

I nod. 'Understandable. They're all terrible individuals. Right-wingers, Audi drivers and people who ask to speak to the manager on a daily basis.'

The look on her face makes me regret my last statement. 'I'm kidding! They're great. Mostly. I'll shut up now.'

'Are you bringing your skater girl? She seemed fun. We could hide in the bathroom together.'

She doesn't do shared bathrooms, I think, smiling to myself. 'Afraid not. I think that was just a one-off. A really fun one-off.'

Sarah sees my brazen grin and laughs.

'Ah . . . the curse of the one-night stand. Never mind,

plenty more fish in the sea ... or reality stars in the *Big Brother* house ...'

'I *knew* Matt would let that slip,' I groan. 'He's such a bloody gossip.'

'I think it's brilliant! I had no idea who she was, but Google tells me she's twenty-five, from Essex, swears by colonics and hates Santa.'

I start to laugh. 'That's nonsense – well, the age part, anyway; she's twenty-nine. I'd rather not slag her off though ... she has a decent heart under all that fake tan.'

'A true gentleman,' Sarah replies, looking at me thoughtfully. She glances at her watch. 'Shit, I need to get back to work. You can finish my fries.'

Sarah pushes her chair out and grabs her bag from the floor. 'Don't forget the milk!' she calls over her shoulder.

The rest of the week flies by, with Izzy in a surprisingly good mood as her boyfriend Antonio is flying over from Madrid for Christmas.

'How long have you been together?' I ask, fluffing up my beard.

'Two years,' she replies. 'He must finish his degree at UCM and then he will live here with me.'

'So, you left him all alone in Spain to come here and be a minimum-wage elf?'

I feel her eye-daggers pierce my face. 'I no just elf. I do little jobs like this between gigs.'

'Gigs?'

'Yes, Mister Nosy, I play violin. I am session musician.'

'I didn't mean to be insulting,' I reply, feeling more than a little embarrassed. 'I was trying to be funny. You play violin? That's amazing.'

'I know,' she agrees. 'But musicians are not rich. We must also eat. Just like you . . . well, maybe not so much as you . . .'

'Well, I hope you have a great time when Antonio arrives,' I say, now feeling like a podgy idiot. 'You must be excited.'

'Very excited,' she says, almost breaking into a smile. 'Christmas is no good alone, you know? You are, how do you say . . . *un fracaso* . . . a failure.'

'Right,' I reply, unsure if that's a dig at my current single status. 'We should probably open up now . . .'

She nods and walks over to the front of the queue where a small boy is kicking the shit out of a plastic polar bear.

I'm happy to see Sarah at lunchtime. We grab a table at the new pancake stack place on her recommendation and I tell her about my faux pas with Izzy.

'I didn't mean to imply she was just an elf,' I say as we take our seats. 'God, she must think I'm a twat. She plays the violin and speaks two languages. I can barely speak one and have no musical ability whatsoever.'

'Three.'

'Three what?'

'Languages,' Sarah replies. 'We have a Parisian barista. Izzy chats to her in French when she comes in.'

'I've never felt less impressive.'

'Oh, I don't know,' Sarah replies, laughing. 'I hear you do a good Scabby the cat voice. That's noteworthy.'

'I appreciate the support, but I think I'm just going to eat myself to death. Can you overdose on pancakes?'

'Definitely. I brought Alfie here last week,' she states, browsing her menu. 'You'll be happy to hear the spicy chicken ones are to die for.'

I frown at the menu. 'No offence, but who the fuck eats pancakes with chicken? Or steak, for that matter? I think I'll stick to the sweet ones. Nutella for me.'

She grins and rolls her eyes. 'I eat them, and you will try them and like them.'

'Oh really?'

'Yes,' she replies. 'And in return you'll give me some of your chocolate ones because it's only fair.'

I chuckle. 'Are you this bossy with Matt? Do you make him eat weird food combinations too?'

She thinks for a moment. 'Nope. But he's a bit of a fussy eater, isn't he?'

'I know!' I reply, laughing. 'He cooks like a professional, but he'll order a plain burger and then add his own ketchup in case they do it wrong. Or he'll be personally offended if there's broccoli anywhere in his meal.'

She grins widely. 'See, this is why you're perfect! You know him so well. You can help me.'

'Help with what?'

'Matt's birthday present! Alfie is getting dropped off here after work and we're going shopping. You *have* to come and help me choose something; I'm at a loss.'

'Hmm, I'm not sure I'd be that much help,' I inform her. 'I mean, we don't even buy each other presents.'

'You're kidding?'

'No! It's just not something that guys do. Same with Christmas presents. We just do food or go out for drinks.'

Sarah waves over the waitress to let her know we're ready to order. 'Well, that's ridiculous and depressing, but it still doesn't exempt you. Come on . . . please? You'd be doing me a huge favour.'

'OK, fine. I'll change after work and meet you at the coffee shop.'

She gives an excited squeal and orders lunch. Turns out spicy chicken pancakes are delicious.

CHAPTER FOURTEEN

Southview Shopping Centre in the evening is an entirely different beast to the one I'm used to seeing during the day: very few children, lots of teenagers flirting with each other from twenty feet away and many flustered-looking adults who have obviously just come straight from the office. Everything is still as shiny and festive as ever, with a large pop-up Christmas market running the length of the ground floor which makes the entire area smell of roasted chestnuts.

After stashing my Santa costume in a locker, I change into my jeans and shirt and head to the café where Alfie and Sarah are already waiting. The thought of sharing my evening with them is a charming one.

'Nick!' Alfie yells, running directly into my legs. 'We're going to get a pretzel!'

'Hey, bud,' I reply, 'that sounds like a great idea, I'm starving.'

'Pretzel after shopping, sweetie,' Sarah reminds him.

'Hey, Nick. Thanks so much for this – you're a lifesaver. If I can sort Matt's birthday present tonight, then I can dash around and do some last-minute shopping for everyone else's Christmas presents tomorrow.'

'No worries,' I reply, running my hand through my hair. That hat makes it so damn flat by the end of my shift. 'Though you know you still have ten days before Christmas . . .'

'Yeah. Well, no; I'm going home to the Cotswolds for Christmas,' she replies as we walk towards the open market area. 'But Matt's doing dinner on the 21st before I go. All of us – present company included. I'm bringing the crackers.'

'Oh really? What if I'm busy?' I reply. 'What if I have a hot date that night?'

'Do you?'

'No.'

She smirks. 'I wish I knew someone I could hook you up with. Sadly, my friends are all taken . . . well, except Tamara but she's not your type.'

I snort. 'How do you know what my type is? I'm a deeply complex and surprising man.'

She grins. 'Obviously. But my intuition tells me that *gay as fuck* isn't what you'd normally go for.' She glances at Alfie to make sure he didn't see her mouth the F-word.

'How long are you away for?' I ask, feeling strangely sad

that I won't see her over Christmas. I'm getting so used to having her around.

'Back after New Year,' she replies. 'Gives Alfie a good break with his grandparents, and well, it gives me a rest too. My bed there has pillows made from clouds.'

I see her glance at Alfie who is three steps ahead, humming quietly to himself.

'I love him very much, but ... you know. It's a lot sometimes.'

I can't even begin to imagine what it's like trying to bring up a child who has lost his dad while you're trying to grieve at the same time. I never knew my dad, but I know my mum struggled, even though she hid it well. I want to tell Sarah that I'm sorry for what she's going through, but I'm also sure that she doesn't need my pity.

'A wallet,' I say, shifting the focus. 'Matt needs a new wallet.'

She scrunches up her face at the suggestion.

'Ugh, that's so boring, no? Like getting socks or something. It's just so ... practical.'

I raise my hand to object. 'I happen to know that he once received a wallet for his birthday, and he adored it. Showed it off to everyone. He still uses it and it's falling apart, so therefore he needs a new one. I rest my case.'

She still doesn't look convinced. 'Really?'

I nod, refraining from telling her that his last wallet was from the only woman alive who has ever broken his heart.

Alfie stops at the pretzel stand and throws his mum a *pleeaassee* look with those big puppy dog eyes of his. She smiles. 'OK, but then we shop. Deal?'

'Deal.'

To his credit, Alfie keeps his word. After wolfing down a cheese pretzel, he happily tags along while Sarah chooses a black leather wallet for Matt and a birthday card which simply reads:

Congrats on getting a card when I could have just texted you!

'I don't want to get all mushy,' she explains before I've even mentioned it. 'Early days . . . you know? Should I get him some booze as well?'

I smile. 'There was no judgement. You are an insufferably good person. Get him some spiced rum, or something else I can steal and demolish when he's not looking.'

Sarah stops to buy a hand-knitted scarf for her mum's Christmas present from Alfie, who is now focused on persuading his mum to buy him hot chocolate.

'Why don't I take him for one?' I suggest as she pays the stallholder. 'You'll get around the shops faster without us tagging along.'

'What a good hubby,' the stallholder remarks. 'I'd hold on to that one, love.'

Both Sarah and I turn bright red, awkwardly informing her that we're not a couple, while I take Alfie by the hand and mutter that I'll meet Sarah at the coffee shop when she's done.

As we near the grotto, I feel Alfie pull me to a stop.

'I need to see Santa again,' he insists with the same look of desperation I saw the first time we met. He looks so adorable in his Rudolph jumper. I wonder if they make it my size.

'Um, the grotto is closed, buddy,' I reply. 'Even Santa has to sleep.'

'But I need to thank him,' he grumbles, shifting from foot to foot. 'My wish came true. My mum is happy again!'

I'm not sure my heart can stand any more cuteness from this kid, whose current need to thank Santa is outweighing his obvious need to pee, but I take a second to momentarily bask in my own success. However, a dull pang in my chest quickly begins to chip away at my smugness. I might have brought Matt and Sarah together but I'm still the same . . . still alone, instead of with someone great like—

I physically give myself a shake before I finish that sentence.

'How about we use the bathroom, get some hot chocolate and then maybe we can buy Santa a card to say thanks. I bet Santa would like that. I'll even hand-deliver it myself.'

Alfie agrees and we thankfully reach the bathroom before I have to buy him new trousers and underpants too.

I sip on my hot chocolate and watch Alfie clumsily write his thank-you card before slipping it into my back pocket, promising to deliver it tomorrow.

'Did you get your mum something for Christmas?' I ask, swirling around the chocolate dregs at the bottom of my cup.

'No,' he replies. 'She says she only needs hugs. They're free.'

'Hugs are good,' I respond, 'but I'm pretty sure we could team up and get her something cool from you to open on Christmas morning. What do you think she'd like?'

Alfie's eyes light up. 'She likes sausages!'

Dammit, why are you only four? I have about a million inappropriate jokes here. I bite my tongue.

'Hmm, they might go off by Christmas morning. Anything else?'

He thinks. 'Mum stuff. Candles, flowers, photos of me.'

My brain immediately springs into action. There's a passport photo booth beside the toilets and a stall where you can get photos made into key rings, mugs, T-shirts, etc. I stand up and hold out my hand.

'You ready to make your mum the best present ever? It's a super-secret mission though.'

'Yeah!'

I can't help but smile as I feel him slip his little hand into mine. I hope this works.

CHAPTER FIFTEEN

'Being born so close to Christmas must have been a real pisser for your parents,' I tell Matt as he pours some crisps into a bowl. 'I mean, the sheer cost of double presents alone. Kids are so expensive.'

He snorts. 'Listen to you, Supernanny. A few babysitting gigs and now you're an expert?'

I laugh. 'Well, that, and the fact that I've met about three hundred kids who want eighty-pound talking bears for Christmas.'

Matt checks his watch. 'Shit, everyone's due in twenty minutes. You sure we have enough beer? Maybe I should get more.'

Matt does this every year on his birthday: panics that there's not enough booze for his party guests, even though everyone brings at least two bottles with them. This year he seems a little more anxious than usual. I know why.

'We're good,' I reply, watching him open and close the

fridge nervously. 'You worried about everyone meeting Sarah?'

'No more worried than you are about seeing your old colleagues . . .'

'Fair point.'

I'm *dreading* it. I've barely seen anyone since I was fired. There are going to be questions. *Where have I been hiding? What happened with Angela? Where am I working now?*

'I swear, Matt, if you've told anyone that I'm Santa, you won't live to see thirty-two.'

He puts down the mixers and holds up his hands. 'I haven't. I promise. I'm the only one allowed to make fun of you. Well, and Sarah.'

'Sarah . . . shit, if she tells anyone about how she met me—'

'We'll say we came into her coffee shop. Bloody hell, mate, relax. I have to deal with everyone making jokes about my shady love life. I haven't exactly been forthcoming about my past. She's going to think I'm a player.'

The buzzer rings. Who the hell comes early to a house party? I open the door with my now sweaty hands and let the wolves in.

An hour later, all guests are present and correct, including Sarah who has been carefully briefed on the whole Santa situation, much to her amusement.

'Why do you give a fuck what anyone thinks?' she asks. 'I thought these people were your friends?'

I pass her a wine and look around. She has a good point. Apart from Greta and Harriet, my so-called friends haven't exactly been blowing up my phone to see how I'm doing.

'I'm telling everyone I'm working privately for a Dubai-based investor. Confidentiality means I don't have to go into detail.'

She playfully kicks me with her foot. 'I think your real job sounds far more fun.'

The leg attached to that foot is perfect. So is the other one. I have a flashback to her standing in the kitchen in Matt's T-shirt. *Whoa, Jesus, Nick, what the hell is wrong with you?* I set down my beer and reach for a can of Coke.

Sarah is looking incredible. I'm not the only one who has noticed either. I keep making awkward eye contact with Matt's friend Kevin, who blushes furiously every time I catch him looking at Sarah's arse.

'Well, um—'

'Sarah, have you met Gabby?' Matt shouts from the kitchen, gesturing for her to join him. 'Gabby, this is Sarah ... my ... eh, my girlfriend.'

Wow. That's the first time I've heard him use the G-word with her. And I was thinking about her arse until he interrupted. I need to get it together and sober the fuck up.

Sarah smiles, but I don't like the way it makes me feel. As she leaves to join them, I force myself to chat with everyone else in the vain hope that it might stop me thinking about how hot she looks. I'm obviously having some sort of early mid-life crisis.

I spy Noel sitting at the kitchen table and scurry across. A married man with a baby on the way is exactly what I need to get rid of this burgeoning horn.

'How are you?' I ask. 'Shame Harriet couldn't make it, is she holding up alright?'

He nods. 'She still has the old morning sickness. They said it should only last about ten weeks, yet she's still gagging into her handbag, all hours of the day. I'm not staying long, I just wanted to see the birthday boy and grab a beer.'

'Where the hell is Harry?!'

I turn to see Matt behind me, obviously three sheets to the wind and with no intention of stopping anytime soon.

'She's sick, mate,' Noel informs him. 'But she sends her love. Are you having a nice birthday?'

'I am!' he replies, reaching into the ice bucket for his next beer. 'I think it's time to crank up the music though. It's my birthday, not a fucking wake!'

We laugh as he staggers back to his other well-wishers. Thankfully, I've managed to bullshit almost everyone to the point where they've stopped asking me about my life, except for Kara, my bitchy old colleague who takes great pleasure in showing me an Instagram photo of Angela and some footballer with his hand on her arse. I guess things didn't work out with Pete from *Love Island*.

'These types go where the money is,' she slurs. 'You were a bit out of your league there, Nick. She'd never have settled for you.'

Settled for me? I take a long swig of my beer. 'Thanks for that, Kara. Say hi to your investment banker for me . . . and his wife . . .'

As I walk back into the living room, I hear her exclaim, 'HE'S LEAVING HER AFTER CHRISTMAS,' but she's soon drowned out by the music. I'm so done with this party, but, given that it's my flat, I can't leave. I could hide though.

Looking around to see whether I could slip into my room unnoticed, I spot Matt in the kitchen with Greta and Phillip something-or-other who joined the firm two days before I was sacked. Greta beckons me over and hands me an envelope.

'Thought I'd drop in your wedding invitation while I was here. March 21st. No excuses!'

'Wouldn't dream of it,' I say, kissing her on the cheek.

'Same goes for Matt. I want you both there, and his girlfriend if she hasn't dumped him by then.'

I laugh and look for Sarah, who's chatting to two women I met briefly earlier. Sarah looks like she's holding her own, but I can spot her fake smile a mile off. I excuse myself and make my way over.

'Sarah,' I say, rudely interrupting them. 'You promised me a dance.'

She excuses herself immediately and allows me to lead

her to the living room floor, where ninety per cent of the party are currently losing their shit to David Guetta.

'Thanks,' Sarah says, 'I was drowning there. Some of the people here ... well ...'

'No problem,' I reply. 'I've just been shown a pic of my ex with another guy's hand on her arse, so I'm ready for a break from the people here too.'

'Ouch,' she responds. 'That's not good. You OK?'

'Totally fine,' I lie. 'We'll just have to dance my troubles away. Though I haven't seen you dance yet, come to think of it ... I've seen Alfie, and he's like the Michael Flatley of four-year-olds, but it might not run in the family. I mean, I can't let my best mate date someone with no rhythm.'

She laughs and moves herself into the middle of the floor and begins drunk dancing like she's been uncaged. It's the greatest thing I've ever seen. I move in beside her and we spend the rest of the evening there, *Soul Train*-ing ourselves up and down the living room, along with everyone else. I try not to notice Sarah looking for Matt, and I try not to get annoyed at Matt for not spending every second he can with this amazing woman. She has no pretention, no self-conscious swagger, she's just her funny, beautiful self.

By the time my head hits the pillow at 4 am, I'm buzzing. I can't remember ever having so much fun with any of the women I've dated, or even my mates. Sarah makes me feel like everything will work out. Like everything will be OK ... but how can it be? Right now, my head is full of images on loop – Sarah in the grotto, scooping up Alfie; Sarah in the black dress; Sarah squealing as she skids around the ice rink; Sarah in Matt's T-shirt in my kitchen; Sarah smiling and holding my gaze for just a second too long over lunch; Sarah grinning and laughing as she dances rings around me in the living room. The woman I can't stop thinking about is in bed right now, asleep next to my best friend. This is all very fucking far from being OK.

CHAPTER SIXTEEN

I reluctantly surface at nine, to the sounds of Matt and Sarah giggling in the kitchen like teenagers. They must have had sex, there is no other scenario which explains why anyone would be this happy first thing. Thank God I slept through any humping noises. She's also wearing Matt's shirt again and if I were him, I'd never let her take it off.

'Morning, sunshine,' Matt says as I slump on to the couch. 'I was just about to wake you.'

I groan. 'Why the hell would you want to do that? I feel like death. Grotto doesn't open until twelve. Let me die in peace, please.'

'Breakfast,' Sarah chirps, like a woman who's impervious to alcohol. 'I have to pick Alfie up from his sleepover at half ten; I thought it would be nice if we all had breakfast first.'

I bury my head into the back of the couch. I'm not in the mood for this. I don't need someone to make me eggs

Benedict when I can just have toast like a normal person. God, eggs. I feel like I might throw up.

'Come on,' Matt insists, hitting me with a pillow. 'I'm buying.'

I grunt in agreement and trudge to the bathroom to wash my face. Being the hungover third wheel was not part of my Sunday plan.

We end up at The Bridge Bar and Grill, thankfully a short walk from our flat and the only place around here that doesn't have a menu filled with hand-raised avocados and free-range cutlery.

I settle for a double bacon bap and free coffee refills while Matt and Sarah order a breakfast platter to share. If they start feeding each other, I'm leaving.

'You're looking less green,' Sarah remarks as she dips a hash brown in ketchup. 'Feeling better?'

I nod. Maybe breakfast wasn't the worst idea in the world. It's amazing what a bit of grease can do.

'I'll survive. At least it's better than those breakfast monstrosities your excuse for a coffee shop sells.'

Sarah laughs. 'The breakfast wraps? I thought you liked them! Fine, next time I'll just bring you one of those weird bran muffin things.'

I make a face. 'Christ, no, the last thing Santa needs is flatulence.'

Matt's looking a tad lost. 'You guys have breakfast together?'

'I throw him a freebie every now and again,' Sarah replies, laughing. 'In exchange for his employee discount at the food court. To be honest, it's nice to have someone to hang out with.'

Matt smiles and continues eating his breakfast, but I can tell he's not exactly comfortable with the whole thing. Personally, I'd have played down our little meetups a bit more, but Sarah isn't secretly pining for me, so why should she?

'Did you see Greta's wedding invitation?' I ask, steering the conversation away. 'I left it on the hall table.'

He nods. 'She cornered me last night. Sarah's coming as my plus-one.'

'Too right,' Sarah asserts. 'It's at Claridge's. I can't even afford to have lunch there . . .'

'At least you have a plus-one!' I exclaim. 'I'm going to be that weird, solo guy who gets pity looks from the rest of the guests.'

'Angela still not returning your texts?'

I scowl at Matt. 'No, and I think that arse-grabbing photo means she's not likely to anytime this century.'

'So, find someone else,' Sarah suggests. 'You must know someone, Matt.'

Matt pauses chewing and gives me a subtle look of abject hopelessness. The only women he knows are either our good friends, the wives of friends, or women he's banged after too many sambucas.

'I'm sure Nick doesn't need my help to get a date,' he says. 'A haircut might help his case, though.'

'Nonsense,' Sarah declares, watching me self-consciously touch my locks. 'That mop of black hair is endearing as hell. It's very appealing.'

'Appalling, maybe,' Matt mumbles, appearing slightly miffed at her comment. Sarah also has very nice hair. I love the way her fringe falls to the side when she wears it up and how—

'Oh bollocks, I need to run,' she says, jolting me back to reality. 'Alfie's not that used to sleepovers yet, so I don't want to be late. Text me if I need to bring anything for Christmas dinner on Wednesday!'

She kisses Matt goodbye and waves at me as she dashes out the door.

Matt is quiet for a moment, casually sipping his coffee, but I can tell it's coming.

'So . . .'

'Yes?'

Here it comes.

'You guys hang out a lot then. You never said.'

I sigh. 'I totally have, you obviously haven't been listening.'

This is technically true. I did tell him that Sarah brought me a coffee. Once.

'What's going on?' I ask. 'I know you're not threatened by your best mate and part-time Santa Claus . . .'

He shakes his head and puts down his cup. 'Of course not, God, you're the reason we met. I just . . . well, I think I really like her. I just hope she feels the same. Is that weird?'

'Not weird, but you sound like a total virgin.'

He laughs. 'Fuck you, you wish you had a girlfriend as hot as Sarah.'

I laugh, a little uneasily, because he has no idea how right he is. 'So much hotter than you deserve.'

Matt stops laughing and sits silently for a second, looking a little glum.

'Christ, you're not pining already. She's probably not even in the Uber yet!'

'It's not that,' he replies. 'It's just . . .'

'What?'

'The wallet.'

'What about it?'

'It reminds me of the one Karen gave me and now I feel like shit for spending half of last night thinking about her.'

'Matt, she broke up with you years ago. Get a grip,' I respond, now thinking that I should be shot for suggesting the wallet.

'I know, I know . . . it's so stupid. Sarah is great.'

'Totally,' I concur.

'Perfect, really.'

'So, don't fuck it up. It's just a wallet.'

He bobs his head in agreement and motions for the bill.

CHAPTER SEVENTEEN

'Matt, if I knew you could cook Christmas dinner this well, I'd have insisted you make this at least twice a week. Can't believe you've kept this talent hidden all these years.'

Our early Christmas dinner is off to a flying start. Alfie has already pulled all the crackers and the *Greatest Christmas Songs Ever Volume 2* plays merrily throughout the flat, which for once isn't festively decorated like two uncoordinated, lazy men live there. Presents have been exchanged, we have a tinsel-covered tree, a laughing, animated Santa and a small boy who is loving every second of it. He whispered earlier that he'd hidden the photo key ring we bought under his mattress ready for Christmas morning. It's funny how that's instinctively the place boys choose to hide things from their mothers. I remind him to make sure he brings it to his grandparents' house.

Matt beams proudly before brushing it off as 'nothing', when in reality, he's outdone himself trying to impress his new girlfriend with his culinary skills. I think he even made his own damn gravy.

'So good,' Sarah agrees through a mouthful of glazed parsnips. 'I won't have to eat for a week!'

'Leave room for dessert,' Matt insists. 'I'm not the only chef in attendance this evening.'

'Chef is a bit of a reach,' I reply. 'It's just a trifle. Nothing fancy.'

'Trifle is Alfie's favourite pudding,' Sarah informs me while he nods enthusiastically.

'Then I think Alfie should get the first bowl.'

I take some dirty plates to the kitchen and open the fridge. Then I close the fridge.

'Alfie?'

'Yes?'

'What's your second favourite pudding?'

Seconds later everyone is in the kitchen, staring at my trifle. My soupy, unappetising, horror show of a trifle.

'Did you drop it?' Matt asks, poking the runny cream with a spoon. A lump of pineapple floats to the surface like a dead body. 'I've never seen anything like it.'

Sarah peers into the bowl for closer inspection. 'Let me guess . . . squirty canned cream and all of the juice from the canned fruit?'

I nod, watching Alfie disappointedly return to the living room in search of more crackers.

She grins. 'I've fucked up a few trifles in my time.'

Matt swirls around the unset jelly with his spoon. 'Kind of looks like he actually fucked it, though.'

Sarah snorts and I consider leaving the planet. I'm mortified. I had one job.

Matt sees my look of despair and slaps me on the back. 'Nothing that Tesco can't fix . . . Alfie! Put your shoes on, I need your help to save dinner, buddy!'

Alfie obliges, excitedly accepting his new mission, and heads to the shop with Matt, while Sarah and I start clearing the dinner plates.

'Well, that's embarrassing,' I mumble, draining the trifle goop. 'I should just have bought something to begin with.'

'Nah,' Sarah replies. 'I'm not so hot in the kitchen either. I once made a date a cup of milky gravy with two sugars because the jars looked the same. I wasn't even drunk.'

I laugh but I still feel like an idiot.

'So only three more days at the grotto?' she asks, wiping the placemats. 'You'll be relieved.'

I throw some cutlery into the sink and pause. 'You know, I thought I would be, but I'm actually kind of sad. I've enjoyed working there. Even with Izzy.'

'I can't wait to be away for two weeks,' Sarah replies. 'Being the assistant manager at Belle Blend isn't as glamourous as it sounds, you know.'

I smirk. 'Try repeating the same thing over and over to children all day.'

'Um, you've met Alfie, right? That's the exact definition of parenting.'

I run the water and let the dishes soak. I'd like to tell her how much I'll miss our lunches and our chats, but now isn't the time. I think never is probably more appropriate.

'So, what now?' she asks. 'Job-wise?'

'Well, I'm guessing I'll start being rejected by law firms again after Christmas. I'd like to get back to the real world. Ideally a job where I don't have to ask everyone how old they are and hope they don't pee on me.'

'Hmm, you say that, but I'm not convinced,' she responds, taking a seat. 'I think fictional characters might be your calling. Easter bunny next, maybe?'

I laugh and join her back at the table. 'Tempting, but no. I don't want to be out of the game too long. Having paid a small fortune in tuition fees to get my degree, it would be nice to use my talents.'

Sarah purses her lips and nods in agreement. 'I know what you mean. When Adam, Alfie's dad, died, I had to put my career on hold. I feel like I'm wasting my training, but let's just say artists don't exactly have a reliable source of income.'

'You're an artist?'

'I am. I wasn't always a barista! That was just a means to an end and I'm predicting that end will be when Alfie's about forty.'

'I'm impressed,' I admit. 'I was so shit at art in school. My teacher used to just sigh at me as soon as I sat down.'

She smiles, twisting the bottom of her hair. 'I was just shit at everything else. Mild dyslexia mixed with hormone-fuelled rebellion was never going to fast-track me to Oxford or Cambridge. Luckily, I got into art college and even had a little show in Camden. Sold a few pieces here and there afterwards. Lily Allen owns three of my paintings.'

I watch her blush as she realises her humble brag, but she has every right to feel proud of herself.

'That's amazing. Seriously. So, you don't paint at all anymore?'

'Nah,' she replies. 'I was too sad to paint for a long time and then I became too busy once Alfie started nursery and I took on more shifts at work. The time just flies by so quickly. When you're solely responsible for a little one, it's hard to find time to catch your breath.'

'You must miss Adam,' I say, and immediately I regret it. We've never talked about Adam before. *Yeah, bring up Alfie's dead dad while she's at her new boyfriend's house for Christmas, that's a sensitive move, you utter prick.* 'Shit, sorry if that's too personal.'

She smiles. 'It's fine. He was a good man ... made me laugh a lot. It's just so fucking unfair. If the other driver had just taken a break ... if Adam had just left half an hour later ...'

'It is unfair,' I agree. Sarah pauses and bites her now trembling lip. 'I'm most sad that Alfie didn't have more time with him.'

I hear her voice trail off as her eyes well up and I put my hand on top of hers.

'My dad vanished before I was born,' I find myself saying. 'And my mum had to raise me alone, which she did like a total champ. I know she wished that I had some kind of male role model in my life, but if it's any consolation, I never missed him. She was all I needed,' I explain. 'It was always just her and me; like you and Alfie, I guess.'

'It wasn't always just us.'

'Of course not, sorry.' I cringe, fumbling around for what to say next. 'I mean, my situation is totally different, but I understand loss. I miss my mum a lot.'

Sarah smiles sadly and asks gently, 'She isn't around anymore?'

'No, she died when I was twenty. Breast cancer.' I take a deep breath as I feel that familiar jolt of sadness in my chest. 'She was already stage IV when she was diagnosed, so there was nothing anyone could do. She didn't even tell me that she was sick; I mean, I understand why, she didn't want me to put my life on hold and come home just to watch her die, but I'd at least have liked the choice.'

'You weren't at home with her?'

I shake my head. 'I was at university. I was with Matt when I got the call and he pretty much held my hand through the whole thing. I'm not sure what I'd have done without his support. He stepped in to help clear her flat, dealt with her landlord and made all the funeral arrangements. He was the one who made sure I remembered to eat, to leave the flat once in a while. Christ, he pretty much made sure I continued to breathe in and out.'

'Ah. I can see why you two are so close.'

I nod. 'He's the best.'

And now here you are, ten years later, and you've been fantasising about his girlfriend for the past week. This thought hits me hard. *What kind of friend am I?* Sarah mistakes my look of remorse for one of sorrow.

'I'm sorry,' she says. 'Life is shit sometimes. It's so hard when parents get sick. Alfie's only got the one set of grandparents and my dad's MS got worse in his mid-sixties and now my mum cares for him full-time. That's why I go to them every year for Christmas; my house isn't exactly wheelchair-friendly.' She trails off sadly.

'Shit, what a conversation for Christmas dinner. I'm so sorry, I didn't mean to upset you,' I say softly, but she shakes her head, gently dabbing the first sign of any visible tears.

'No, it's not your fault. If anything, you've made things far more bearable lately. I should be thanking you.'

She leans in to hug me and I reciprocate, feeling her grasp tighten ever so slightly as I do. It feels like the most natural thing in the world. As we pull apart our eyes meet, just as they have dozens of times before. Only this time we're not sitting across from one another at a crumb-covered shopping-centre table, we're inches apart, and I can still feel her arms around my neck. Her eyes drift down to my mouth. I can barely breathe.

'THE ADVENTURERS RETURN!'

Jesus fucking Christ, my heart leaps from my chest as Matt and Alfie burst through the front door, congratulating each other on their successful pudding mission. Sarah springs away from me like I'm a ticking bomb.

'Wow. Success then?' she says, her voice breaking. 'What did we get?'

Alfie carefully carries the box and sets it down in the kitchen. 'Chocolate cake,' he informs us. 'They only had tiny trifles, but this cake is huuuuge.'

'Good job, buddy,' I say, my brain as scrambled as my trifle. 'Cut me a piece, I'll be right back.'

The seclusion of the bathroom is exactly what I need, but once I've locked the door, I flop down on the side of the bath, my head in my hands. What is wrong with me? Here's Sarah having a vulnerable moment and I'm all, *she's totally checking me out* when she probably was doing nothing of the sort. Oh, fuck this, go eat your cake, Nick, and grow up.

Dessert was evidently worth the wait, with Alfie eating two pieces before falling almost immediately asleep on the couch, his head in Sarah's lap. She's been acting like nothing's happened ... because it didn't. Whatever is going on in my head, it certainly isn't going on in hers.

'I hear you're off to Matt's parents' house for Christmas. That'll be nice,' Sarah says, breaking a slightly awkward silence.

'Yeah,' I reply. 'This will be ... God, the ninth year. Can't believe it's been that long. His family are super nice, they really should adopt me already. I've dropped enough hints.'

Matt laughs, calling me 'Hard Knock Nick'.

Sarah's laughing makes Alfie stir and she announces that she'd better take him home.

'We're getting an early train tomorrow and I still have some packing to finish.'

'Thanks for my bourbon,' I say, grinning. 'I'm chuffed.'

'Well, thank *you* for Alfie's robot thing. It'll keep him entertained while he's away.'

'My pleasure. Have a great Christmas. Bye, buddy!'

I watch as she gets Alfie's coat on, then I disappear to the bathroom to give them some alone time. As I hear the door close behind Sarah and Alfie I feel a pang of both sadness and relief. Being around her is becoming more difficult than I could have anticipated. Matt starts clearing the living room table as 'Last Christmas' begins to play. I turn it off immediately before Matt starts reading too much into the lyrics. I've had enough misplaced emotion for one evening.

CHAPTER EIGHTEEN

'And that, my little elven helpers, is a wrap!'

Everyone stares at me blankly.

'Get it? Because of the wrapping paper and the fact that we've finished . . . forget it.'

Grumbling to myself, I turn to collect the unused gifts while, around me, last-minute Christmas Eve shoppers panic-buy themselves into a frenzy. Izzy pulls across the rope and officially closes the grotto while Geraldine hovers around, reminding everyone that uniforms must be left in her office before we leave.

'A word, Nick?'

Nope. There's a word, Geraldine. Just. Fuckin'. Nope.

I put down the gifts and walk over, my head sweating profusely under my hat. 'Everything OK?'

'Yes,' she replies, expressionlessly. 'Just wanted to thank you for all your hard work over the past few weeks.'

'Oh,' I reply, surprised. 'No worries. It's been . . . an experience.'

'Izzy specifically mentioned that you were a valuable addition this year. So, next year, if you want it, we'd be happy to have you back.'

Izzy said something nice about me. Holy shit, I'm just knocking these Christmas miracles out of the park.

'Thank you,' I reply. 'I'm hoping to be back in full-time employment by then but . . .'

. . . Aaand she's already walking away.

'Does everyone who works here have zero social skills?' I ask no one in particular, but Laura overhears and laughs.

'Hey Santa – high five!' she demands, and I feel obliged to comply, my padded gloves hitting her hand with a dull thud. It's very anticlimactic.

'So, what are you doing for Christmas?' Laura asks, taking off her hat. I'm dying to take mine off but, as much as I want to burn my entire costume, there are still kids around.

'Quiet one,' I answer, continuing with gift duty. 'The usual.'

'Just you and your girlfriend?'

'No girlfriend,' I respond, ripping apart a selection box then openly eating a Snickers. I don't even care anymore. 'I'm single.'

As I hand her a Mars Bar, she looks perplexed. 'Single? But the woman from the coffee place. I thought—'

'I told you,' Izzy interjects loudly as she walks past. 'See! Everybody think this . . . Laura think this . . .'

'She's just a friend,' I say indignantly. 'And she happens to be dating my best friend.'

'... I think this,' Izzy continues, waving her hands around and paying no attention to me, 'Christine thinks this, even the security man Charles with the stupid beard think this ... oh, and the woman with the bad eye who make the vegan soap, what's her name—'

'I'm leaving now,' I interrupt, but she's still talking. 'Have a great Christmas, everyone.'

I march myself back to the staffroom, annoyed and a little embarrassed. Was I that obvious around everyone, or do people just have nothing better to do than gossip? I grab my clothes from the locker and move into the men's bathrooms to change out of this hot, itchy suit for the last time.

When I return, I bump into Laura, who looks a tad embarrassed.

'I didn't mean to offend you or anything,' she begins, but I stop her, reassuring her that I'm fine and just want to get home.

'Have a drink with me,' she suggests. 'There's a nice pub around the corner.'

'Thanks for the offer but honestly, I'm tired and—'

'Stop being so old! I mean, it's not like you're rushing off to meet your girlfriend ... Live a little, Grandpa.'

I can't help but laugh. In that squeaky voice, her sassiness is quite charming.

'Sure, why not,' I reply. Matt is off picking up the hire car to drive us to his parents' and then out with his work colleagues until God knows when. Maybe a drink is exactly what I need.

'A private detective? You're shitting me. I'm not even sure that's a real job.'

Laura nods, trying to guide her straw into her mouth, while she props up the wall. We've been in the pub for almost three hours and still haven't found a seat. I'm slightly miffed that she's far drunker than I am; as hard as I try, I can't seem to let my hair down.

'Yep. I want to investigate shit,' she explains. 'Like Jessica Jones but without the superpowers.'

'Right,' I reply, pretending to know who the hell Jessica Jones is. If she has superpowers, I bet Alfie would know. I wonder how he's doing . . .

'And if it all goes tits up, maybe I'll just be an elf for the rest of my life!'

'There are worse things to be,' I respond, swirling the last of the beer in my bottle. 'Another drink?'

She peers at her glass. 'Maybe a cocktail,' she considers. 'Something strong, I'm not really feeling anything from this gin.'

The fact her eyes are darting in different directions leads me to believe that the gin is, in fact, working just as intended. I smile, thinking about how cute Sarah is when she's tipsy. She does this thing with her hair where—

'Earth to Nick . . .'

Laura's voice snaps me out of my momentary trance, and I notice her wandering eyes are now fixed firmly on me. She really wants that cocktail, I guess.

I push my way to the bar, but get stuck behind at least seven people for what feels like forever. With only fifteen minutes until Christmas Day, everyone is in high spirits, but I don't feel quite so merry. Laura has been a great distraction, but it hasn't stopped Sarah drifting in and out of my mind. It's like a miserable sense of longing and I need to snap out of it, but not here. I need to go home, get a reasonably early night before the drive to Matt's parents' house in the morning. Giving up on ever getting a drink before midnight, I about-turn and make my way back to Laura.

'No one is getting served anytime soon,' I tell her. 'I think I'm just going to call it a night.'

'Great idea,' she replies. 'My place or yours?'

I'm genuinely surprised when she says this and choke on the dregs of my beer. 'Oh! No, I meant—'

She prises herself off the wall and tries to pull on her coat, missing the arm several times before she successfully slips it on. Even if I wanted to take her home, she's far too wasted. I take out my phone and open the Uber app.

'What's your address? Maybe we can share?'

She presses herself up against me and giggles.

'Santa, baby . . .'

Oh fuck, she's singing. I glance around, hoping that this moment isn't being shared by anyone else. 'OOOOK . . . I just need—'

'Put a stable under the tree . . .'

'I think it's *slip a sable*, but whatever, I just need your address . . .'

'And hurry round the chimney tonight . . . be doo be doop.'

OH, DEAR GOD, this is horrible. People are starting to stare. I take her arm and try to guide her towards the door but instead she holds on to my jacket and plants her mouth firmly on mine. I briefly consider keeping it there, so she won't be able to sing again, but in the end I gently pull away and step back.

'Laura, you're a great girl but I'm just not looking for anything . . .'

'Santa babbbbyyy . . .'

'Laura, are you hearing me? I'm going home. Alone.'

The smile on her face suddenly drops. 'Seriously? It's Christmas!'

'I'm sorry . . . Look, it's late, I've just ordered an Uber, let me drop you—'

She starts to cackle. 'Did I just get turned down by a shopping-mall Santa? That's a new fucking low. God, why are men such dicks?'

'Wow, OK,' I reply. 'So, I'm going to go . . .'

'Good. Shove your Uber up your arse, I live at the end of the road above the chippy, not that you'll ever know.'

'You literally just told me.'

I hear her announce that I *probably have a knob like a cocktail sausage anyway* in front of the whole pub as I slink away, confused and slightly wounded by her drunken outburst. My knob is at least a bockwurst.

Stepping outside, I check my phone and see that no one has accepted my Uber request yet. This is just perfect. It's minus three and I'm going to have to walk home.

Sticking my hands in my pockets, I begin my journey, my boots crunching into the newly formed ice on the pavement. This time last year I was a corporate lawyer, kissing my beautiful girlfriend Angela at a party in Kensington with a free bar. Now I'm an out-of-work Santa Claus who's going home alone to an empty flat.

As I quicken my pace, my phone vibrates in my pocket.

Merry Christmas, Nick! Love, Sarah and Alfie xx

My internal yelp of delight at receiving her text is quickly replaced by a very audible yelp of surprise as I slip and fall flat on my back. Jesus Christ, ice, why do you hate me so much? What did I ever do to you?

'You alright, fella?' I hear a voice ask from across the street. I give them a thumbs up as they walk on, but the pain radiating from my arse makes me suspect otherwise.

I lie there momentarily, wondering how tonight could get any worse, as the faint sound of 'Jingle Bell Rock' drifts out from a nearby flat and into the night air.

Merry fucking Christmas indeed.

CHAPTER NINETEEN

'She actually sang "Santa Baby" to you . . . in the middle of the pub?'

'Yup,' I respond as Matt and I walk up the garden path to his parents' house. Their garden is perfectly tended, even in winter, with frost-covered conifers and little bare holly bushes, the berries evidently ravaged by hungry birds.

'It was just so awkward,' I continue. 'I didn't know where to look. The whole night was a disaster, mate, even before I broke my arse.'

Matt puts down his bags at the front door and rings the bell. A cheery *ding-dong* sound chimes out, nothing like the harsh buzzer we're forced to endure at home. I peer through the living room window and see the twinkle from the Christmas tree lights along with the warm glow from the fire, making me feel like an orphan from a Dickens novel. I can almost hear the Victorian carol singers. The Buckleys own a large five-bedroom house in the Surrey countryside. It's obscenely picturesque and was undoubtedly a wonderful place to grow up. Mum and I lived in a two-bedroom ground-floor flat with a damp problem and neighbours who never quite grasped the concept of keeping it the fuck down. Even though Matt hasn't lived here for years, he still has that ruddy, country-boy glow about his cheeks.

'Sarah sends her love,' Matt informs me, pressing his face up to the frosted glass on the door. 'Alfie's having a ball apparently. He's running wild.'

'You've spoken to her?'

'Just a text. I'll call her later.'

I don't mention that she texted me last night too. He knows she has my number for babysitting duties, but I don't want him to read anything into it. Perhaps I shouldn't either.

Finally, the door opens, and we're greeted by Matt's mum, Maureen, who's wearing the fluffiest white jumper I've ever seen, and their golden retriever Harvey, who *gruffs* at us indifferently.

'There's my boys!' she exclaims, beaming. 'Oh, I'm so glad you're here! Quick, come in, it's chilly!'

I beam back as she ushers us in. Since my mum passed, Maureen has ensured I never feel like anything other than part of the family. I get birthday cards, Christmas gifts and they even included me in their family celebratory dinner after Matt and I graduated.

'Merry Christmas, Mum,' Matt says, kissing her cheek. 'You look lovely. New jumper?'

'Gift from Dad,' she replies, giving a twirl. 'I'm rather pleased. How are you, Nick?'

She hugs me tightly as I tell her I'm great, omitting pretty much everything that's happened in the last six months. We drop our bags at the bottom of the stairs and head into the living room.

'James, stop fiddling with that gadget, the boys are here.'

Matt's dad places his Amazon Echo on the arm of the couch and slips off his reading glasses. The whole house smells like cinnamon and berries with faint notes of soggy Harvey.

'Sorry, love, just trying to sync that thing up. Merry Christmas!' he says, hugging us both. 'Was the drive OK?'

'Terrific,' Matt replies, as he sits on the couch. 'Roads were dead . . . Mum, did you get Dad an Alexa for Christmas? That's practically another woman.'

'I did!' she replies, shaking up the pillows beside me on the couch. 'I thought it might be fun! Gives him someone to talk to other than me and Harvey.'

I laugh as James considers this and then nods in agreement. You can tell they adore each other, and I've never heard either of them raise their voice in anger since I've known them. Matt told me once that they had wanted a huge family but only had one successful pregnancy, resulting in him. You can tell that they had enough love and kindness for twenty more and I've been lucky to receive even a breath of it. When Matt eventually gives them grandkids, I think they might burst with happiness.

Matt's mum pushes some bowls of nibbles towards me while Harvey decides to sit directly on my foot until I scratch his head. It's the same every year.

'House is looking very festive, Mrs B,' I say, grabbing a smoked salmon blini, 'thanks for having me.'

'Our pleasure, Nick,' she replies. 'Wouldn't be the same without you. Matt, give your dad a hand with that thing, will you?'

She toddles off to the kitchen while I watch Matt take over the set-up of his dad's new toy. I imagine that this responsibility befalls every child whose ageing parents have received technology made after 1993.

After much mumbling, I hear Matt say, 'Alexa, what's the weather?'

Matt's dad's face lights up as his new device tells him that it's minus two with a fresh breeze, despite it being information that could also be obtained by stepping outside.

'Put some music on!' Matt's mum yells from the kitchen. 'Something Christmassy!'

'Not "Jingle Bell Rock",' I request, and my arse aches in agreement. 'Anything but that.'

Matt turns to look at me, a grin slowly appearing on his face.

'Alexa, play "Santa Baby".'

'So, Nick. Tell me about this girl Matt is seeing, because it's like pulling teeth trying to get anything out of him. You know what he's like.'

Matt picks up a little Christmas pudding salt shaker, rolling his eyes like a stroppy teenager. 'Really, Mum? I'm right here.'

There's enough food here to feed an entire army: turkey, beef, cocktail sausages, three kinds of stuffing, pickles, potatoes, home-made cranberry sauce, and veg prepared in ways I can't even pronounce. They even have the *good* Christmas crackers, not the ones that fail to bang and contain terrible jokes and choking hazards.

'Sarah? She's cool,' I reply, spooning some more sprouts on to my plate. 'I mean, who knew Russian brides were so affordable!'

Matt's dad laughs out loud while his mum looks momentarily horrified.

'He's kidding, Mum,' Matt quickly interjects, glaring at me to help reassure his mother. 'She's an assistant manager in a coffee shop ... she studied in the Cotswolds which is where she's spending Christmas with her family.'

'Oh, the Cotswolds are lovely,' Matt's mum interjects,

now considerably less aghast. 'Your dad and I have been there several times. Beautiful churches.'

'You'll like Sarah, Mrs B,' I confirm. 'She's a great mum—'

'She has a child?'

I grin as Maureen's eyebrows rise far above the rim of her glasses.

'Well, that's . . . unexpected.'

Matt nods. 'Alfie. He's four. They're both fantastic. I'm very happy, Mum, you can relax. This one's a keeper.'

'That's great news, son,' his dad says. 'We look forward to meeting her.'

As I watch Matt's mum grin from ear to ear, I can't help but feel gutted. Having the whole family now invested in this relationship makes my stupid heart hurt. It makes their relationship even more solid. As much as I want to be happy for him, inside I want to be the one boasting about Sarah, because no one else, not even Matt, could possibly do her justice.

'And you, Nick?' she asks, pouring me some more wine. 'How are things with you?'

'Um . . . good,' I reply, glancing at a smirking Matt who knows that it's now my turn under the parental microscope. Christ, I feel about fifteen again. 'Not much to report! These sprouts are a triumph, Mrs B, did you—'

'Don't be modest, Nick!' Matt insists, his smirk now morphing into something that resembles payback for the

Russian brides remark. 'I'm sure they'd love to hear all about your new work situation!'

'Did Kensington Fox finally promote one of you boys?' James asks.

I smile politely at Matt's dad and shake my head. 'Not quite ... I'm no longer working there. Funny story, actually; you see—'

'Not only did he get food poisoning and throw up on a client's wife,' Matt informs them, 'he also took the rap for some junior's filing mistake, so he got the boot. Noble, but ultimately stupid.'

If Matt was my actual brother, I'd have given him a dead arm by now. Possibly a wedgie.

'Oh, my goodness!' Maureen exclaims. 'Sorry to hear that, Nick. So where are you working now?'

'The North Pole,' Matt mumbles through a mouth full of turkey. 'He's Santa.'

'Oh, behave,' his mum scolds, 'that's ridiculous. You boys and your jokes.'

'Ridiculous, yes, but true nonetheless,' I confess, my face rapidly becoming the colour of the cranberries. 'Southview Shopping Centre ... well, until yesterday – there's not much use for a Santa after Christmas Eve. So, I guess I'm officially out of work again! Yay, me!'

A hush falls over the table as I reach for the roast potatoes and for a moment, I start to panic that I've just ruined everyone's dinner with my depressing tale of Christmas unemployment. Even Harvey gives a little whine from his bed in the corner of the dining room.

Nice one, Nick. Maybe bring up your mum later for some real festive cheer!

'Well, Nick,' James finally says. 'I guess it's safe to say . . . you're a bit of a lost *Claus*.'

Matt snorts into his wine and the laughter that follows is a welcome relief. I've never been so pleased to hear a dad joke in my entire life.

After dinner, I help clear the dishes while Matt and his dad go outside for their annual festive cigar. I tried to smoke one three years ago and it made me greener than the Christmas tree. I like helping Maureen clear up anyway, it makes me feel like I'm somehow earning my keep.

'Is he really happy?' she asks, scraping a plate into the bin. 'I do worry, you know – this girl has a son and—'

'He's fine, Mrs B,' I reply. 'You should see them all together . . . they are like a proper little family. I actually introduced him to Sarah: she works at the shopping centre too, and Alfie came into the grotto. He's a great kid. And honestly, Matt's happy. You don't need to worry about him.'

She laughs. 'I will never not worry, it comes with the territory . . . but this Sarah, does she have her head screwed on properly?'

'Oh, she's very down to earth,' I interrupt, almost defensively. 'Sharp as a tack. She isn't—'

'She isn't *her*, Nick.' Maureen's face looks strained as she sighs and folds over a dishtowel.

'Karen?'

She nods. 'And that's what worries me.'

I understand her concern – sometimes it feels like Karen's the bloody Voldemort of the Buckley household. Even after three years, her name is still tiptoed around, like somehow actually saying it out loud will summon her directly in front of Matt to break his heart again. Christ, he can't even see a fucking wallet without pining.

It wasn't hard to see why Matt was so smitten with the tall strawberry-blonde he sat next to at his very first lecture; she was stunning. But for him it was more than that. She was his equal: his tennis-playing, career-driven, frustratingly stubborn equal. With Karen, he'd met his match.

Matt's mum pulls out a stool at the cream kitchen island and motions for me to join her.

'You remember how Matt was when she left for New York,' Maureen continues. 'I've never seen him so shattered. I dread to think what would have happened if you hadn't moved in with him.'

I nod. Matt had been there for me after Mum died, so there was no way I was going to let him deal with his heartbreak on his own. I knew Matt needed company – that being on his own in the flat that he had shared with Karen was the very last thing he needed. Matt isn't the type to show vulnerability, but he thought Karen was the one, and losing her hit him really hard. I still shared a flat with Greta and Harriet, and Harriet's sister had been looking for a room anyway, so getting out of the lease wasn't a problem. I moved in with Matt the day after Karen left and became his rock, propping him up until he was standing firmly on solid ground again. It took time but we got there.

'He got through it,' I insist. 'He's moved on.'

'Getting *through* something isn't the same as getting over it,' Maureen replies. Mrs B is so bloody wise. 'It would have been entirely different if they'd split up because they weren't in love anymore, but she was just on a different path.'

'Sarah is good for him,' I say firmly, not sure whether I'm trying to reassure her or myself. 'You've seen how his face lights up when he speaks about her.'

She bobs her head in acknowledgement and smiles, trying to mask her visible concern. 'I hope you're right. It's a whole other ball game when there's a child involved . . . I just don't want him to let anyone down, if he's not ready for that.'

'Don't worry,' I reply. 'Sarah is no idiot, and neither is Matt. He's the best . . . in fact, they both are.'

The conservatory door opens and Matt's deep, hearty laugh floats through the house.

'You're a good boy, Nick,' Mrs B says, standing up. 'We

all think the world of you; Matt's lucky to have such a good friend.'

As she leans in for a hug, I feel like I've been punched in the gut. Matt's been more than a friend to me; he's my family. They all are. I'm the one who's lucky and I swear to myself that I won't let what I feel for Sarah override my loyalty to Matt. Regardless of what that little voice in the back of my head is telling me, Sarah isn't my Karen. She is not the one who got away, because she was never mine in the first place, and if Matt can get over the love of his life, then I can get over the best thing I never had.

The next morning, Matt takes Harvey for a walk and I join him. His parents live a few minutes' walk from a huge open field where everyone walks their hairy best friends. I don't really get dogs. They just seem like a whole load of work, only to be slobbered on in return. Cats are more my vibe. Well, technically reindeers have been my vibe for the past few weeks, but a cat seems like a more realistic choice for a Londoner. I don't see Rudolph fitting into our two-bed.

'I spoke to Sarah this morning,' Matt says. 'Sounds like they're having a blast. Alfie asked for you, but I didn't want to wake you.'

'Aw, I wouldn't have minded,' I reply, picking up the stick that Harvey has dropped at my feet. 'I hardly have a barrage of people wishing me Merry Christmas ...'

I throw the stick, and Harvey gallops after it, but he's intercepted by a plucky little boxer who grabs it first, returning it to a woman in a bright orange jacket. Matt gasps.

'*No way*. I don't believe it.'

'Well, it's a stick. It's kinda what dogs do.'

Matt waves at the woman who's now walking towards us, smiling.

'Kirstie Jardine,' he says under his breath. 'God, I haven't seen her since high school.'

'Matt Buckley, as I live and breathe!' she exclaims, her face slightly ruddy from the cold air. 'How the bloody hell are you?'

'I thought that was you,' he replies, going in for a hug. 'I'm good, how are you? Jesus, it's been years!'

I watch in amusement as Matt seems to regress back fourteen years to the cocky, cumbersome teenager he once was, joking about his school years and their mutual friends. By the way they're coyly looking at each other, it's obvious they used to have a thing. Fucking hell, can't I have just one day where I don't feel like Matt's third wheel?

'I'd better run,' Kirstie eventually says, taking her thief dog by the leash. She removes the stolen stick from his mouth and hands it to Matt. 'So lovely to see you! Say hi to your mum and dad for me.'

'Will do,' he replies. 'Take care!'

As Matt watches her walk away, I notice his eyes glaze over, just for a second.

'Uh-oh,' I say, snapping him back to reality. 'Don't fall too far down the rabbit hole, mate.'

He smirks. 'Nah, I'm good. Just, she still looks bloody amazing. Kirstie was my first . . . real . . . girlfriend—'

'And by "real" you mean you boned? Popped your cherry, stamped your v-card, bumped her ugly?'

'Shut up! There was nothing ugly about it. She was the hottest girl at school: smart and funny and popular, and oh my God, she did this insane thing with her tongue—'

'Whoa, mate! I really, really don't need to know.' I mime vomming and Matt shoves me.

'Seriously, though. Weird to see her with a wedding ring on – she's an actual grown-up now. In my head she's still sixteen. She was the only girl I ever loved . . . you know, except for Karen.'

Karen's name works its magic and there is an awkward silence as we trudge along.

'Ghosts of girlfriends past and all that . . .' Matt finally says with a sad smile, and I wonder about what Mrs B said last night.

'Could be worse, Matt – mine just ghosts me.' I smirk, trying to lighten the mood.

Matt laughs and flings the stick again for an impatient Harvey. 'Your luck will change, mate. Maybe you should try Tinder or something?' he suggests. 'Meet someone who isn't a shirt-stealing sociopath, or a part-time elf.'

'Tinder? Not only no – *hell* no!' I reply, taking over stick duties. 'Don't you remember the girl with the neck tattoo? It was literally prison ink – and I was genuinely scared for my life. She asked if I wanted to see her knife collection. And then there was the one who tried to mount me at the cinema. I was asked to leave halfway through *John Wick* because she wouldn't get off my lap. And those were just the ones I met up with. There were the hundreds who rudely ignored my carefully crafted openers. Like what was so off-putting about my face that they couldn't spare a "Hey"? Online dating is way too brutal. How people actually manage to sort through the psychos and the hookers and find relationship material on Tinder will never fail to astonish me. But, I'm not even that bothered right now. I need to focus first on getting a job sorted, now that my reign as Saint Nick is over.'

'I was just talking about a shag, not a full-blown relationship, mate. I think all that babysitting and Santa shit has killed your mojo. Your right hand must be knackered. You need to get back out there.'

Rather than remind him that my mojo is still very much alive and creating havoc – between fraternising with horny ice-skating instructors and dodging overly friendly elves, it's been an eventful month – I just tell him he's probably right and that I'll look into it, knowing full well that I absolutely won't. My brain won't stop taunting me with thoughts of Sarah – her mouth, her smile, the way it felt when she hugged me at Christmas dinner. He's right about my hand though – if I'm not careful I'll get a repetitive strain injury. That would make for an incredibly awkward doctor's appointment.

When we return to Nick's parents' house, they've prepared a huge breakfast which is very welcome. Countryside walking always makes me ravenous, like that feeling I used to get as a kid after swimming. Fortunately, every meal at Matt's house is like a Hogwarts banquet.

'I haven't put ketchup on your rolls, sweetheart,' Maureen tells Matt as she places an enormous plate of pastries on the table beside the towering stack of bacon and vat of scrambled eggs. 'I know how particular you are. Nice walk, Nick?'

'Yes, thanks,' I reply. 'I'd forgotten what fresh air smelled like. It's cold out there though, I think my face is frozen.'

'Oh, that reminds me,' Matt's mum informs us, 'Lionel and Kitty are coming over at two and Kitty has had a little too much Botox—'

'She looks like she's had a stroke,' Matt's dad interjects. 'I'd avoid mentioning it.'

'Oh, it's not that bad, James,' Maureen protests. 'She just looks like she's had a dental block. Hopefully it will have settled by the time we go on our cruise.'

'When are you off?' I ask through a mouthful of bacon roll. God, I love being here.

'Twenty-ninth. Just a little jaunt round the Canary Islands for New Year.'

'Who's taking the dog?' I ask, watching Matt carefully move his mushrooms away from his scrambled eggs.

'My sister Yvonne,' she replies. 'If she spoils him as much as she spoils those foxes, he'll have a ball.'

'She has pet foxes?'

'No, she just feeds every animal that ventures into her garden. It's like a bloody Hitchcock film with the amount of bird feeders she has.'

'We have to get back after breakfast, I'm afraid, Mum,' Matt advises her. 'I'm working tomorrow, need to return the car . . . lots to do.'

'Aw, shame,' she replies. 'It's been so lovely to see you both. Maybe next year I'll be laying a couple of extra places . . .' She winks at me and raises her eyebrows at Matt.

Matt gives a little chuckle. 'We'll see, we'll see . . .'

I leave the Buckley house armed with a new dressing gown and slippers set, some toiletries and as much left-over food as we can carry. It feels weird knowing that I have nowhere to be tomorrow. No kids to enthral, no Izzy to appease and, unfortunately, no Sarah to eat lunch with. Thankfully it also means I won't have to see Laura ever again.

The Boxing Day traffic is quiet but steady, the motion of the car making me sleepy enough to nod off briefly. Matt notifies me that this is unacceptable car companion behaviour by rolling down the window my head is resting on. He finds this far more hilarious than I do.

'What are you doing for New Year?' he asks as I attempt to get comfortable again. 'Basement is having their annual party – some roaring twenties-themed event. Might be alright?'

'Maybe,' I reply, 'though no one else will be there. Greta is away visiting her fiancé's family at their McMansion, Harriet is busy growing a human, no one from work remembers that I exist, and Sarah won't be back from her parents' house. I might just stay home.'

I've been working hard to ignore any thoughts of Sarah and although I've been somewhat successful, random musings or memories of her still pop up like hiccups when I least expect it. She texted me to thank me for her Christmas present, saying she'll treasure it forever. I know she means the key ring photo of Alfie's hot chocolate-covered face, but I like the thought that, maybe, there's a one per cent chance she'll treasure it because of me too.

'You of all people should be pumped for New Year's Eve!'

'Why?' I ask. 'New Year's Eve is the biggest let-down since the invention of Kinder Eggs. It's all wrapped up nice and shiny on the outside, but inside it's just full of disappointing shite.'

'Because it's a chance to say goodbye to this shitshow of a year!' he replies. 'Honestly mate, I see big things in your future. Next year is going to be ace for you. Start like you mean to go on!'

'What, alone, skint and hungover?'

'God, you're depressing when you're tired. You're going. End of story.'

'Ugh, fine . . . but you're buying the tickets.'

'Deal.'

I smile and close my eyes again. Maybe he's right. Maybe next year will be ace. It certainly can't be any worse than this year.

CHAPTER TWENTY

'I'm still not feeling this party,' I announce, fastening my braces. 'It's cold outside. I could get pissed and throw up here for free.'

'You could,' Matt agrees, 'but there's zero chance of you getting a shag here. Unless you get creative.'

'I'm dressed like a fucking reject from *Bugsy Malone*. Besides, there's more to life than sex, mate,' I reply and then we both laugh because that's utter bullshit. 'Just promise me you won't try and get me pity-shagged. I'm perfectly capable of doing that on my own.'

We head off at 10pm, navigating the freezing cold in ill-fitting three-piece suits from the retro charity shop on Primrose Hill. Three years ago, Matt, Harriet and I dressed up as Charlie's Angels for a Halloween party and won free drinks all night. That outfit was far more flattering than this is. Totally worth the chaffing. Also, the added bonus of keeping a phone in your bra – much more secure than a pocket.

Inside the venue, it seems that other people have decided to mix it up a little. I've never seen so many flappers with full beards and women in sexy Gatsby get-ups. The place is heaving so Matt and I both head to the bar and get two drinks each, knowing that soon, the battle to get to the bar will make the *Games of Thrones* final showdown look tame in comparison.

We find two seats at a table near the smaller dance floor, which is playing remixed dance versions of classic twenties songs. I've never heard 'Tiptoe Through the Tulips' with a disco beat, but I'm not hating it. This night might be more fun than I first thought, despite the seam of these size-too-small trousers aggravating my balls.

Four drinks down and Matt goes to get another round. It's an hour before the bells and the place is officially jumping. I'm glad I decided to come tonight; it feels like I haven't been properly out in ages. Thankfully the teenagers sitting beside us are in the minority and everyone else here looks like they've definitely gone to IKEA willingly at some point. I laugh as I watch a short man in an even shorter skirt dance like his feet are on fire. Everyone is getting increasingly drunk, increasingly bold and increasingly sweaty.

Matt returns with four shots and a face like a cartoon baddie.

'Don't look!' he says, taking his seat. 'You'll never guess who's here . . .'

'Why can't I look? Who is it?'

'Just guess.'

'Um . . . Jodie Comer?'

'From *Killing Eve*? No. You need to stop watching that shit. Guess again.'

'Gimme a clue. Is it someone off the telly?'

'Yes . . . kind of . . . do not say Sandra Oh.'

'Fuck, I dunno. Someone off *EastEnders*? Claudia Winkleman?'

'Angela.'

My eyes begin panic-scanning the room, until I spot her at the bar. She's standing in the middle of a gaggle of girls and she's staring right at me.

'Oh shit.'

'Yep,' he replies. 'I told you not to look.'

I watch her slink over towards me, drink in hand. She has decided to stick to convention and is wearing a red, fringed dress complete with a feathery headpiece. I really wish she didn't look so good.

'Fancy seeing you here,' she remarks. 'Wouldn't have thought this was your kind of place. No reindeers.'

'I was here last year,' I reply, with a sigh. 'But you know that, considering you were with me.'

'Oh yeah,' she responds, shrugging. 'Must have slipped my mind. How are you, Matthew?'

'Still going by Matt,' he answers frostily.

'Fabulous . . . enjoy your evening, boys.'

I don't respond; there's no point. She's already walking away.

'You alright?' Matt asks, passing me a shot. 'Honestly, Nick, you're well rid.'

The throat burn from my tequila makes me wince, but I manage to force a smile.

'I'm fine,' I reply. 'It's just weird that one minute you're with someone and the next they're acting like they barely know you. You've got a good one with Sarah, mate. Hang on to her.'

Matt slides another shot across the table. 'The night is young, my friend. Here's to being rid of Angela, getting drunk and getting pizza on the way home.'

I cheers him and let the tequila do its worst.

CHAPTER TWENTY-ONE

'Nick, *Nicholas* . . . you need to go.'

That voice makes one eye shoot open and I immediately wish I was dead. You have got to be shitting me.

After my fourth tequila, the rest of my New Year's Eve is a bit of a blur. I remember dancing to a house version of 'I Got Rhythm' with a very tall woman. I remember trading my hat with a bald man for his cigarette holder, and I remember not being able to find Matt after the bells. However, I do not remember the events leading up to this moment.

'Angela? How the hell—'

She hits me with a pillow, trying to speed up my revival. 'Get up!'

I bolt upright, my head spinning. All I can taste is booze. Angela paces beside me in her yellow dressing gown like an agitated lemon.

I feel underneath the duvet. No underwear. Fuck, this is bad.

'You have to go *now*, and this never happened,' she insists. 'I don't know what I was thinking. Why do I drink vodka? Nothing good ever happens when I drink vodka.'

I rub my hands over my face. 'Jesus, fine. I get it. Where are my clothes?'

'Probably in the hall where you left them, just hurry up.'

'What's the bloody rush?' I ask. 'I could use a coffee, at least. Some food? I feel like garbage.'

'Nick, I am having people over this afternoon. They cannot see you here.'

I climb out of bed butt naked and walk into the hall, grabbing my crumpled clothes.

'By "people", I take it you mean your new boyfriend? I saw the Instagram posts.'

'That's none of your business.'

'I'll take that as a yes. Didn't take you long to move on, did it?'

'For your information, Dale is not my boyfriend, he's just a friend.'

'Dale?' I start to snigger. 'Jesus, that's not even a proper name, it's a landform.'

She watches me pull on my trousers and sighs. 'Nick, I don't know if you were hoping for some sort of reunion here but—'

'Oh, for God's sake, a reunion?' I exclaim. 'I was just hoping for a bit of toast. You really do flatter yourself, Ange; the amount I had to drink, you could have been anyone.'

'Like Sarah?'

I stop fastening my trousers. 'What?'

'Sarah. You mumbled the shit out of her name in your sleep.'

I feel my cheeks burn. Thank God I wasn't passed out anywhere near Matt.

'She's just a friend,' I mutter, lifting my phone out of one of my shoes. My braces are missing in action.

'I didn't ask who she was,' Angela informs me, 'I just wanted to make it clear that nothing between us has changed. I'm glad we've both found new friends, though.'

'God, you're infuriating,' I reply. 'Please be nicer to your next pushover.'

'OH, I WILL! Wait. He's not—'

'Bye, Angela.'

Uber ordered; Angela practically drop-kicks me out of her flat, shoes in hand. On New Year's Day, rides are limited so I'm forced to hang out in a freezing cold hallway for forty minutes before it eventually arrives. A tiny part of me wants Dale to show up and see me here, but in my current condition I'm in no state for any kind of confrontation. I just want to get home and forget this ever happened – but not before I kill Matt for not dragging me away from her the moment the tequila kicked in.

As I do my walk of shame from the Uber to the flat, Matt's already holding the flat door open for me, grinning.

'Mate . . .' he begins, his laughter already bubbling over.

'Don't!' I reply, pushing past him towards the bathroom. 'Just get the kettle on.'

I throw my clothes on to the floor and run the water, hoping to wash away any remnants of last night's blurry hook-up. God, is that lipstick on my—

'Can't believe you did that!' I hear him yell from the hall. 'There must have been at least a thousand other women there.'

'THE REAL QUESTION HERE IS HOW COULD YOU LET ME?' I yell from the shower, his laughter still showing no signs of subsiding. 'Ugh, I feel violated.'

'Dude, I couldn't find you for the last hour and then I saw your face glued to hers in the taxi queue. You looked completely into it. I wouldn't cock-block my best mate.'

The words 'best mate' make me wince a little knowing that I've been sleep-talking about his girlfriend. It's making me feel like even more of a shithead. Sarah will be back in a couple of days and hopefully she will have grown tentacles and had a personality bypass because I need something to turn me off.

Matt makes some French toast while I dry off, informing me that Dale is a footballer whose track record with blondes is worse than his.

'According to his Twitter he was in Soho last night. There's a photo of him at some homelessness charity event.'

'So, if they're not dating, why did she want rid of me

so quickly?' I ask, walking into the living room. I've never been so glad to get into my dressing gown in my life.

'Maybe she wants to date him but thought if he saw you there it would scupper her chances.'

'Yeah, maybe.'

'Why do you care?' Matt asks, handing me a plate of slightly singed French toast. 'You don't want her back, do you?'

I throw my towel over the back of the chair and sit. 'Hell no. I think she's just given my ego a kicking for the second time. I'm more annoyed with myself than with her.'

'She needs attention,' Matt says, pouring some maple syrup on to the side of his plate. 'She doesn't care where it comes from. She's also a gold-digger. No offence, but to someone like her, without your salary, you're not worth the fake tan.'

'God, that's depressing. I hope Dale sees through her quicker than I did.'

Matt continues scrolling through Twitter as we eat, making sure he gets even amounts of syrup on each piece of French toast. Then he suddenly stops, mid-bite.

'Mate. You're going to want to see this.'

'What?'

Matt hands me the phone to reveal a photo of Angela and me kissing outside the club.

'If Angela was looking to keep this quiet from Dale, she's fucked up big time.'

CHAPTER TWENTY-TWO

By the time Sarah and Alfie return from her parents' house, Angela has called me forty-seven times and left me over twenty voicemails. The picture of us has been feverishly retweeted by people who give a shit about that kind of thing and I'm mortified. I didn't like being pictured with her when we were dating, and I hate it even more now.

'She's attractive,' Sarah remarks, looking at her photos. She's brought Alfie over so she and Matt can have their first cinema date of the new year. 'Good hair ... strong eyebrow game.'

Matt laughs as she hands him back his phone. 'She's desperate to get Nick to publicly announce that they're not back together and that it was just a friendly, platonic kiss.'

'I'm not getting involved,' I interject. 'She can sort out her own mess.'

'Dale's already been seen hanging out with some woman who was on *The Voice*,' Matt continues. 'I think she's flogging a dead horse now.'

Sarah and I glance at each other before laughing. 'Is celebrity gossip just a hobby or a real passion, Matt?' she asks. 'What's Harry Styles up to these days? Or Adele?'

'No idea,' he replies, grinning. 'I'm only interested in Z-listers who bother my friends. Speaking of Nick's exes, before I forget, I can't go to Greta's wedding anymore. Work are sending me to Washington for four days. Some acquisition bullshit. In fact, I'll be on the flight home while you're all getting drunk.'

'Oh bugger,' Sarah says, not quite managing to hide her disappointment. 'That's a pity.'

'You're joking? Wait . . . Washington DC or Washington Newcastle?' I ask.

'There's a Washington in Newcastle?'

'So, DC then,' I reply. 'That sucks. You know that Harriet isn't going either, but she has her pregnancy as an excuse. Greta will murder you, you realise that.'

'Yeah. I feel bad. I'm actually pretty gutted to be missing it, but there's nothing I can do.'

'You should feel bad,' I insist. 'Now I'm going to have to hang out with people I hardly know, and Sarah here won't get to steal something from Claridge's.'

Sarah laughs, but I can tell she's disappointed.

'So, take Sarah as your plus-one,' Matt suggests. 'Everyone's a winner.'

Sarah and I look at each other and then back at Matt.

'Won't that be a bit . . . weird?' she asks. I nod in

agreement. Taking your friend's girlfriend as your date isn't exactly normal wedding etiquette.

'Why? I don't want to be the reason my two best people miss out on free food and wine. Go and have fun.'

'But—'

Adamant that he won't take no for an answer, Sarah and I both finally say yes to Matt's plan. I can tell that Sarah feels awkward, but probably not for the same reason I do.

'Shall we go?' Matt asks. 'Film starts in forty.'

'What are you seeing?'

'There's a special screening of The Babadook showing,' Sarah informs me. 'Who doesn't love some horror in the afternoon, right?'

The look on Matt's face tells me that the answer is him.

Sarah hands Alfie his snack and settles him down on the couch. He's brought over the Lego set his grandparents gave him for Christmas and I know I'll be stepping on one before the afternoon is through.

'Be good,' she says, kissing him on the top of the head. 'Matt and I will only be a couple of hours.'

She's changed her hair over Christmas. It's slightly shorter, just above her shoulders, and it's all straight and glossy. I like it but it's not quite the repulsive, tentacle-clad metamorphosis I'd hoped for. I'm starting to realise that Sarah could turn up with a Mohawk and face tattoos and I'd still be smitten the moment she smiled.

I say goodbye and dive into helping Alfie build his

masterpiece, which he tells me is a truck but looks more like a skip on wheels. It makes me nostalgic for my childhood – me playing with Lego in my bedroom while Mum busied herself with housework for an hour before I inevitably messed up the flat again. I was never lonely as an only child, but I often wondered what it would be like to have a sibling. Someone on hand to play with or fight with or just vent to when Mum was being unreasonable by asking me to put my dirty washing in the machine.

'I wish I was going to the cinema,' Alfie states. 'But Mum says I can't see scary movies until I'm eighteen.'

'Your mum's right,' I reply. 'You don't need that stuff in your head.'

'But I already know who Chucky is.'

I raise an eyebrow. 'You do, huh?'

'Yep. Darren told me. He's a doll who will stab you if you're not his friend and he said that Chucky can hide in your wardrobe and jump out while you sleep.'

Darren sounds like an asshole.

'Well, I'm very glad that Chucky is just a made-up character, then,' I reply. 'His movie was boring anyway; you're not missing much.'

Alfie turns back to his Lego, obviously not convinced. Nothing worse than an adult trying to convince you that something which is clearly fun, isn't.

'I'll tell you a secret. Matt hates scary films and even *he* wasn't scared of Chucky,' I inform him. 'I'm surprised he agreed to see one with your mum. He'll be hiding behind her the whole time.'

Alfie giggles. 'That's silly. Mum loves scary films. Do you like them?'

'Not really,' I reply. 'It's hard to be scared of things that aren't real, you know? I'd much rather watch a cool animation, or see someone save the world!'

Complete lie. I adore horror movies. Having the bejesus scared out of me distracts me from how mind-numbing real life can sometimes be, and the fact that Sarah loves them too makes me like her even more. I once made Angela sit through *The Fog* and she was so horrified she didn't speak to me for three days after. Maybe if I dress like a murderous pirate and vape outside her window, she'll finally stop calling me.

Sarah and Matt return three hours later to find the best fleet of Lego trucks the world has ever seen.

'Wow, you two have been busy!' she remarks. 'I wish I had stayed here to play. The film was so boring.'

Alfie looks delighted by this news, while Sarah mimes that it was fucking awesome. Matt declines to comment but he's definitely a shade lighter than when he left.

CHAPTER TWENTY-THREE

'Happy New Job, Nick!!'

Behind an assortment of oversized balloons, I see Alfie beaming at me, while Sarah clutches a bottle of champagne, her hair wet from the persistent February showers we've been having.

'Wow!' I reply, ushering them in. 'Thank you! It's perfect timing, I've just this second run out of giant inflatables.'

Alfie heads straight for the PlayStation as Sarah hands me the wine, yelling at him to take off his shoes.

'Every time,' she mumbles under her breath as she removes her coat. 'I don't know why he thinks the shoes rule doesn't apply here.'

'Probably because Matt doesn't take his off either,' I reply, putting the bottle into the fridge. 'But he's emotionally younger than Alfie, so he has an excuse.'

Sarah pulls out her usual seat at the table. 'So, *Mr I've Just Been Hired*, you must be feeling very pleased with yourself!

I was saving that champagne for Valentine's Day, by the way, but this is a far worthier occasion.'

I laugh. 'I'm more relieved than pleased to be honest. It's been touch-and-go, but Greta finally came through for me. I mean, it's temporary to cover maternity leave, but it's better than nothing.'

Relieved is an understatement. When Greta called this morning to say I'd be offered the position at Portman Brown LLP, I'd shouted *fuck* over and over for about a solid five minutes and punched the air repeatedly.

'However,' I continue, 'I'd like to state for the record that I don't regret the eight months of humiliating rejection it took me to get here.'

She grins. 'It's character-building, right?'

'Something like that.'

I bring Alfie some apple juice as Matt arrives home, carrying a bag full of ingredients which will soon be used to create my celebratory meal. He says hi to Alfie before kissing Sarah hello.

'Glad you could make it,' he says, placing the bag on the kitchen worktop. 'Bit of wine and risotto to celebrate our boy's good news!'

'Yep,' she replies. 'You'll be happy to finally have him back in that posh-boy, wanky lawyers club, I'm sure, sweetheart. You can all get together and talk about cricket and totty again.'

She sticks her tongue out at me as I fake a gasp of offence.

'Only place he belongs,' Matt replies, laughing. 'He's much happier when he has private health insurance and a superiority complex.'

'You both see me standing here, right?' I ask while they continue talking about me.

Sarah moves from the table and stands beside Matt to help chop the onions. 'Actually, I could see Nick doing something far more noble. Humanitarian work, saving old ladies from burning buildings, performing risky surgeries to remove brain tumours or . . . a teacher, perhaps? He's so good with Alfie, I could totally see him shaping young minds.'

Matt turns to look at me. 'Weirdly, I see where you're coming from, Sarah,' he remarks, squinting at me. 'Fancy swapping boardrooms for classrooms, buddy?'

'I appreciate the career advice, but I'll pass,' I reply. 'I have zero interest in anyone else's kids. Alfie is the exception.'

Matt's chicken risotto is a big hit, and everyone properly toasts my new position – even Alfie, who holds his tumbler high. Eventually he gets bored of the adult chat and Sarah lets him take his dessert to the living room to watch a movie, making him promise not to spill. I whisper that he's only allowed to spill over the stains I've already made, and he chuckles before vanishing with a bowl full of warm apple pie and ice cream.

'I'm too full for apple pie,' Sarah insists as she starts to clear away the dinner plates. 'Shall I make some coffee?'

Matt takes the plates from her and frowns. 'You clear tables and make coffee all day. Besides, you're the guest here.'

'True, but you make coffee at my house.'

'I know. You're a terrible host.'

As they playfully bicker over beverage duties, I slip off to the living room and check on Alfie, who has wolfed down his dessert, his eyes glued to the movie channel.

'What're you watching, bud?'

'*Aladdin*,' he replies. 'It's my favourite!'

'Nice! I'm just going to sort a few things—'

'I have it on DVD. My mum knows the songs, but she doesn't have time to watch it with me that much. Will you watch it with me?'

Ugh, the emotional pull is strong with this one. How can I say no? Even though I have a million things to do, I tell Alfie to scooch up, and join him on the couch. He snuggles in and begins telling me the plot, while I nod along, pretending this is new information.

When Sarah appears half an hour later, Aladdin and Jasmine are flying high over Agrabah on a carpet and Alfie is fast asleep.

'Well, that's adorable,' she remarks quietly, staring

down at us. 'He looks so comfy. You're like his human pillow.'

'Post-Christmas weight,' I reply, pointing to my belly. 'Once I hit the gym again, I'll be far too ripped to cuddle. It'll be like snuggling up on a steel washboard.'

She snorts as I pretend to flex the arm that's not wrapped around Alfie.

'Good for you,' she replies. 'You'll have the gym bunnies clean-eating out of your hand in no time.'

Sarah wakens Alfie and helps him put his jacket on while I try to remember where I put those weights that I ordered from Amazon last year.

'Penny for them?' Sarah says, redirecting my attention. 'You look concerned.'

'I'm good,' I reply. 'Just thinking about getting my shit together, you know. New job, new me, lose a few—'

'Uber is here,' Matt interrupts. 'I'll carry Alfie down, he's dead on his feet.'

'Night, Alfie, see you soon,' I say as he nestles into Matt's shoulder. Sarah picks up her bag and leans in to hug me.

'Don't be so hard on yourself,' she says softly. 'You're wonderful just the way you are.'

I watch her leave and continue to stare at the door once she's gone. I miss them already.

I drag my infatuated arse into my room and lay out my clothes for the morning. I'm not particularly nervous about tomorrow – in fact, I'm looking forward to getting back to the real world, with a real job, where I can use my training. Then again, the significant salary drop, and their huge staff turnover, makes me question this company's legitimacy.

Even Greta was reluctant for me to take the position, but understood that having no money was completely untenable, so working for a firm which is notorious for playing hardball with everyone, especially its staff, was still better than remaining unemployed. Plus, judging from the job spec, I should be able to do this with my eyes closed. This might be exactly what I need to take my mind off Sarah and focus on building my career again.

CHAPTER TWENTY-FOUR

Portman Brown LLP boasts an impressive postcode near Bond Street station in the heart of the city, but from the outside, it doesn't quite match the imposing exterior of Kensington Fox or any of the other magic-circle law firms in London.

The right-hand side of the street is undeniably charming with converted, clotted-cream-coloured Victorian town-houses, which wouldn't look out of place in a Richard Curtis film, but the left side, *my side*, is half building site, half purpose-built office space in a fetching shade of prison grey.

My heart sinks as it dawns on me that my days of working in a bazillion-square-foot, glass-structured modern office, complete with restaurant, gym and rooftop terrace are well and truly over. Shit, are those actual bars on the windows? What the hell have I let myself in for?

I take a deep breath and pull open the heavy brown doors, which lead into the small IKEA-inspired lobby, where a receptionist calls ahead to the second floor to let them know I'm on my way up.

'You Nick?'

The lift doors have barely had time to close behind me when I'm ambushed by a frowning woman in black hipster glasses who's clutching a pile of manila envelopes.

'Um, yes, that's me. I'm due to—'

'This way.'

I follow her along the side of a large open-plan office painted in shades of blue and lighter blue, which looks more like a call centre than a law firm. It smells like fifty different types of takeaway breakfasts and even at 9am, the place has clearly been buzzing for hours. At the back of the room I see four private offices overlooking the floor and a large boardroom to the top right which is currently occupied by three men, all with folded arms and the same glazed expression.

'Your desk,' hipster lady informs me, stopping beside a vacant workspace at the end of the room. She reaches down and snatches up a solo photo frame, featuring a bride and groom which was obviously left by the last occupier.

'Dump your stuff and I'll take you to see Sophia.'

'Um, my agency told me to report to Marion Thomas. I thought *you* were—'

'Marion no longer works here.'

'Oh.' I get the feeling some poor sod is now missing a wedding photo. We march over to the offices at the back.

'I'm Kim, by the way,' she finally offers, knocking on the third door. 'Office manager.'

'Nice to meet you, Kim. So, who is Sophia?'

'For fuck's sake, WHAT DO YOU WANT, KIM? I haven't even had my coffee yet!'

I glance through the office window to see a woman with poker-straight black hair, manically waving us in.

Opening the door, Kim smirks. 'Sophia, this is Nick, Rachel's maternity replacement. I'll be at my desk.'

I enter and take a seat in front of a woman in her late forties who clearly has no idea who I am and would prefer to keep it that way.

'Christ, I didn't even know Rachel was pregnant, never mind on maternity leave.' She picks up her phone and angry-dials an extension. 'What agency are you from?'

'GL Recruitment. Greta arranged everything with—'

She holds up a hand to shush me. Her fingers are very long, with unnervingly sharp nails emerging from them like a manicured shiv. 'Kim, can you come back in here and just deal with this?'

Sophia places the receiver back, opens a drawer and takes out a tub of coffee sweeteners, while Kim enters the room again.

'I'll leave it to Kim to run through everything with you, but we don't hand-hold here. Everything we deal with is business critical, so we expect you to hit the ground running.'

'No problem.'

'Good.' She opens her laptop and begins typing, while Kim subtly motions for me to follow her. I feel a little stunned; not quite the welcome I had hoped for. At Kensington Fox, they'd have taken me to lunch.

Kim expertly throws some files on to a desk to her right while I tag along behind her like a lost puppy. I draw looks from the rest of the staff who try to size me up as I pass.

'I'm sure you've done your research,' she begins, 'but to recap, we deal with four main areas here: Corporate, Commercial, Property – all on this floor – and of course, our lovely Personal Injury lawyers, who are all based on the first floor when they're not out chasing ambulances during their lunch breaks. Ground floor has eight client meeting rooms – book those through me. The coffee machine here sucks and the Nespresso machine is for partners only, but there's a Starbucks on the corner.'

'Who's on the floors above us?'

'An advertising agency has the top three; above them, some tech company. If you smoke, you'll no doubt bump into most of them in the back courtyard. I try to avoid that area, it's like a fucking meat market for the morally challenged.'

We reach the far end of the office where she opens a door into a large room filled with endless boxes of files and cabinets. She bangs the side of a stalled printer which whirrs back into action.

'Closed cases from the past three years are stored here;

anything older is off-site but can be brought over within the hour. Everything must be signed out.'

She closes the door and leads me back to my desk, lifting paperwork from completed filing trays as she goes. I'm exhausted just watching her. She sees my slightly uneasy look.

'You worked at KF, right?'

'Yeah, five years.'

She nods. 'I used to work at Clifford Allen ... damn, I miss their canteen. Look, this place is like karma for whatever sins you committed in your past employment, and God knows, most of us have. My advice? Buckle down, put the hours in and *don't* piss off Sophia.'

I look over at her office and see Sophia standing at her window watching the floor. I wonder if she can hear us.

'Got it. Thanks.'

Kim grunts and hands me a key to the locked drawer on my desk. 'So, now that's out of the way, I want you to go to Starbucks and grab a strong coffee for yourself and a Diet Coke for me, while I set up your logins and email. When you get back, I have a breach of contract case for you to get started on.'

'Sure, no problem,' I reply, grabbing my coat from my chair. 'Won't be long.'

She walks me to the lift, and I step inside, pressing the ground floor button. I hate this place already.

*

'Jesus, I thought you'd run off,' Matt says from the kitchen as I enter the living room and throw myself down on to the couch face first. 'You want a beer?'

I give him a muffled *yes, please* in response, my entire body beyond grateful to be home. It's gone 11pm and I haven't even had dinner.

The clink of the beer bottles makes me pull myself up into a slouching position which I intend to stay in for as long as possible.

'So?' Matt asks. 'How was your first day?'

I stare blankly ahead as I take a long swig from my Budweiser.

'That bad, eh?'

I take a second swig and place my bottle on the coffee table with a thunk. 'If Satan ran a law firm, it would be this one.'

Matt doesn't look surprised at this news in the slightest. 'Yeah, I'd heard they can be a tad merciless. Their billing hours are notoriously high but—'

'Information that might have been useful before today, mate . . .'

'But they're successful!' he insists, trying to make me feel better. 'Remember Felix Thingamajig who started with us at Kensington? He worked there before he went solo. Made more in bonuses than he did on salary.'

'Didn't he get disbarred?'

'That's not the point.'

'Well, temps don't get bonuses,' I inform him. 'I'm only contracted to work 9am–6pm but apparently *showing initiative* and *going the extra mile* goes a long way towards not being quickly replaced by someone else.'

Matt scrunches up his face but remains silent. We both understand that this a terrible working practice, but we also know that this is the world we chose to work in. At Kensington, we'd pull all-nighters, competing with other associates in order to get head pats from senior staff.

'Fuck it,' I say, attacking my beer again. 'I'll tell Greta to keep looking for other opportunities, maybe something better will come up.'

'I hear Build-A-Bear are hiring . . .'

'Up yours,' I reply, while secretly thinking that it's not a bad idea. 'Anyway, I'm off to bed.'

Matt says goodnight while I slump off to the bathroom to wash the very long day off. If I can survive working with screaming children, I'm almost certain I can handle a few cantankerous lawyers.

CHAPTER TWENTY-FIVE

'Is this dress too "meh" for a wedding? Or is it too weird? Maybe it's too weird. I don't want people to be all "hey, there's Matt's girlfriend, the thrift shop weirdo".'

I laugh as Sarah stands in front of the mirror, pinching at the fabric on her bluey-green dress. I personally think she looks beautiful. Classy, even. Hot. I remove my gaze and continue knotting my tie.

Matt's girlfriend. Not yours. You don't care how she looks. Play it down.

'It's definitely a look,' I tell her. 'You remind me of a retro peacock.'

She looks appalled.

'No, I mean the colours! And the way the skirt poofs out. You look fine!'

'I should change.'

'No time. We should have left twenty minutes ago. Greta will end me if I'm late.'

As neither of us are particularly flush we choose to

get the Underground, feeling decidedly overdressed as we take a seat in a carriage filled with Adidas and skinny-jean wearers. Sarah sits beside me and begins smoothing down her hair. I quietly chuckle.

'Flyaway hairs are nothing to laugh at,' she informs me, grinning. 'My ability to frizz at any given moment is legendary.'

'I wasn't laughing at you!' I reply. 'You just remind me of a woman who works in my office, Kim. She gently pets the top of her head constantly like it's a show dog.'

'I feel her pain. How's work going, anyway? Matt says they're all savages in that place.'

I laugh. 'In our industry, it's widespread, not just in my office. Let's just say, I've quickly become reacclimatised to finding loopholes and making rich people's lives easier. Kensington Fox wasn't any more virtuous; it just had more natural light.'

'I still think you're meant for greater things,' Sarah says, rummaging through her bag. She brings out her phone and checks the screen. 'I should probably text Brandon's mum, shouldn't I? Make sure Alfie's OK.'

'You only dropped him off a couple of hours ago! I'm sure she would text you if he wasn't. Besides, the signal is non-existent down here. You'd have more luck just yelling.'

She makes a face and puts her phone back in her bag, before clutching it anxiously.

'He'll be fine,' I say supportively. 'He's done sleepovers before.'

This is the one part of parenting that makes me nervous about having kids. Worrying about someone else twenty-four seven must be exhausting.

We arrive at Bond Street and make the short walk to Claridge's, where Sarah finally caves and sends a short message to Brandon's mum before we go inside. Thankfully she responds almost immediately, reassuring Sarah that Alfie's playing in the garden with Brandon and can be heard giggling as she types. Sarah returns her phone to her bag looking marginally less worried.

'Sorry, I just—'

'No need,' I interject. 'You ready?'

With one final dress adjustment, the doorman ushers us in and Sarah follows behind.

Knowing Greta's intolerance for organised religion, I wasn't in the least bit surprised that she chose not to have a church ceremony – however, this was far grander than the basic, yet tastefully unfussy, civil ceremony I had pictured in my mind. Maybe because the last wedding I had attended was Harriet and Noel's registry-office and pub-crawl extravaganza, where everyone put in a kitty and we all ended up eating fish and chips in the middle of Camden at three in the morning. I'm grateful it isn't a church, however. I haven't stepped in one since Mum's funeral and I have no great longing to do so anytime soon.

Sarah and I are led into a pink and white, champagne-filled reception area, complete with dignified pianist and at least one hundred close friends and family. White roses seem to be the flower du jour, arranged in glass vases all over the room, and I'm handed one for my lapel, as I appear to be the only boutonnière-lacking male at the party.

'Christ, this is like another world,' Sarah says quietly as she straightens my flower. 'That woman's shoes cost twice my monthly salary.'

I follow her eyes towards the feet of a woman wearing blingy-looking sandals with a white feather hanging off the front. Sarah is wearing red shoes with a thin purple heel.

'Yours are nicer,' I reply. 'I mean ... what's with the feather? It looks like she kicked a bird on her way in.'

Sarah laughs and looks away.

'Anyway, her toes look weird,' I continue. 'Are they meant to cross over like that?'

'The price women pay for fashion,' she says, sipping her champagne. 'I have hobbit feet hidden inside these bad boys; I can't judge anyone.'

A server in a crisp white shirt offers us smoked salmon canapés which I gratefully devour, having missed breakfast in favour of getting an extra hour in bed. With Matt in Washington, I've enjoyed having the flat to myself, but I usually rely on him to feed me. Remembering that dinner isn't until five, I chase the server down and grab some more.

'You scrub up very well,' Sarah informs me. 'I don't think I've seen you in evening wear before.'

I smile. 'Ah yes, you've only seen me in casual attire. This must be quite the treat for you. Like hanging out with a real-life Littlewoods catalogue.'

She laughs heartily. 'You forgot the festive, jolly-old-man-wear, but I can't really talk. I feel like I've come in fancy dress.'

The more I look around the room, the more I'm certain that Sarah chose *exactly* the right dress to wear today. As gorgeous as the women here are, they all look the same – like they're all painted by the same numbers in marginally different shades. Sarah looks exactly like she is – beautiful, colourful and completely original.

'Shall we take a selfie for Matt?' she suggests. 'I feel bad that he's missing this!'

'Sure,' I reply. I feel bad that he's barely crossed my mind at all – but of course, he's still clearly on Sarah's. I take out my phone and we *cheese*, before WhatsApping the photo to his phone, which is currently somewhere over the Atlantic.

'So, if this is the preshow party, where are they having the main event?' Sarah asks. We don't have to wait long to find out. The doors on the left-hand side swing open to reveal another larger room and we're cordially invited to take our seats for the ceremony. It's so bloody classy, I can't help but be impressed.

'Wow,' Sarah exclaims, admiring the pristine white and gold décor. 'This is beautiful.'

God, she's adorable. She's literally enchanted by everything she sees here and it's completely genuine.

We're directed towards the bride's side of the room, where I spot Greta's mum and older sister Imogen, sporting giant hats, along with the groom who's looking surprisingly relaxed for a man about to marry Greta. She's at least worth a light sweat. I wave politely at them all as Sarah and I take our seats.

I recognise a few faces from their engagement party, but it seems to be mainly family and friends from outside our little uni circle. Harriet must be so pissed off she's missing this. She lives for a good knees-up. I surreptitiously send her a copy of our photo and send my love before turning off my phone.

Before long, a hush comes over the room and two violinists, along with the pianist, begin to play the wedding march. As the doors open, I see two little dark-haired flower girls, dressed in yellow, commence the procession, followed by Greta with her dad. I instantly get goosebumps all over. She looks exactly like I thought she would: tight-fitting white lace gown, her hair delicately curled, and a glow that radiates beyond the walls of this magnificent function room. I beam with pride as she walks slowly past, smiling unabashedly, until a hand clasping mine grabs my attention.

A single tear rolls down Sarah's cheek as she squeezes my hand and then lets it go. My momentary confusion soon subsides when it dawns on me that she's thinking of her wedding, and her late husband. Shit. I never even considered this might be tough for her.

'You alright?' I whisper, leaning in. 'If it's too—'

She swiftly wipes her cheek and shakes her head. 'I'm fine. Just wobbled. She looks so happy.'

Greta reaches the top of the aisle and kisses her dad, who then steps aside to let Will take his place. As he looks at her like she's the only woman alive, a lump appears in my throat. *Good for you, Greta*, I think to myself. *Matt was right. Our girl did well.*

'Dear friends and family. We have come together today to celebrate the love of Greta and William, who have decided to live their lives together as husband and wife . . .'

CHAPTER TWENTY-SIX

After a whirlwind of cheering, group photos, mingling and drinking, we make our way to the next part of the wedding, where Greta and Dr William Cashflow have hired out the ballroom for the meal. We're greeted in the ballroom reception area by a harpist, more champagne, and the cerise pink-clad mother of the bride who looks like she's about to implode with joy.

'Well, you look splendid, Mrs Lang!' I say as she hugs me. 'It was such a nice ceremony.'

'Wonderful, wasn't it, Nick? I'm so glad you could come! I hear Matthew is otherwise engaged; such a pity, really.'

'I know; he's gutted not to be here. This is Sarah, by the way. Sarah, this is Greta's mum.'

'Ivy,' she informs her. 'Pleased to meet you, dear, your dress is wonderful. Grab a drink, seating chart is just inside the door.'

We enter the ballroom, scooping up champagne flutes as we go, and are met with a sea of white linen tablecloths, fresh flowers and a black starlit dance floor which has probably been installed by God himself.

'This just gets better and better,' Sarah remarks as she gazes in wonder. 'My reception was nowhere near as grand as this – but then again, we were twenty-five and skint. Where are we sitting?'

I wonder what Sarah looked like in a wedding dress, imagining her walking up the aisle towards me. Gathering myself, I scan the list of twelve tables, eventually finding our names.

'Table four,' I inform her. 'You ready for some scintillating small talk?'

'Always,' she replies. 'And by always, I mean never.'

We find our place cards, nodding politely to the other couples already seated at the table, vaguely recognising two of them as Will's guests at the engagement party. 'Nick,' I say, introducing myself. 'This my friend Sarah.'

Sarah gives them a little wave and takes her seat.

'Kelvin,' replies the man wearing a far nicer suit than mine, 'and my wife, Shondra.'

The other couples are both from Will's side of the family: cousin James and his wife Lynne plus his Gen-Z niece Emma with her boyfriend Louis. Without a doubt one of them has a YouTube channel.

'Have you seen Greta yet?' I ask, scanning the room again. 'I wanted to say hello before she gets swamped by everyone. I barely got a chance to say hi during the photos.'

'They'll probably do the grand entrance in a moment,' Shondra replies. 'We couldn't make it to the ceremony so I'm dying to see her dress.'

Sarah quietly sips her champagne, taking it all in. I've been a plus-one to several weddings, and it's always awkward as hell at first, but I get the feeling she's still a little upset after the ceremony.

'You sure you're alright with all of this?' I ask quietly. 'I mean . . . at the ceremony you seemed . . .'

She smiles warmly. 'I am . . . I haven't been to a wedding since, well, my own. It all kind of just . . . hit me . . . y'know?'

I nod. I'm more than aware of how grief can just blitz-attack when you least expect it.

'Ah, of course. Listen, if it's too much we don't have to—'

'I'm good,' she interrupts, placing her hand on mine. 'But it's kind of you to offer. I'm not overly sad, just maybe a little sentimental.'

'Understandable,' I reply, secretly hoping she will just leave her hand on mine for the rest of the evening. 'Sometimes life is just a great big boot in the balls. Weddings remind me that I'm probably the only single man on earth.'

'Jesus, now who's being glum. You need to cheer up, Nick; who knows, your future wife might be here tonight, but she is hardly going to approach you if you're the weirdo crying in the corner!'

Her eyes dart around the room while my gaze stays firmly on her.

A hush comes over the room as the arrival of the bride and groom is announced, and Greta and Will enter to a rapturous applause, taking their seats at the top table beside their immediate family. As happy as I am for Greta, it all reminds me of how far behind everyone else I am. No immediate family, no spouse, no girlfriend, no kids. Jesus, I need to get a move on.

Dinner is outstanding as expected; I chose the lobster risotto to start, followed by lamb with barley and parsnips, then a chocolate fondant to finish. Sarah went with the same dessert but had scallops with caviar to start and an inventive-looking duck dish with grilled pears for her main course. I google the wine, feeling my eyebrows shoot up into my hairline when I see the price tag. Sarah and I both pull faces at how bloody delicious everything is. It's perfection, even down to the waiting staff, who are all trained with military precision, expertly placing and clearing plates like stealthy catering ninjas.

Will's niece Emma seems to have taken quite the shine to Sarah, quizzing her on her dress and something involving coffin nails which I'm sure is less morbid than it sounds. The rest of the table are chatty enough, but it's not a patch on the riot I would have had with Harriet and Matt here too. As the coffee arrives at the tables, I hear the sharp feedback from a speaker as the bride's father Mike is introduced to give the first speech.

'First of all, I want to welcome you all and thank you for joining us on this very special day,' he begins. 'I know that some of Will's family have travelled from as far as Australia to be here and it means the world to all of us.'

A small collective cheer from the Australians in the room makes everyone smile, while Greta's dad wipes his leathery forehead with a napkin and sips his wine.

'Now, being an MP, I'm not entirely averse to public speaking, however, Greta has asked me to keep this short – probably because we have a lot of speeches to get through, but also probably for fear I might filibuster for hours with her entire life story and keep the band waiting.'

I see Greta and her mum both laugh and nod in unison.

'So instead, I'll just thank Greta for being Greta. Her mother and I are unbelievably proud of the woman she's become. We wish her and Will nothing but happiness, love and the humour to deal with whatever life throws their way. We love you both.'

Mike is now in tears. God, even I'm starting to tear up a little. Sarah whoops in support of the man, who's now being hugged tightly by his daughter, along with the rest of the room.

Next up is Will, who receives a rapturous applause before he's even said a word. He stands there, basking, like he's just won an award.

'Thank you, Mike, for those kind words. On behalf of my *wife and me* –' the room cheers – 'I want to say how thrilled we are that you could be here to share our special day. I would also recommend that you keep your glasses charged as I intend to toast a lot of people in the next few minutes. Starting with my parents, Diana and Hunter . . .'

Hunter? Is his dad a gladiator?

Will keeps to his word, pretty much raising a glass to everyone who is here, who couldn't be here, who works here and even family members who died before being here was even an option.

'And finally, to my beautiful partner in crime, Greta.' He takes her hand and she gazes into his eyes, like there's no one else in the room.

'Thank you for choosing to take the tube on that rainy morning five years ago. Thank you for taking a chance on the man who offered you his umbrella on the way out. Thank you for being the first face I see in the morning and the last I see at night . . . and most of all, thank you for agreeing to be by my side as we navigate this crazy, beautiful little thing called *life*. You are the skip in my step, the light in my eyes and the song stuck in my head. Thank you.'

As everyone puts their hands together, I see Sarah purse her lips, desperately trying to stop the corners of her mouth from shooting upwards.

'Well, that was truly beautiful, wasn't it?' I say to her, grinning. 'The emotion . . . the poetry of it all . . .'

'Stop it.'

'I mean, what new bride doesn't want to be compared to a stuck record during a wedding speech?'

She breaks, promptly pulling a napkin to her face to hide her laughter. 'Oh God, we are terrible people. *Crazy, beautiful*, terrible people.'

Shondra glances over at Sarah who's almost hiding under the table. 'Is she OK?'

'Overwhelmed,' I reply, rubbing Sarah's back as she shakes with laughter. 'She'll be fine.'

Sarah finally regains her composure as the next of the speeches continues. Five speeches later, it's time to cut the cake, which is served with even more coffee. With an hour to freshen up before the dancing begins and the evening guests arrive, those who are staying in the hotel retreat to their rooms, while Sarah and I take a breath of fresh air in the hotel garden.

'God, I feel so bad for laughing,' Sarah says, as we take a little walk. 'I feel like such a jaded old bastard these days.'

'Don't beat yourself up,' I respond. 'You're human. That level of cheese is hard not to smirk at.'

'You dated Greta, right?'

I nod. 'Years ago.'

'Interesting. So that could have been you up there, almost plagiarising Queen.'

'Doubtful,' I reply, chuckling. 'Our relationship was very

brief and very uneventful, which is probably the reason we've remained friends.'

'No broken hearts?'

'Exactly.'

Sarah gives my answer some thought. 'So, when did you know that something was . . . well, missing? I mean, not all love is like BAM! It can grow over time.'

'True,' I reply. 'But who wants to spend the next sixty years getting there? Or worse, just settling because it's better than being alone. You saw the way she looks at Will . . . she never looked at me that way.'

'Well, you deserve that too,' Sarah says softly. 'You deserve to be looked at that way.' She unfortunately is studying the ground as she says this.

'You're right,' I reply. 'And one day, when I least expect it . . . I will find my very own Will.'

She grins. 'I have no doubt. Let's get back in; that Dom Pérignon isn't going to drink itself.'

Greta and Will's first dance is a surprising one. Knowing Greta as long as I have, I didn't expect some cringey, choreographed dance routine, but neither did I expect her to choose 'You Make My Dreams Come True' by Hall and Oates.

'Why are you laughing?' Sarah asks as I snort unexpectedly.

'It's just . . . Greta is a ballad kind of girl. I was expecting

Etta James or some grand romantic number. This is, well . . . fun!'

She grins, watching Will eighties-bop his new wife around the floor. They are radiating happiness as he twirls her round.

'We had "Annie's Song". My middle name is Annie so . . . actually seems a bit weird now, having a first dance solely dedicated to the bride. It should really be a team song.'

'Nice, though,' I reply. 'Though you can't dance like *that* to "Annie's Song".'

I gesture towards Greta who is gleefully stomping her expensive shoes into the equally expensive floor. God, she's like a different woman with Will. He obviously brings out a side in her that I never could.

'What would you choose?' Sarah asks me. 'For a first dance? I reckon you'd go for . . . something super cool like Bowie or The White Stripes. I've seen your Spotify playlists.'

I laugh. 'No, actually. It would be something simple. Like "Should I Stay or Should I Go" by The Clash.'

She frowns and socks my arm. 'I should hope you aren't even considering going anywhere the day you get married. I see now why you're single.'

'. . . or maybe "God Only Knows" by The Beach Boys. Not that I've ever given it much thought.'

She looks surprised. 'Well, you've managed to redeem yourself just in time; that's romantic as fuck.'

'I can be romantic.' I smirk. 'I'm like the Barry White of the legal world. I can make a woman feel like she's walking on clouds.'

'Unless you have a beanstalk in your trousers, I'm calling bullshit.'

I laugh a little too loudly, drawing daggers from Shondra, who's living her best life via Greta's dress. Thankfully, Greta's mum and dad have now joined them on the dance floor, and everyone is gearing themselves up to do the same.

'I think I need more booze before I hit the floor,' I confess. 'You up for another?'

'Definitely,' she replies. 'Something with a double in it. This dress only works when I don't give a fuck.'

I walk towards the bar, trying to remain upbeat. While I might already be having the best time with Sarah, deep down I know that this is as far as it goes. No matter how funny she is or how beautiful she looks, I'm here on a purely platonic basis.

'Nick! At least one of my good friends made the effort to be here!'

'You look beautiful,' I reply, smiling at the bride, 'and you know they'd be here if they could. But unless you want Harriet throwing up on your dress . . .'

Greta, now slightly tipsy on wine and adrenaline, and also without shoes, pulls me in for a hug before grabbing a seat at our table. 'I've been dying to grab a chat with you all day! Did you get some cake? You must try the cake.'

Sarah holds up her slice, wrapped in a napkin for confirmation. 'I'll share it with Alfie.'

'Oh, take more for him!!' she replies. 'There're four tiers, we're not on rations. I'm so glad you came with Nick; he's the more fun one, anyway, Sarah.' Greta winks.

'So, Mrs Howard, where to on the honeymoon?' I ask, also feeling slyly glad that Sarah is here with me.

'Howard-Lang,' she corrects, 'and we're off to the Maldives tomorrow night. Two weeks of sun, sex and drinks with umbrellas. So excited.'

'Sounds amazing, Greta. You deserve it,' I say, leaning in to kiss her cheek. 'I'm so happy for you.'

She hugs me back. 'Thanks, Nick. You're such a lovely man. Whoever you choose is a lucky woman.' She breaks away, smiling at me. 'Oh, Shondra, take a pic of us, will you?'

Greta motions for me to hand over my phone as we all huddle together and say cheese for the camera, me in the middle and Sarah's arm wrapped around my back.

'Aww, that's lovely,' Greta remarks as we look at our photograph. 'You look so pretty, Sarah, Matt will be kicking himself when he sees this.'

'Thanks,' she replies, 'but there's only one beauty in this photograph.'

'Nice of you to say,' I respond. 'It's about time my magnificence was recognised.'

Greta laughs before announcing that she needs to pee.

'I've been holding it forever. These Spanx are too much hassle to whip up and down willy-nilly.'

'Ugh, just go,' I reply, scrunching my face up. 'I really don't want to hear about your willy-nilly.'

'Have fun, guys. Remember, grab some more cake and find me before you leave, OK?'

We nod as she legs it to the bathrooms. I forward the photo to Greta, Matt and Harriet.

'Will you send me that pic too?' Sarah asks. 'It's great. I need more pictures of my friends.'

Yuck. Friends. Fuck the friend-zone, I want to be in the sex-zone. Or even the fully clothed-spooning-zone. Anything but the friend-zone.

Sarah suddenly springs to her feet. 'I love this song. Get your arse on the dance floor immediately.'

I happily follow her to the sound of 'Crazy in Love', prepared to spend the rest of the evening sweating it up on the dance floor with the rest of the well-dressed drunkards. We dance for a solid two hours, only stopping to make emergency trips to the bar for water and another tequila shot.

'I had fun tonight,' she yells into my ear, as I bite into my lime. 'A really great time. Thank you.'

'We still have two hours left!' I laugh, dragging her back to the dance floor.

'I know,' she replies. 'I just wanted to let you know. I'm sorry you got stuck with me and couldn't bring someone special.'

'Don't be daft,' I reply, grinning. She's doing the robot. I can't keep a straight face.

Fuck. The urge to tell her that I *did* bring someone special is almost overwhelming. That I'm here with the only woman in the world that I want.

'We're mates. I'm very happy you're here.'

Three songs down and we take a seat. Sarah bypasses the champagne in favour of water.

'I hear it's your birthday in a couple of weeks,' she says, fanning herself with a napkin. 'Any plans?'

'Matt's trying to get me to have a party, but to be honest, I'm a bit done with crowds at the moment. I'd like to do something fun. Something silly. It's not every year you turn thirty-one.'

'Theme parks will be open again for the summer soon,' she suggests. 'They're so much fun. An entire day screaming and eating food you'll see again ten minutes later . . . Silly enough?'

'I haven't been to a theme park in years. That's not a bad idea. Think Alfie would be up for that?'

'Um, yes, but it's your birthday, don't feel obliged to—'

'Perfect then. I'll let Matt know.'

She grins broadly. 'You sure you want us tagging along?'

'You'll need to. Matt's not the best on wild rides. I'll

need a coaster companion. He can go on the kids' rides with Alfie.'

She agrees immediately, clapping her hands excitedly like a five-year-old. I just hope Matt is as keen as we are.

Several shots later, the DJ announces the final song of the evening. Sarah drags herself to her feet again, kicking off her shoes, while I wince in exhaustion.

She frowns, one hand on her hip, the other stretched out towards me. 'I'm not doing the last dance alone – on your feet, soldier!'

I begrudgingly agree and she hauls me up, just as 'Knocks Me Off My Feet' by Stevie Wonder starts playing. Sarah looks faintly embarrassed – clearly, she wasn't betting on a slower number. I smile, hoping it reaches my eyes, and take her hand, pulling her in close for the obligatory rock back and forth of untrained dancers. After a moment of awkwardness, her head eventually settles against my chest and I feel myself struggling to swallow, hoping she can't hear me gulp. Why does her hair smell so goddamn amazing? It takes all of my self-restraint to resist burying my face in her curls. I wonder if she can feel how fast my heart is beating. Just then, as I'm gazing at the top of her head, she looks up at me and, suddenly, our lips are just centimetres apart. When she meets my eyes, I spring back like I've been scalded, afraid that if I stay touching her for a second longer that I won't be able to resist kissing her.

I cough uncomfortably. 'Sorry, just gotta go to the men's

room. Grab your shoes, yeah? I'll call us an Uber when I get back.' I literally flee.

Having retreated to the men's room to gather my composure again, I let my face fall against the cold wall tiles, gross bathroom germs be damned. I cannot keep getting myself into these situations with Sarah. It's physically fucking painful.

CHAPTER TWENTY-SEVEN

'I hate you,' Matt says, his hands gripping the overhead restraint of the roller-coaster. 'I absolutely fucking hate you.'

Matt's initial enthusiasm about spending my birthday at Thorpe Park seems to have dissipated somewhat.

'You don't have to go on anything too wild,' I'd informed him. 'Just fancied doing something a bit different this year, you know. Instead of just getting another hangover.'

'Oh, don't worry about me,' he'd replied, looking distinctly green. 'I'll go on anything. Faster the better.'

'But when we went to Blackpool, you almost cried when—'

'Mate, that was six years ago. I had food poisoning. I was just feeling emotional that I'd been coaxed into going to bloody Blackpool. Nothing to do with the rides.'

On the train ride here, he'd excitedly told an eager Alfie about the attractions the little man would be tall enough to go on, along with tales from yonder years of when his own dad would take him to the rides at the local cattle show fair.

'High on the big wheel, wellies on, great view of the countryside. Good times.'

Sometimes I think Matt missed his calling as a farmer.

'I thought you said he hated rides?' Sarah had whispered, while Matt and Alfie watched YouTube videos from previous theme park visitors. 'He seems totally up for it.'

'Maybe I misjudged him,' I replied, knowing full well that I hadn't. Ninety per cent of this was bravado for Sarah and Alfie's benefit and probably ten per cent was amnesia from the trauma suffered on the Big One at Blackpool Pleasure Beach.

'You don't have to do this, you know,' I inform him, albeit redundantly, since we're now locked in and ready to go. 'I said I'd go on by myself.'

'What, and look like a pussy in front of Alfie and Sarah? No chance.'

'I don't think—'

'I blame you for this. Actually, not just for this . . .'

I tell Matt to relax and try to enjoy it as the last safety checks are done, giving Sarah and Alfie a quick wave as they look on. Alfie looks irritated that he hasn't quite reached the four-foot-three minimum height requirement but watches keenly as the ride hisses into action.

The initial force by which the coaster rockets off surprises even me, but Matt's loud yelp makes me laugh more than it should. The momentum carries us past greenery and through a small tunnel before facing a steep hill which we slowly climb, giving me a chance to glance over at Matt, who now has his eyes firmly closed and is either cursing or praying under his breath.

'Dude, you're missing the view.'

'Shut the hell up.'

'I thought you liked views?'

'I swear if I die, I will haunt the fuck out of you.'

As we finally reach the top, a fearless few in front raise their arms and we hurtle down, arses leaving seats and stomachs dropping, eventually culminating in a particularly impressive high-pitched scream from Matt. After several loops and corkscrews, we come to a halt and Matt finally opens his eyes.

'You still with us?' I ask. His face isn't even a colour anymore; it's practically transparent.

He shakes his head. 'I'm expected to walk after this, yeah?'

He wobbles off and we exit, where Sarah and Alfie stand waiting, ready for post-match analysis.

'That was soooo fast!' Alfie declares. 'Was it scary?'

Matt nods sheepishly. 'Well—'

'He didn't even scream! I don't know how anyone can be that brave, but he was. I was terrified!'

'Wow!' Sarah declares. 'Impressive! I'd need a general anaesthetic to get me on that ride. What a champion!'

Alfie beams at Matt like he's just saved the planet. It's the least I can do; after facing his coaster fears for my benefit, Matt's practically a hero anyway.

'Matt . . . can you come on the little roller-coaster with me? That looks a bit scary too.'

'Sure, buddy,' he says, taking Alfie's hand. 'Love to.'

As we walk past the merchandise stall, Sarah laughs and stops me, gesturing towards the screens on the wall.

'He didn't even scream, you say?'

It takes me a second to find it, but there, in glorious HD, is a petrified, open-mouthed, shrieking Matt.

'Woman, keep walking,' I say, moving along. 'He'll freak if he sees that.'

'What, like this?'

Sarah tries to replicate his photo face and I howl with laughter. Fortunately, Alfie has managed to drag Matt far enough away that he doesn't see me clutching my sides.

'He's having a ball,' Sarah informs me as we watch Alfie skip alongside Matt. 'Thanks for inviting us, birthday boy.'

'You're welcome,' I reply. 'You've made an old man very happy. Probably not what most adults would choose for their thirty-first, but I'm having the best time.'

'Pfft, I painted my kitchen for my thirty-first,' Sarah retorts. 'This is the kind of adulting I'd rather be doing. Though I had a baby at home. You just have a Matt.'

'What? I thought you were younger than me, like late twenties?'

She laughs. 'God bless you and your terrible eyesight. I'll be thirty-four soon.'

'So, Matt's your toy boy?' I say, grinning. 'Lucky him.'

'Piss off!' she replies, chuckling. 'Three years is nothing! I'm not some coffee-serving cougar.'

As Matt takes Alfie on to the Flying Fish ride, Sarah points to a nearby attraction which looks relatively tame compared to the coaster I've just been on.

'We're going on this,' she insists. 'I feel the need to sway wildly.'

I look up at the current passengers, most of whom are screaming their heads off, which seems excessive for a ride which only swings back and forth.

We take our seats on the back row, next to a couple of young teens who are already whooping excitedly. She giggles as the ride begins to rock throwing her head back as it peeds up. It's a joy to watch.

'Hands up, bitches,' someone yells, and everyone follows suit, including Sarah and me, now both laughing like drains as our stomachs exit the carriage.

After a quick juice break, Alfie decides we should all go on the dodgems, which happens to be my least favourite ride in the park.

'Um, maybe I'll just watch . . . take pictures?' I suggest,

but Alfie's having none of it, insisting I ride with him. Trying to explain to a four-year-old the concept of whip-lash is pointless.

Matt and Sarah take one car, leaving me squashed in beside Alfie, who's grabbing the steering wheel like a tiny Michael Schumacher. As the buzzer rings to start, Alfie floors the accelerator, squealing in delight as we head straight first into Matt and Sarah, who visibly jerk forward with the force.

'Let's see if you can just drive around the track without hit—'

A kid in a baseball cap blindsides us and I feel my chest thud against the seatbelt. Alfie giggles and powers us off again. How the fuck is this fun?

Forty crashes later, I stagger off, wondering if my internal organs are still where they should be. Fortu-nately, both Sarah and Matt appear to be pretty banged up and declare that they're never going on that again, before I do. Alfie, remaining unscathed, bounces off towards a food stand.

Two hours later we're fed, happy and slightly soaked from the water rides. This part I don't mind so much, given that a small child threw up on my foot earlier and now, post-water ride, my shoe appears to be somewhat puke-free again. Matt and Alfie decide to have one last go on the junior roller coaster while Sarah and I head to SAW, a ride based on the horror movie.

'This looks brutal,' Sarah remarks as we take our seats. 'Have you seen that bloody drop?'

'One hundred feet,' I reply, smirking. 'Say goodbye to that burger you had earlier. Oh look, there's that little puppet shit, Billy. That can't be good.'

Before I can say anything else, the ride takes off, twisting our way to the foot of the climb.

'Oh fuck,' Sarah declares, as we tip back and begin our ascent. 'Here we go.'

Gravity is doing its best to pull us back headfirst to where we started. Sarah reaches over and grabs my left hand. With one last look at each other, we tip over the edge and hurtle towards the ground like Thelma and Louise, but with far more screaming. We loop, we invert, we bang our heads off the sides of the chairs, but we hang on to each other. Even in a death grip, I feel like her hand fits perfectly in mine. As we finally come to a stop, the restraints lift, and we're forced to break apart.

'Goddamn, that was intense,' she says, climbing out. 'Sorry about the whole hand thing, I panicked up there.'

'Not a problem,' I reply, 'though I haven't been gripped that tightly since Nadine Foster took me round the back of the Sports Centre.'

'I cannot believe you just made a hand-job joke in a kid's theme park,' she replies, taking out her phone. 'You're going to hell ... oh, Matt's just texted, they're waiting by the Dome.'

'He's been good with Alfie today,' I say as we walk across. 'You must be pleased they're getting on so well.'

'Of course,' she replies, 'though I'm a little reluctant to let them get too close . . . just in case. I don't want men coming in and out of Alfie's life. He needs stability.'

'Matt's the epitome of stable,' I assure her. 'Completely level-headed . . . like a human spirit level.'

She gives a little laugh. 'I know, but I'm not naïve, Nick. Relationships either last forever or they end . . . there really is no in-between and the majority fall into the latter. Besides, I have a habit of making things way more complicated than they need to be . . . I never seem to get it quite right.'

'Hmm, you're talking to King Fuck-up here,' I reply; 'I'm the last one to judge.'

'Don't you talk about my friend like that!' Sarah insists, nudging me. She waves over at Alfie who's munching on some candy floss, while an exhausted-looking Matt is slouched on a nearby bench. 'I happen to think he's pretty special. I won't hear a word against him.'

'I think you're pretty special too,' I respond but my words fall on deaf ears as she skips off to hug Alfie and Matt, leaving me to follow behind.

When we arrive home, I'm ready just to collapse in front of the television but Matt, Sarah and Alfie have other ideas.

'Happy birthday, Nick,' Alfie chirps as he presents me

with a beautifully wrapped present, which of course I rip to shreds immediately.

'Wow!' I exclaim, marvelling at the gift inside. 'I've always wanted a yellow bathroom speaker shaped as a submarine! How did you know?'

Sarah laughs as a puzzled Alfie looks to her for an answer. 'A little birdy told me how wonderful your shower singing is,' she informs me, glancing at Matt. 'So, Alfie and I thought you might want something to play your tunes through.'

Matt smirks, slowly shaking his head. 'Abysmal! I said his singing was abysmal! He's going to be a nightmare now.'

'Stop hurting my delicate feelings,' I say, inspecting my new toy. 'Besides, you were the one playing Destiny's Child the other morning . . . would have been rude of me not to join in.'

'Yeah, alright, Beyoncé,' he replies, looking slightly embarrassed. 'Anyway, this is from me.'

I frown as he hands me a small silver package. 'What is this? We don't do gifts. We've never done gifts.'

He shrugs. 'You've had a hell of a year. I'm making an exception.'

I tear open the paper suspiciously, hoping it's not something horribly inappropriate that will scar Alfie for life. Inside is an Armani watch.

'Mate . . . you shouldn't have,' I say, admiring the dark

blue sunray dial and leather strap. 'Seriously. This is way too much!'

'No,' he replies, 'what it is, is better than that Argos-looking piece of crap you own. Oh, don't get all teary-eyed, just put it on.'

My stomach sinks as I unbox the watch and wrap it around my wrist. Matt deserves a better friend than me.

CHAPTER TWENTY-EIGHT

Harriet and Noel have moved into a charming three-bed-roomed semi in Brighton, which gives me two hours on the train journey to plough through some of the work I've taken home for the weekend.

'Need a hand?' Matt asks, watching me rub my fore-head. 'What are you working on?'

'Ugh, don't even ask,' I reply. 'Some bullshit merger that sounds fishy as hell. I need to have it ready by Monday.'

'Want a beer?' Matt pulls a tin of Heineken from his rucksack. 'Still cold.'

'It's eleven thirty,' I reply. 'I think I'll pass.'

He laughs. 'Don't act like a few weeks ago you weren't drinking Baileys for breakfast.'

'True,' I reply, 'but I wasn't a formidable, dodgy-merger-organising lawyer back then. Jesus, I never thought I'd miss being Santa.'

'You've only been at this new firm a couple of months

mate. Give it time. Kensington Fox was hard going the first few weeks, remember? You'll settle in.'

Doubtful, I think to myself. Compared to this place, Kensington Fox was practically a summer camp. At least there we were respected. I don't think my boss has even learned my name yet, given that she just calls me 'you, over there'.

Matt puts in his AirPods and begins swigging his morning beer while I try to focus. I don't want my entire weekend at Harriet's to be spoiled by work.

Soon-to-be dad Noel picks us up from the station in his boring yet dependable Hyundai and drives us to the most middle-aged, white-picket-fenced street I've ever seen in my life. We pull up outside a mixed-brick semidetached with a moving truck parked outside.

'They're dropping the last of the boxes,' Noel informs us. 'You'll need to excuse the mess. Just head in, I'll be there in a second.'

Harriet's ginormous bump greets us first as we step inside. I'm shocked by how big she's grown. Behind me I hear a concerned-sounding Noel beg the driver to be careful with his computer desk.

'Yay, you're here!' she says, leaning in sideways for a hug. 'Sorry it's a tip, we thought we'd be far more organised by now. I can't lift anything, so Noel's been left with most of it.'

'Jesus, Harry,' Matt exclaims, 'are you having twins? There must be at least two fully grown humans in there.'

'Nope, just one,' she replies. 'And before you ask, we don't know the sex. I want to be surprised.'

'Surprised that it's twins?'

'Shut up, Matt.'

Apart from a few boxes, the house is actually tidier than ours, which is somewhat embarrassing. Even a heavily pregnant woman and her anxious husband are more diligent than we are.

'Wow,' I say, as we walk into a living room straight out of *Homes & Gardens*. Jesus, they even have an open fireplace. 'This is impressive.'

'Nice floors,' Matt remarks. 'The last time I saw this much hardwood was in Nick's browser history.'

'Shocking, eh?' Harriet replies. 'Who'd have thought I'd end up barefoot and pregnant in suburbia with a fucking conservatory and monoblocked driveway. They did leave us the hot tub, though I'm not stepping foot in it until it's been fumigated. I know what these middle-class Brightonians are like: it's all pampas grass and bowls of car keys; fuck knows what they did in there.'

'It suits you,' I tell her, peering through the window in search of swinger paraphernalia. 'God, with Greta married and Matt meeting Sarah, it looks like I'm the only one still to become a functioning member of society.'

'Ah, yes!' Harriet exclaims, throwing her gaze at Matt. 'I heard about this new woman! This baby has made me miss all the good gossip. I demand to know everything!'

'Let me get my coat off, Harry,' Matt replies. 'Besides, Nick's Angela fiasco is far more interesting . . .'

I roll my eyes as Harriet focuses back on me. He is the master of deflection.

We order in Chinese food for dinner, as Harriet has recently developed an insatiable craving for wontons with duck sauce and plain fried rice. We sit in their half-decorated dining room, eating out of the takeaway containers.

'That Angela one was always a bit sketchy,' she informs me. 'Anyone who actually chooses to be on *Big Brother* needs their head seen to. I'll never understand the need to be famous. I don't even enjoy doing author interviews.'

'I like how everyone waits until now to tell me they hated her,' I reply, gnawing on a spare rib. 'You're supposed to have my back. This information would have been useful beforehand.'

'We do have your back,' Harriet replies. 'But we're not your mammy, we're your friends. We respect your decision to date horrendous women but reserve the right to then make fun of you when it all goes tits up. It'll be the same with Matt's new girlfriend.'

''Scuse me but she's not horrendous,' Matt interjects. 'She's actually the nicest woman I've ever dated and therefore you cannot slag her off.'

'I'm not sure whether that says more about you or her,'

Harriet replies, laughing. 'But I look forward to meeting her.'

Damn. Harriet is even more blunt than usual tonight.

'How's the new job, Nick?' Noel asks. 'Nice to be back in the rat race?'

'Exhausting, actually,' I reply. 'I'm putting in minimum fourteen-hour days at the moment. My boss is—'

'Exhausting? Try moving to a new house and working and lugging around a bowling ball twenty-four seven,' Harriet snaps. 'And having to pee every thirty seconds when you're trying to work . . . you bloody men don't know you're born.'

Noel almost chokes on his chow mein. 'Harriet! There's no need to—'

And now she's crying. Big fat tears detonate from her eyes and make their way down her cheeks. 'I'm s-s-sorry,' she says, picking up a napkin. 'I have no idea what's fucking wrong with me. I'm vile! Fat and vile!'

Noel gets up and hugs his wife. 'You're not vile, sweetie. You're pregnant. The hormones must be—'

'What the fuck would you know about my hormones? How many times have you been pregnant? God, I could murder a glass of red!'

'I . . . I . . . uh . . .'

'Sweet Jesus, Harriet,' Matt exclaims. 'The rude just jumped right out of you, didn't it? Do I need to call a priest? Nick, take away her cutlery before she fucking devours us all.'

Harriet's crying morphs into a mixture of sobs intermingled with hearty laughing. She grabs Noel's hand and kisses it. 'Forgive me. I'm an arsehole. And I need to pee. I'll be right back.'

We hear Harriet trudge upstairs to the bathroom.

'Sorry, guys,' Noel says sheepishly. 'She's been like this all week. I wanted to cancel this weekend, but she insisted.'

'It's fine,' Matt insists. 'She must be getting fed up by now. When is she due?'

'Now, pretty much,' he replies. 'Well, next weekend, to be exact. But they say first babies are notoriously late.'

'Are you excited?' I ask him, getting back to my meal. 'Must be weird, knowing that any day now you're going to be a dad.'

'It's fucking terrifying,' he confesses. 'Not that I'd admit that to Harriet.'

'Maybe not right now,' I reply with a smirk. 'But she's obviously nervous too.'

'Sarah told me that the baby stage is actually the easiest stage,' Matt informs him. 'When they start to walk and fall into furniture and stick their fingers in power sockets, that's when the real work starts. She says the baby stage is just making sure you don't drop them and surviving on three hours' sleep.'

'Sarah has a kid?'

Matt spins around in fright. 'Fucking hell, Harriet, did you fly downstairs on your broomstick?'

She laughs and sits back down at the table. 'The stairs don't creak when you've just lost fifteen pounds' worth of fluid. My question still stands though.'

'Yes,' Matt replies. 'She has a four-year-old son, Alfie.'

'Wow,' she replies, returning to her wontons. 'A single mum, eh? Never pictured you as the fatherly type.'

'Why?' he asks. 'I'm great with kids. Alfie and I hang out all the time.'

She crunches into her wonton and shrugs. 'I dunno. You just don't give off that vibe. Nick does. I can see him running around the park with six kids. You, I picture owning the park.'

'Six kids?' I start to laugh. 'Do I look like a Mormon?'

'Moron, maybe,' Matt says under his breath.

I smile. It's true that I'd like a big family, probably because I come from such a small one, but maybe just three kids. Six is bankruptcy waiting to happen.

'Greta will be next anyway,' she informs us, 'judging by the amount of shagging she did on honeymoon. She's coming down to see the house next month.'

Noel almost chokes again.

'Yeah, that's not something she shares with her male friends,' Matt declares, 'but you're probably right. How the hell did this happen? We're adults. I remember when we got pissed every night and barely made our 11am uni lectures.'

With the smaller bedroom currently being made into a nursery, Matt takes the bed in the other spare room while Noel makes up the sofa for me in the living room. I could have shared with Matt, but fuck sleeping next to him after a few glasses of wine. His snoring can be heard from space.

While it's been lovely catching up with Harriet, it's given me a much-needed kick up the arse. My life will pass me by if I don't start living it . . . *properly* living it.

CHAPTER TWENTY-NINE

'Nick, where the fuck is the brief? How long does it take to prepare one fucking brief? I'm surrounded by fucking idiots, I swear. Is that the paperwork for the merger? I need that finished before you leave too. The client is coming in first thing tomorrow.'

'Sure, Sophia,' I reply, glancing down at the clock on my PC, 'but I really need to be out of here by half six at the latest. It's my friend's—'

'Leave them on my desk before you go or don't bother coming back tomorrow.'

Sophia Goddard, the only woman alive who makes me genuinely miss having Geraldine as my boss, proceeds to dump her half-empty coffee cup on my desk and walk away, shouting at her phone to call *Alan*. I have no idea who Alan is, but I guarantee he hates her too. Where Geraldine was a stone-faced, unwavering guardian of all things customer service, Sophia is a cold, detached shark of a woman who demands nothing less than everything, and sometimes even that isn't good enough. Last week she asked me to rework a thirty-page proposal over the weekend and then promptly binned it in front of me because she'd decided to go with the original after all. I'm only halfway through the six-month maternity cover and I cannot wait for it to be over.

I turn my attention back to my paperwork, now aware that I have only two hours to batter through before I'm due to meet Matt, Sarah and Alfie for dinner. It's Sarah's birthday and I've been looking forward to this all week.

At six forty-five, I'm finally finished and place three folders on Sophia's desk on my way out. She went home ages ago, but there are at least five members of her team still working, their desks scattered with papers and half-eaten sandwiches. I say goodnight and catch a black cab outside.

When I arrive twenty minutes late to the Thai Palace, I quickly spot Alfie, who has his face pressed against the huge fish tank in the corner of the room. Behind him to the left sits Matt, looking at his menu, while Sarah has her eyes firmly fixed on her son. Alfie notices me first.

'Are you choosing a fish to eat for dinner?' I ask him and he throws his arms around my waist. He chuckles.

'You can't eat those fish; those fishes are pets.'

'Hmm, I dunno, that white one looks quite meaty.'

'Finally!' Matt exclaims. 'I've just texted you.'

'I'm sorry,' I say, kissing Sarah on the cheek before

pulling out a chair. God, she smells nice. 'I got away as soon as I could. Happy Birthday!'

I hand her a birthday card with a picture of a cougar wearing a tiara and she laughs, proudly standing it upright on the table.

'Aw, thank you, and don't worry,' Sarah insists, 'I'm just glad you're here! Feels like we haven't seen you in ages.'

I place my suit jacket on the back of the chair and pour some water. 'I know. Work has been so hectic; it's kicking my ass and my boss . . . well . . .' I make a weird growling noise to express my loathing.

She frowns. 'That good, huh?'

I shake my head. 'Worse. Think *Jaws* with bleached veneers and a spray tan. Honestly, it's relentless. I mean, at least when I was at Kensington Fox, I used to love what I did, even if it was hard work, but this new job is miserable – I'm starting to think that I was genuinely happier passing out gifts to snot-nosed children.'

'Yes, maybe, but you were definitely poorer,' Matt reminds me.

'True . . . but right now all I'm doing is ensuring rich twats stay rich despite breaking several laws, and some of the mergers and acquisitions I'm doing are seriously dodgy. When I got into law, I wanted to make a difference. Yes, naïve, I know, but it's true. The work I'm doing right now doesn't make any difference, at least not one that matters – in fact, no, scrap that, it probably makes the world worse. Either way, it's completely soulless.'

'So maybe it's not the career that's the problem,' Sarah suggests. 'Maybe it's just this job?'

'Well, you were hardly changing the world at Kensington Fox and you were happy there, right? And I mean, what else could you do?' Matt asks. 'Work for a non-profit? Those gigs pay peanuts.'

'Money isn't everything, sweetheart,' Sarah says, quietly. I'm not sure if that's a subtle dig that she earns less than both of us, but I get the feeling it might be.

A waiter brings across some wine and we order, while Sarah dives into her bag and brings out a colouring book and pencils to entice Alfie away from the fish tank.

'I can't believe he's starting school in a few months,' she laments. 'He won't be my baby for much longer.'

Matt hugs her and laughs. 'If my mum is anything to go by, he'll always be your baby. Just don't mention his bed sheets between the ages of, oh, thirteen and twenty-eight. He'll never forgive you.'

Alfie sits down and begins to scribble furiously, his little legs swinging off the edge of the seat contentedly.

'Oh, speaking of babies,' Matt continues, 'Harriet had a girl this afternoon! Noel called me.'

'Amazing,' Sarah asks. 'What did they call her?'

He hesitates. 'Hmm, I think they called her Irish.'

'Irish?' she repeats. 'They called their kid something Irish, you mean? Like Niamh or Siobhan or something?'

'No, her actual name is "Irish". That's what Noel said.'

I cock my head to one side. 'You're lucky you're pretty, mate. They called her *Iris*. Numpty.'

He pauses again. 'That would make more sense.'

I scroll through to find my text from Noel confirming that the new baby's name is indeed Iris. For an extremely smart man, sometimes Matt lives in a world of his own.

As we eat, I notice how Matt's more involved with Alfie than ever now. His once awkward demeanour has now been replaced with a more hands-on, confident approach that Alfie responds well to, as does Sarah who observes them interacting with a burgeoning delight. Fuck me, it stings. I'm watching a family flourish right in front of me and all I can selfishly think is how I wish it was me instead of Matt. I thought seeing less of Sarah would help me move on but it's useless. Even the briefest of meetings sets me right back to square one. Every time I see them together my heart breaks all over again. I haven't been happy for a long time and while I'm around them all, I never will be. It's time for me to go. I need to move on. I need a fresh start.

CHAPTER THIRTY

Telling my best mate that I planned on moving out was far more emotional than I thought it would be.

First there was shock, which was also very much like denial:

'Mate? What the fuck? You're not serious?'

'I need somewhere cheaper, Matt,' I'd replied, biting into my toast and suddenly feeling terribly guilty that I'd just ruined Matt's breakfast. He hesitated for a moment before a huge grin spread across his face.

'Shut up, you twat, you're not going anywhere.'

'I am! What, did you think we'd live together forever like Bert and Ernie? I need a change, mate. I can't stay here doing the same thing over and over and expecting anything to be different.'

Then came anger. Only louder:

'*What the actual fuck, Nick? What the fuck does that even mean? What is supposed to be different? I cannot believe you're doing this.*'

Matt's chair screeched back as he stormed off into the living room, while I just sat there at the kitchen table, wondering if I was going to be leaving sooner than I thought. Perhaps via the window.

He stayed silent for what seemed like forever before he thundered back into the kitchen and the bargaining began.

'Look, if you need a bit of time to build up some savings, I'll cover your rent for a bit. Don't be hasty – we can definitely sort something out..'

'I need to do this on my own,' I'd replied. 'You're going in a whole new direction with Sarah, it's just a matter of time before you move in together. Concentrate on yourself, mate, and I'll be fine.'

I accompanied him to the living room, just as depression hit.

'Man, I feel sad as fuck,' he said. 'Prick. It'll be weird not having you here. What will I do without you? We're like the two musketeers.'

'The musketeers come in threes, buddy. But I'm not dying. I'm just moving out. You'll still see me, dude.'

Matt smiled weakly and grabbed me in a huge bear hug.

'You know what I mean,' he said, sniffing. 'I'll just miss you. But I get it. Do what makes you happy.'

And finally – acceptance.

He left for the gym about an hour ago and I still feel at odds with the whole thing. Saying it out loud has made it more real and although planning a new future for myself is exciting, leaving everything behind is daunting. I'm going to see Greta first thing tomorrow before work to see if she has any positions further afield. Reading, maybe? Winchester perhaps . . .

'How about Slough?'

Greta turns her screen around to show me a position she has for a corporate solicitor focusing on Equity and Acquisitions.

I frown. 'I was hoping for something a little more virtuous.'

'Right . . .'

'And a little less Slough-based.'

She snorts. 'OK. Now when you say virtuous, are we talking priest or missionary worker? Lawyers Without Borders?'

I smirk. 'Maybe something non-profit . . . I'm not sure, just something where I make a difference.'

She bobs her head and continues scrolling. 'That's admirable, Nick. Good for you . . . OK, here's one. Legal aid lawyer for a homeless charity. Based in Oxford. Salary's actually pretty decent. Start date in three weeks.'

I read over the job spec and get a little rush of excitement. She sees my face and smiles.

'Shall I forward your CV?'

'Yeah,' I reply. 'Let's go for it.'

I leave Greta's office and stride through Covent Garden feeling positive and hopeful. Oxford isn't that far, so I'd still be able to visit Matt, and I might even be able to afford something more spacious than a room in a shared flat. Today is a good day; a step in the right direction. A step closer to leaving everything behind and ... fuck, is that Angela?

I stop abruptly and turn to look at the menu in a restaurant window, surprising the woman inside who's setting up tables. As I peer to my left, I see her stop to chat to someone before continuing in my direction. It's definitely her; she's wearing the white poncho I bought for her in Marbella. We haven't seen each other since New Year's Eve, and I was more than happy keeping it that way.

Shit. I have two options: I can turn and bolt in the other direction or I can walk past her and hope that she's feeling just as awkward about this as I am. Steeling myself, I turn and continue walking towards her. We're almost side by side before she makes eye contact, but I keep walking.

'Nick!' she exclaims as she realises that I'm not stopping. 'I thought that was you!'

Dammit. I slowly come to a halt and turn to face her.

'Hey, Angela. How are you?'

She runs her hand through her hair and then rests it on one hip. 'Oh, you know, can't grumble. How are you? You're looking well.'

'Thanks,' I reply, nonchalantly. 'I'm doing well.'

She waits for me to return the compliment then realises it isn't coming. She narrows her eyes. 'So ... how is the North Pole?'

I don't react. 'I'm sure it's fine, though I'm on my way to Bond Street.'

'You're working on Bond Street?' she asks, her tone now breezy. 'Wow! Impressive! Well done, babes, I knew you could ... wait ... is that ... is that a Tom Ford suit?'

'It is,' I reply, checking my phone. 'Must dash, I'm late. Nice to see you.'

I stroll off as she tells me it's nice to see me too. She's only saying that as she thinks I'm worth bothering with again. I smirk at the Tom Ford comment. This suit is one hundred per cent Marks and Spencer. Funny how having pound signs in your eyes can skew your vision.

When I get into work the office is already buzzing, but thankfully my fake dentist appointment covers my late arrival. Still, Sophia looks at her watch as I pass, and glares just to remind me that I'm permanently on thin ice – no one is safe here. I take a seat and begin trawling through the files that have magically appeared on my desk overnight. Half of this stuff isn't even in my remit, but I plough through because I'd quite like at least one glowing reference to give to a new employer that doesn't say 'does a decent "ho-ho-ho"'.

By 7pm, I feel like I've stayed long enough to cover my early appointment and any other sins Sophia feels I might have committed. I've promised Sarah and Matt that I'll babysit tonight, so that gives me an hour to get to her place. Just as I'm leaving, I get a text.

Hey babe, really was great to see you again. Maybe we can do drinks soon? I miss ya 😔 Ange xoxo

I've had enough of this woman. We broke up months ago and she is still fucking haunting me. Screw this.

Fuck you and your sad face emojis and your fucking xoxo bullshit. I'm done.

I block her number, pick up my things and head home. I should have done this months ago.

'Did it feel good? Telling her to eff off?' Matt asks while we wait for Sarah to finish helping Alfie get ready for bed.

'It did . . . for about a minute. Now I wish I'd just ignored her. She revels in the drama.'

'Who revels in the drama?' Sarah asks, joining us in her living room.

'Angela,' Matt informs her. 'Our boy here finally blocked her. Told her to bugger off.'

'Good for you,' she replies, 'clean slate and all that.'

I nod. 'Hopefully . . .'

Matt slaps me on the back. 'It's hard to move forward when you're dragging the past behind you.'

Sarah frowns. 'OK, Plato . . . what does that mean?'

'I'll explain in the car, we need to get a move on.'

I say goodbye then pop in to see Alfie, who's already

out cold at eight thirty. Being careful not to wake him, I tiptoe back out and grab a Coke from the fridge, feeling somewhat guilty that I'm glad he's asleep, but fuck it, I'm tired too. I settle down on the couch and flick through the TV channels, determined to keep my eyes open.

Sarah and Matt arrive back from their date earlier than expected to find me completely invested in the latest episode of *Killing Eve.*

'Hey,' I say as they walk into the living room. 'She just killed that guy from The Mighty Boosh; I am shook! Everything alright? It's not even ten yet.'

'Sarah's not feeling very well,' Matt informs me, rubbing her back. 'Thought it best we call it a night.'

'I'll be fine,' she replies. 'Probably just a bug. Was Alfie OK?'

'Yeah,' I reply, 'good as gold. Can I get you anything before I go?'

'I can stay if you want,' Matt adds. 'I don't mind.'

She shakes her very pale head. 'No, but thanks. You two get off. I don't want to infect you if I have picked something nasty up. I just need to sleep. I'll call you tomorrow.'

We both say goodnight and head outside where the taxi is waiting.

'Fancy a drink?' Matt asks as we climb in. 'Or are you planning on binge-watching the entire *Killing Eve* box set tonight?'

'I can do both,' I reply, grinning. 'I'm a man of many useless talents.'

I haven't been in Bar Black since Greta's engagement party last year, but now that I'm working again, I can safely order a beer without checking my bank balance first.

We order drinks then find the last available table near the back of the room. It looks like there's a hen party here or some kind of cackling women's support group. Either way, they're operating at full volume.

'I'm starving,' Matt says, 'I'm totally getting chips on the way home.'

'Shame you had to cancel dinner,' I reply, swigging back my beer. 'She did look sick, mind you.'

He nods. 'Weirdest thing, we had a glass of wine at the bar while they were sorting our table and she was fine. Then she suddenly asked if we could go because she felt ill.'

'Maybe the wine didn't agree with her?'

'Probably. I'll call her tomorrow. Bring her some soup or something if she's still under the weather.'

I pout. 'You never bring me soup when I'm sick.'

'There's not enough soup in the world to cure what's wrong with you. Be right back, I need a slash.'

As I wait for Matt to return from the bathroom, I'm tempted to text Sarah and see if she's alright, but I decide that's not my place, no matter how much I want it to be.

Besides, I don't trust myself not to accidentally send a kiss at the end of the message like a fucking love-struck wanker.

The next morning, I make it into the office for 7.30am, thinking that I'd be one of the first here, but I see that everyone else also has their try-hard hats on. Jane Bridges, the tall woman with enormous hair who started a week after me, looks exhausted. In fact, they all do. The more I get to know some of my colleagues, the more I realise that they're just as full of shit as I am. The tough veneer they exhibit is deceptively fragile and could crack at any moment. Of course, there are always a few who thrive in this kind of environment, like Sophia ... or Duncan Walker, who sits near the water cooler and calls everyone his posse. Or Matt ... is Matt actually a sharky wanker?

Just as I'm starting to wonder how I ever thought that this was the world I wanted to exist in, my mobile rings.

'Nick, it's Greta. They want an interview! I think you're in.'

CHAPTER THIRTY-ONE

The last (and only time) I was in Oxford, I was eight years old and being reluctantly dragged around the Botanic Gardens by my mum and three of her excessively perfumed friends. I don't remember that much about the day trip, apart from being bored as hell, but I do remember how much my mum longed for a garden of her own when we returned. High-rise flats don't really lend themselves to horticulture, but she filled our flat with as many reduced-price flowers and houseplants as her budget would allow.

For my second trip, I'm infinitely more excited to be going to Oxford, if a tad nervous – not just about the interview, but about the fact that this job could literally change my world. New direction, new town, new life – it's quite overwhelming to think about, so I put in my earbuds and drown myself out.

The train arrives at nine thirty-five, giving me plenty of time to find the office I'm interviewing in at ten. Google Maps informs me that it's a nine-minute walk away, so

I grab a quick espresso at the station and head out the main entrance.

Not having to navigate the same pavement with seventeen thousand other people is the first tick on my Oxford vs. London list – that and the fact that it's incredibly pretty. London isn't an *ugly* city as such, there's just so fucking much of it and it's everywhere.

I follow my map, passing a mixture of historic-looking buttery-coloured brickwork buildings, shops and new builds before I finally arrive at Homelessness Action, whose offices look very modern, but not at all imposing.

'Good morning! How can I help you?'

The receptionist smiles at me like she's genuinely happy to see me, while behind her, a staff of at least twenty people occupy an open-plan office. I count at least seven happy faces and see a woman wearing a Nirvana T-shirt – I'm already getting good vibes.

'I have an appointment with Joseph Dalton at ten.'

She taps on her keyboard, finding my appointment and nods. 'Nick? Great. Please take a seat and I'll let Joe know you're here.'

I thank her and sit on a huge purple couch, wondering if I've come to the right place. If someone wore a band T-shirt at my current office, Sophia would have them fired or maybe even thrown from the roof. This is all very disconcerting. Even the ring from the phones sounds chirpy.

A man in a blue shirt and swinging lanyard approaches me, holding out his hand.

'Nick. Joe Dalton. Thanks for coming in.'

We shake hands and I follow him through the office and into a large pale green meeting room, complete with yucca plants and a water cooler. Joe opens his folder, revealing my CV and I take a deep breath.

'Impressive,' he remarks, his pen scanning down the pages. 'First class degree, a year at Rose Allen, then five years at Kensington Fox. You were lead on the Broadshore merger, right?'

'Yes,' I reply, slightly unnerved by the fact that this particular piece of information isn't on my CV. Broadshore was a particularly tricky healthcare client who threatened to move their business to other firms on a daily basis. He's obviously done his research. 'It was an interesting project.'

'Why did you leave Kensington?'

'It was time,' I lie. 'I think it's important to expand one's horizons.'

'One's horizons' . . . When have you ever spoken like that? Are you the Queen? Is that what we're doing now?

'And you're currently at Portman Brown . . . I hear they're a tough crowd.'

I nod. He has no idea. 'It can be, but you know . . . work hard, play hard.'

As the words leave my mouth, I want to immediately cram them back in there. *Moron. Absolute fucking moron.*

He places his pen on the table and leans back in his chair. He reminds me of Matt Damon, if Matt Damon was five foot six and almost completely bald. This is going horribly; I just want to leave.

'You've seen the job description; obviously we're not a huge organisation like Shelter or Crisis, but we need someone to assist with everything from advising on the Charities Act, to dealing with the trustees, to giving legal advice to drop-ins who may be facing homelessness. You're obviously more than capable of doing the job with some in-house training.'

'I'm sure I can get up to speed relatively quickly with the appropriate policies,' I respond eagerly, hoping he's forgotten everything I've previously said. 'I'm used to working over many different legal disciplines.'

He smiles and closes over his folder.

'This won't be like any other place you've worked before. I need someone who can deal with Joe Bloggs – who's been sleeping outside Tesco for the past year – just as competently as they deal with the business side. Our focus is people, Nick. Real people with stories and families and problems, some of whom you'll have walked past on your way to the office. While you'll have an important role to play here just like everyone, from Briony on reception to the street fundraisers we have pounding the pavements, I prefer to hire people who are willing to share their stories, just like the people we help.'

'My story?'

Joseph nods. 'Tell me about yourself, Nick. What's not on your CV?

Stuff that makes me look bad, Joe, that's why it's not on there. Next question?

I shift uncomfortably in my chair. 'So . . . um, unfortunately I'm not that interesting, but I'm sure I can apply what I've learned in my previous roles to bring something unique and . . .'

Oh God, did his eyes just glaze over?

'Perhaps a fresh perspective on the current policies which . . .'

I see him subtly glance at his watch. What the hell is this? Why does it matter what my damn story is?

'So, I think that's probably all—'

'Santa!' I blurt out. '. . . I used to be Santa.'

He raises an eyebrow. 'Go on . . .'

By the time I've told Matt Damon all about my job at Southview Shopping Centre, I know I've blown it. An interviewer who goes from impressed to bored to mildly amused doesn't exactly instil confidence. And neither does a candidate who just told you his calling was to play Santa.

'I appreciate you being so candid with me. Sounds like quite the experience,' he says, still smirking. 'And while you're being so open, I have one last question for you.'

Why am I still sitting here?

'Kensington Fox. Why did you *really* leave?'

I pause and look at the table. Here goes . . .

'I left Kensington Fox because they asked me to.'

As I look up, I see Joseph nod, waiting for me to continue.

'I think I became disillusioned by the nonsense which came with a job like that. I became complacent. And while arguments could be made that my dismissal wasn't *entirely* my doing, they were absolutely right to let me go. Although I regret the way I handled things, I wouldn't change anything because it's shown me that I'm capable of being better . . . of doing things I never thought possible, and I know I could bring that to the role here. I think everyone deserves a second chance.'

Joseph shakes my hand and says he'll be in touch, but my gut feeling tells me otherwise. I thank him for his time and walk back to the station, knowing that the next time I hear from him will be by letter with a short, sharp rejection, possibly followed by a recommendation for a therapist.

That evening, I agree to watch Alfie again so Sarah and Matt can finish the date they barely started the other night. I'm happy to; the last thing I need is to be sitting at home wondering if my interview went as horribly as I think it did.

'I thought we'd watch *Jumanji*,' I say to Alfie. 'I hear the new version is really good.'

'Can we have popcorn? We have some in the cupboard.'

'Fine by me,' I reply. 'But check with your mum first.'

Tell me about yourself, Nick. What's not on your CV?

'Yes, popcorn is fine, just make sure he brushes his teeth,' Sarah yells from her room.

Alfie runs to the kitchen while I try and shake off the voices in my head and stop them running over my interview relentlessly. Matt notices the look on my face.

'Will you stop worrying already? I'm sure it wasn't nearly as crap as you imagine.'

'Mate, I told them I thought it was my calling to work as Santa!' I say quietly. 'My way of giving back to the community. It was like I couldn't stop talking utter garbage. MY CALLING. What kind of idiot says they were destined to work in a different industry at a freaking job interview?'

He smirks supportively. 'I'm not sure working as a Santa counts as an industry? But they're do-gooders. They'll eat that shit up. Better than saying no one would hire you . . .'

'Nick! I can't reach the popcorn!'

I leave Matt and join Alfie in the kitchen where he is on his tippy toes, straining to reach the top shelf, even though it's a good metre out of his grasp. I can't help smiling as I lift it down for him. I ask him to get two bowls from the dish drainer while I microwave the popcorn.

It's not often I hear of lawyers playing Santa Claus.

'Ready!' Sarah announces. 'Sorry, I couldn't find my earrings.'

'No problem,' Matt replies. 'You look great. We should head out though, reservation is for seven.'

I yell bye from the kitchen as they both rush out the door. I don't need to see how great she looks, I'm already aware. Besides, I have enough going on in my head without adding Sarah in some slinky dress to the chaos.

I settle down on the couch with Alfie, divide up the popcorn and turn on Netflix.

'Mum says Mrs Grainger will be watching me when you go away,' Alfie says quietly, as we watch the film. 'I don't want her, she never plays with me. She just talks to her cats.'

'Your mum told you I was going away?'

He nods. 'She said that you might get a job far away. Don't you like us anymore?'

'Of course, I do, buddy!' I exclaim, my stomach plummeting as I notice his bottom lip beginning to wobble. 'It's just that sometimes grown-ups need a change.'

He stares at me blankly.

'Right . . . I'll try and explain it better. You enjoy nursery, right? It's fun. You know everyone, you know where all the good toys are.'

He nods.

'But eventually you'll leave and start school. Not because

you hate nursery, but just because you're ready to move on to something different. You'll still keep all of your old friends, but you'll make new ones! You'll have new challenges, new toys and become a big boy who can do more things for himself. That's what I'm doing. I'm trying to be a big boy too.'

He ponders this before saying, 'I don't want you to go. I don't want Mum to be unhappy again.'

I pull him in for a hug. 'Aww, Alfie, why would she be unhappy again? Look at all the fun she's having with Matt now and the stuff you guys do together. That's what has made her happy. Besides, I promise that wherever I move, I'll only be a car ride away, so I'll drive up to come and see you all the time. Deal?'

Strictly speaking, this isn't a false promise. Even if I moved to Aberdeen, it would still only technically be a car ride away, but Alfie seems satisfied anyway. He smiles and agrees which makes me feel a little better, though I'm still somewhat disconcerted that Sarah's been speaking to Alfie about the possibility of me leaving but hasn't directly mentioned it to me. Maybe the only effect it will have on Sarah is disrupting her childcare arrangements. The thought of not seeing her regularly anymore kills me and I know that's exactly why I need to go. However, after today's interview, I have a feeling that it might be a while before it happens.

Kensington Fox. Why did you really leave?

Jesus fucking Christ, why did I go with honesty? Why didn't I just stick to the whole expanding one's horizons, bullshit? Or that I wanted to try something new? Anything except that pile of melodramatic drivel. I should call Greta and see if Slough is still available.

Saturday morning begins with a plate of Matt's famous French toast. It's been two days since my interview and my cringe level has gone from a strong ten to a much more manageable four. There are lessons to be learned here and once I figure out what they are, I'll be sure to implement them. Matt hands me the maple syrup while he turns on LBC radio.

'Do we need to listen to this?' I whine, drenching my breakfast in sugar. Matt loves radio phone-in shows – almost as much as French toast – but I hate them with a passion. It's like the radio version of Facebook.

Matt takes a seat, grinning. 'How can you not love this shit? Angry members of the British public, ranting down the phone for the whole world to hear? It's music to my ears.'

'I'd prefer actual music to my ears,' I mumble. Thankfully, my phone rings and I move through to my bedroom just as Geoff from Kent starts talking about Brexit.

'Nick. Joe Dalton here, sorry to bother you so early. Our

Saturdays here get hectic later in the day. I hope I'm not interrupting your breakfast?'

'Oh . . . hello! No, no problem at all.'

'Great, just wanted to give you a quick bell to let you know that I was very impressed with your interview.'

I feel my face contort in confusion. 'You were? I mean, thanks. Thanks very much.'

'The fact that you've experienced just how quickly circumstances can change is a quality I feel would be infinitely beneficial for this role. And if there is anything we believe in here, it's second chances. So, I'd like to offer you the position.'

I slump down on my bed, stunned and apparently, mute. In what world was that interview a success?

'You still there? Nick?'

'Yes,' I respond, clearing my throat. 'Sorry, can you just repeat that?'

I hear him chuckle quietly. 'Job's yours, Nick, if you're still interested. We'd be looking for you to start in a couple of weeks, if that's feasible?'

'I think so,' I reply. 'I'll make it work.'

'Excellent, you've made my morning. I'll get all the paperwork sent over to GL Recruitment when Sigita is back on Monday. If you need help finding accommodation, she'll be able to recommend some letting agencies.'

'Sounds great,' I respond. This whole conversation feels

like a dream. If Matt wasn't in the next room, I'd swear he was pranking me.

'Very pleased to have you on board, Nick,' he replies. 'Speak to you soon. Have a great weekend.'

I hang up the call and return to the kitchen table. The look on Matt's face tells me he already knows what I'm about to say.

'You got it then?'

'Two weeks,' I tell him. 'They want me to start in two weeks.'

He slices into his French toast. 'Or ... now hear me out ... you could start *never* and just stay here.'

'Hmm, kind of ruins the whole "new start" thing I have planned.'

He nods and continues eating but I can tell his heart's not in it. God, he looks so ... *sad*. I sit back down at the table, pick up my fork and stare at my food.

'I'll leave the room empty for you ... just in case you change your mind,' he muses. 'You might get there and hate it. I mean, it's full of smug Oxford University students and fucking Harry Potter bullshit. You'll go crazy.'

'You like Harry Potter!'

'I like *Alien* too. Doesn't mean I want to live in space.'

I smile tentatively. 'Come on, mate, you're supposed to be happy for me.'

Matt nods. 'I am, Nick. Truly. It's just, well ... the end of an era. I'll miss this ... I'll miss you.'

'I know, mate, and I'll miss—'

As he pulls me in and hugs me tightly, there's no need to finish my sentence. There's nothing I can do or say that will make any of this any easier. All I can do is hug him back.

CHAPTER THIRTY-TWO

'Can I have some quiet, please! Now, as you all know, I met Nick at university and we've been through a lot together. The good . . . the bad . . . the downright embarrassing and occasionally ugly – we've survived it all.'

I smile as Matt commands the attention of our flat, which is bursting at the seams with familiar faces: Greta, Noel, Harriet, Sarah, of course, plus Izzy and the guys I worked with last year at Kensington Fox – all tipsy, all happy and all here to wish me well for my new job in Oxford.

'But, as he's decided to fuck off and do legal aid at a bloody homeless charity, I thought it might be a good idea to have a little whip-round before he goes. We all know how much those poor sods earn.'

Everyone who is not a lawyer smiles politely while the lawyers laugh at Matt's joke, including me. My salary isn't exactly life-changing, but for someone, my job just might be.

'So please, raise your glasses and wish the best man I know all the success and happiness life can bring him. He truly is Saint Nick. Though this time the wardrobe will be a little more flattering.' He winks at me and I laugh. 'To Nick!'

Hearing the room toast me makes my eyes well up. Even Alfie is holding up his little juice box. It will be strange leaving all this behind, but for the first time in ages, I'm looking forward to whatever the future holds.

'Speech . . . SPEEECHHH!'

I laugh and take a quick swig of my beer, agreeing to say a few words. Thank God I'm tipsy, it'll make this less painful.

'I'm rubbish at this kind of thing, but thank you for coming, everyone,' I begin. 'I honestly didn't expect so many of you to show up, but I'm very grateful you did. Would have been a shit party otherwise . . . oops, sorry, Alfie.'

I see Sarah jokingly place her hands over Alfie's ears, while everyone chuckles.

'You all know that the past year has been challenging, to say the least, but I feel like things are finally moving in the right direction . . . Anyway, I'm only a couple of hours away, so there's really no excuse not to come and visit me when the overwhelming urge to see my face becomes too much to bear.'

I turn to Matt and raise my glass, a lump in my throat already forming.

'And Matt ... what can I say, brother? You are the yin to my yang, the piña to my colada and, well, without me, you'd never have met the lovely Sarah, so I expect a seriously large and very expensive housewarming gift.'

Matt laughs and wraps his arm around Sarah, giving me a thumbs up. Sarah in turn puts her arm around Alfie, who looks exhausted. I'm going to miss their faces most of all.

'So enough from me. Please drink the flat dry. Cheers, everyone!'

Half an hour later, Sarah announces that she'll have to get Alfie home, and I follow her into my room to help her find their coats among the monstrous pile which has accumulated on my bed. As we dig through, Alfie gets a second wind and decides to bounce manically on my bed. It's the most action it's seen in months.

'That's a lot of boxes,' Alfie remarks, pointing to the back of the room as he trampolines.

'It really is,' I reply. 'I have a lot of stuff.'

'Can Nick take me to the zoo tomorrow?' he asks, dive-bombing someone's expensive leather jacket. 'They have gorillas and a penguin beach!'

'Not tomorrow, bud,' Sarah replies, finding Alfie's coat. 'Nick is moving away, remember? That's why his things are boxed up. This is his goodbye party.'

Alfie stops bouncing and slinks off the bed. 'But I don't want him to go,' he mumbles. 'I want Nick to stay.'

I sit on the bed beside him and help him with his little coat.

'Do you know what's even better than a zoo?' I ask. He shakes his head, glumly.

'A farm. They let you feed the animals and ride on tractors and I hear you can even cuddle baby rabbits. When you come to visit me, we can all go together!'

His face suddenly lights up. 'Do they have penguins?'

I laugh. 'No, but you can race goats. Do you have good running shoes?'

He nods enthusiastically. 'Mum! Can we go, pleeeasse?'

'Absolutely,' she replies. 'Honey, go and say goodnight to Matt, we need to get home.'

As he scurries off to find Matt, Sarah smiles. 'You've done your homework, I see.'

I grin. 'Of course. I'm not just moving there for the shiny new job; their epic farm scene was the determining factor. Who doesn't want to race a goat?'

Sarah finally finds her own jacket and slips it on.

'Better get the little guy home,' she says, moving in for a quick hug. 'Take care, Nick.'

'You too, Sarah.'

As she turns to follow Alfie, she hesitates at the bedroom door.

'He's not the only one who doesn't want you to go, you know. I'm really going to miss you, Nick.'

'We'll still see each other,' I reply, smiling and hoping

it masks my sudden urge to cry. 'I mean, you're Matt's girlfriend. There's no way he—'

She steps closer, her face now visibly upset. 'Is that all I am, Nick?' she asks. 'You just see me as Matt's girlfriend . . . nothing more?'

'Well, we're friends too. Right?'

She doesn't reply, but her eyes never leave mine. My heart feels like it's going to pound right out of my chest.

'Are we? You really think we are *friends*?'

What is she asking me? I search her face for a clue, but she's searching mine just as intensely in return.

'Sarah, I don't know what—'

'Yes, you do,' she replies, her voice trembling. 'I need to know, Nick. I need to know, before you leave, if I'm just a friend or—'

My mind is racing. Does this mean she feels the same way? What the fuck is happening?

Sarah steps forward again and I gulp. I find my hand reaching out and touching her face of its own accord. She is openly crying and she has never looked more beautiful. She is literally breaking my heart right now. All I want is to hold her, but . . .

'I . . . Sarah . . . I don't know what to say . . . I'm sorry. I don't understand . . . I can't . . . Matt—' My voice breaks on the last word.

'My hat!'

Alfie's voice surprises us both and I snatch my hand

from Sarah's face, stumbling back against the bed, as Alfie and Matt burst into my bedroom.

'I forgot my monkey hat . . . Mum, why are you sad?'

I feel my face begin to burn as Matt stands in the doorway, watching Sarah surreptitiously wipe away her tears.

'Everything OK in here?' he asks. His face is unreadable, his voice emotionless.

Sarah nods. 'Just me being silly. You know how I get with goodbyes.'

'She's trying to blackmail me with tears,' I quickly respond, 'but the lure of the bright lights of suburban Oxford is just too powerful.'

He pulls Sarah in for a cuddle. 'Don't get upset over this fool. He'll be back annoying us before you know it.' His tone is jokey, but his expression is blank, and his eyes haven't left my face. I feel like they are burning through me. Does he know? Has he finally realised that I have been pining after his girlfriend for nearly as long as I've known her?

'I know,' she replies, sniffing. 'It's just hard to find a good babysitter these days.'

She laughs and I smile, but inside I'm dying. We're both lying to Matt's face and I couldn't feel any shittier if I tried.

Sarah leaves swiftly after, Matt walking her and Alfie downstairs, leaving me to go back to the party where I find Harriet and Noel sitting at the table. Harriet's on the apple juice as she's breastfeeding.

'I'm going to have to admit defeat,' she says reluctantly. 'My nips are leaking like crazy. You alright? You look a bit pale.'

'I'm fine,' I lie, trying to keep the tremble out of my voice. 'Just a bit overwhelmed. Where are you staying?'

'Travelodge up the road,' Noel replies. 'Mum's there with Iris. Pop by tomorrow before we go and you can meet her.'

'Your mum?'

'Iris,' he replies, laughing. God, my brain has officially turned to mush.

'I'm driving up to Oxford in the morning, but I promise I'll come and visit soon,' I say, hugging them both. 'I appreciate you coming through to see me, though. Means a lot.'

'Well, we wanted to meet Matt's girl too,' Harriet confesses mischievously. 'That was worth the train journey. She's so sweet, I'd never have believed it! Didn't think I'd see him this happy ever, after . . . well, you know.'

'Yeah, he's found a good one,' I reply, flatly. 'There's hope for us all, eh?'

I see Harriet and Noel to the door and wonder when the rest of the party will fuck off, too. As much as I appreciate everyone coming to send me off, I just want them to go. I need to leave now.

CHAPTER THIRTY-THREE

Waking up with a hangover is vile enough, but combined with guilt and confusion, I think I'm just about ready to be put down. I pull my pillow around my head and sigh deeply. I should never have had that bloody party. I should have just left. No fuss. No sentimental bullshit. No reason for Sarah to—

'Van will be here at ten,' I hear Matt yell from the hall, his tone unusually icy and flat as my pillow springs back into shape. Fuck. My mind races back to last night; his face when he saw Sarah and me . . . Sarah's face as she asked me how I felt about her . . . *fuckfuckfuck*. The irony that I decided to leave London to avoid this very thing happening isn't lost on me.

My phone informs me that it's 9.35am, leaving no time to shower, so I drag myself up and throw on some clothes, manoeuvring round the boxes which are ready just to chuck in the removal van. Matt stays in the living room, boundaries set firmly in place by his oversized headphones while I quickly use the bathroom and grab some breakfast, though in the end I barely touch it. Even without the hangover, I'd be in no mood to eat. Everything just feels wrong.

By the time the van arrives, Matt's barely said two words to me. This isn't the final-morning, 'Goodbye, London' send-off I'd hoped for. I can't bring myself to ask him what's wrong because we both know the answer already and then I'd need to lie to him again. Tell him what he saw was nothing and that he's reading too much into it. God, I'm such a coward, but I'd rather leave for Oxford with my best friend mad at me, than with no best friend at all.

The annoyingly upbeat movers bring down my bedroom furniture, while Matt and I deal with the boxes and bags that have been cluttering up my room and the hallway for the past week. At least he's helping me move and not just throwing my bags from the window with a loud *fuck you*. I give my bedroom a final once-over; it looks so stark now: furniture gone, pictures taken down and packed away, every trace of me removed and crammed into cardboard boxes. It's almost like I was never here.

We trudge downstairs and step outside, the morning sun instantly warming the top of my head while I drag the last three bin bags to the van. On a day like this, Matt and I would normally be nursing our hangovers in a beer garden somewhere. My stomach twists as I wonder whether that will ever happen again.

'All set then?' Matt asks as the removal men close the van doors. 'If you've left anything, I can send it on.'

'Yeah,' I reply, trying to remain as chipper as the knot in my stomach will allow. 'I think I've got everything.'

He nods, shuffling from foot to foot while his hands remain firmly stuck in his pockets like a kid who'd rather be anywhere else but here. I've known Matt for eleven years, but I've never felt like such a stranger.

'Ready when you are, pal.'

As I wave at the driver, signalling I'll just be a second, Matt takes the flat keys from his pocket, jangling them as an indication that he's also ready to go. 'Have a safe trip.'

'Thanks. I'll give you a call later, maybe?'

'Sure,' he replies, shrugging. 'I'll be around.'

I didn't think it was possible for my heart to sink any lower, but it now appears to be somewhere near my knees. He turns and retreats towards the flat.

'Matt! Please, we can't just leave things—'

He stops and turns to face me, rubbing the back of his neck. I can't tell whether he looks angry or confused but as he moves swiftly towards me, I steady myself, prepared to accept whatever's coming my way. Matt throws one arm around me and pulls me in with a hug that feels almost threatening at first – but slowly he brings around his other arm and it becomes something more tender.

We stay like that for a few seconds before Matt pulls away, sniffing loudly and dabbing his eyes with sleeve of his hoodie. My own glistening eyes cause him to smile reassuringly. He slaps me playfully on the arm, giving himself a shake.

'You take care, Nick, you hear me. Don't be a stranger.'

'I won't,' I assure him. 'God, this is all so weird. Can't believe I'm actually doing it . . . wish me luck?'

He grins and backs up towards the door. 'Nah, you don't need luck; you'll crush this.'

'Thanks, mate.'

'You still need a haircut though . . .'

I laugh and swivel around, giving him the finger as I climb into the rental car parked behind the removal van. I'm aware that I'll be stuck on the motorway in wall-to-wall traffic for the next two hours, but I honestly don't care. It doesn't matter. All that matters is that Matt and I are good. Thank God, we're good.

It's nearly 1pm by the time we reach my new flat in Headington and I'm so grateful that, from the outside at least, it looks exactly like the pictures provided by the letting agents. A small brown-brick, one-bedroom, ground-floor flat in a modern development about five miles from my new office. God, *my new office*. I feel a rush of excitement, quickly followed by a jolt of anxiety, because for the first time, I'm on my own. No roomies, no bill sharing, no passive-aggressive fights over the washing up – just me.

Collecting the keys from a lockbox by the door, we quickly unload the contents of the van into the flat, which apart from white goods is completely unfurnished. Once the movers leave, I wander aimlessly from room to room, wondering what the hell to do next. Even with my bedroom set in place, it's just so empty. The thought of turning this blank canvas into a home is a daunting one, but it's clean and newly painted, and once the living room furniture I've ordered arrives, I'm sure it'll feel less of a mammoth task. Probably. Jesus, I'm thirty-one and I've never been accountable for every single thing in a flat. Fuck, I've never even had to buy a spatula. It was always just . . . there.

I open up Spotify and shuffle some music while I park myself on the edge of my unmade bed. I can do this; I just need to be organised. Make some lists. Find the nearest supermarket so I don't starve to death. It's not rocket science – people do this shit every day.

As I begin to unpack my clothes, I hear 'Without You' by David Guetta playing in the background and it stops me in my tracks. This was the song I danced to with Sarah at Matt's birthday party and for a second, I'm back there, laughing and drinking and falling for her. Christ, if things were different, maybe . . .

I let my thoughts trail off as I sit back on the bed and put my head in my hands. Whatever happened last night, whatever feelings exist between us, it's over now.

CHAPTER THIRTY-FOUR

'Everyone, this is Nick. Nick, meet everyone.'

I raise my hand and greet my new colleagues, feeling horribly overdressed in my dark blue suit. Even my boss, Joseph, is wearing Converse.

He takes me around the room, introducing me to at least thirty people I won't remember the names of in half an hour, except for office manager Sigita, a Lithuanian woman with pink hair tips who was incredibly helpful when it came to short-notice flat hunting and sorting out my contract.

'So, this is the main hub,' he informs me, 'but we also have quieter offices to work from at your disposal, just through the doors to the right of reception. We prefer to work as a team here – hierarchy and closed-door policies in this type of environment can be counterproductive. Meeting rooms at the back here, as well as the kitchen. Coffee?'

'Please,' I reply, my head spinning slightly as I try to absorb everything. I'm not used to the people I work with being this approachable, especially management. Please don't let there be some weird catch, I'm almost looking forward to wearing jeans to work tomorrow.

Coffees in hand, Joseph takes me into meeting room two and begins my induction.

'So ... I know we ran through the job spec at your interview,' he says, gesturing for me to sit, 'but I wanted to dive a bit deeper into what we do here.'

'Of course,' I reply.

'A home isn't a luxury,' he begins, taking the lid off his coffee. 'It's a basic human need. We work with a diverse group of people, from rough sleepers to people in shelters to families being threatened with eviction, and everything in between. We deal with landlords, the local council, the police, social workers, the Addictions Advisory Service, the NHS, and many other organisations who specialise in dealing with the homelessness crisis we have in Oxford.'

'Sounds like something I can really get my teeth into,' I reply. 'I'm excited to get started.'

'Glad you said that,' he says, handing me two files. 'It's all hands on deck at all times. While you'll mainly be working with Martin Goodwin, our main charities' legal adviser here, it's important you get to grips with the meat and the bones of what we do.'

Taking a sip of my coffee, I open the first file. Maria Cooper, twenty-nine, two kids. Eviction notice from her landlord.

'Landlord is a real piece of work,' Joseph informs me. 'I think her rental agreement is worth having a look over, as well as his dodgy letting practices.'

I nod and open the next file. John Parker, seventeen.

'This kid needs help,' Joseph says, before I've even begun to read through. 'Both parents are addicts, and he's been crashing on floors for the past year. Got caught with a tiny amount of weed, an amount that they wouldn't bat an eyelid at if it was a student carrying it, but they still arrested him. Due in court on Wednesday.'

My face drops. I'm not a barrister. Does he expect me to go to court? Fuck, I think I'm way out of my depth here.

'Don't stress too much,' Joseph says, obviously noticing my expression. 'Christina and Gordon, who you just met, have about fifty years of court experience between them – everything from criminal to civil cases and beyond. Use them, learn from them, pick their brains. They'll do the same to you, believe me.'

I breathe a small sigh of relief and smile.

'No two clients are the same here, Nick, and we need everyone to pull together to make this work. It's the most challenging, affecting, mentally draining job you will ever do, and I guarantee the most rewarding. So . . . you ready to help change some lives?'

I smile and nod enthusiastically. Goddamn, his speech was impressive. I feel like a superhero. Alfie would be proud.

CHAPTER THIRTY-FIVE

'Nick, I have a Matt Buckley for you.'

'Thanks, Briony,' I reply, placing my phone on speaker. I'm in the back office, halfway through my lunch, and I'm ravenous. I haven't stopped since I got in at 8am.

'Hey, mate,' I say, biting into my BLT. 'You well?'

'Why aren't you answering your phone?' he asks sternly. 'I've been texting and calling.'

'Calm down, Dad,' I reply, chuckling. 'I've been in a meeting all morning. What's up?'

'It's Alfie's birthday next week and he's insisting that we go to that farm you told him about. Do we need to book tickets or anything? I don't want to leave it too late.'

'What farm? I don't remember telling him . . .'

Do you know what's even better than a zoo? A farm. They let you feed the animals and ride on tractors and I hear you can even cuddle baby rabbits.

'Ignore me,' I continue. 'I totally remember.'

Matt laughs. 'Seven weeks in Oxford and you're already

losing your mind. Shit, I need to run, my client's just walked in. Send me the link to the place and mark the date down in your diary.'

My chest tightens a little. 'I'm invited?'

'Of course!' he replies. 'Alfie insists. Think he misses you. No idea why, but he's been having sleepovers in your old room. Anyway, catch ya later.'

Matt hangs up and I slump back into my chair, cursing under my breath. I wasn't prepared to see any of them again, not yet. I thought that time plus fifty-six miles would equal a speedy emotional recovery, but it's been harder than I thought. If Alfie's been sleeping over, they must be getting serious. Suddenly I'm no longer hungry. Fuck, even the thought of seeing Sarah again makes me anxious, but it would look suspicious if I don't go and I'm not giving Matt any reason to doubt me.

I wipe my clammy hands on my jeans as I await the arrival of Matt, Sarah and Alfie, ignoring the wary looks from the passing parents at the overly sweaty single man by the entrance, as they make their way into the petting zoo. I wish I was perspiring just a little less – it's definitely adding to the 'about to bundle a child into a van' vibe. Given that it's almost eighty degrees and I made the mistake of wearing a long-sleeved shirt, I must look as uncomfortable as I feel, but it's not just the heat. I'm more nervous than I thought I'd be, given that it's now been eight weeks since I've seen any of them, although I've kept in touch with Matt almost daily. Neither of us has mentioned my leaving party and it seems we both intend to keep it that way.

With Sarah, it hasn't been so easy. I haven't heard from her since that evening – well, other than a stilted 'good luck' text on my first day, which I replied to with an equally stiff 'thanks'. Everything that was said and left unsaid that night had to remain firmly in the past, for both our sakes. Sometimes at night, alone in my bed, I replay that conversation over and over in my head, imagining everything I could have said or done differently. I imagine Sarah's face as I tell her that I love her, that I've never felt about anyone the way I feel about her. I imagine her telling me that I'm the one, that I can't leave because she is hopelessly in love with me. I imagine what her lips would feel like on mine.

And then, inevitably, Matt interrupts my fantasy and suddenly it becomes a nightmare as I picture my best friend's face as he walks in to find me kissing his girlfriend or professing my love to her. It doesn't matter that it isn't real – every time I feel myself burn with shame and guilt.

Not being in touch with Alfie has made me feel like the biggest arsehole on earth. He's such a good kid and doesn't deserve to be ignored but that was one promise that I just couldn't keep, not while I was avoiding his mum. This one, however, I can keep, which just leaves

Sarah and I to suck it up today, for what I'm expecting to be an absolutely tortuous afternoon together.

I spot Matt first, towering over the family in front of him, Sarah and Alfie eventually emerging beside him, holding hands. She's wearing a yellow sundress and ankle boots and for a moment, my heart beats just a little faster. I'm not sure what I was expecting, but it appears my longing hasn't subsided as much as I'd hoped for, or at all.

'Nick!' Alfie yells, running towards me. He's wearing an oversized blue badge with the number five on it. I smile widely and wave.

'Hey, bud,' I reply as he swoops in for a hug. 'Happy birthday! Have you grown taller? You're practically a giant.' I squeeze him hard. God, I've missed his face.

'Almost an inch,' Sarah responds. 'We measured him on the wall last week.'

She doesn't make eye contact with me for long, instead shifting her focus to Matt while linking into his arm. My stomach sinks as he kisses the top of her head. *Why did I think this would ever be a good idea?*

'You're looking well, mate,' Matt remarks as we go in for a hug.

'It's great to see you, man, I've missed you.' And it's true, I've missed them all, perhaps more than I've let myself admit over the last two months.

'Is that for me?' Alfie asks, pointing to the colourfully

wrapped present I've been clutching for the past ten minutes.

'Sure is!' I reply. 'Do you want to open it now or wait until we—'

He's already excitedly tearing at the paper and lets out a rapturous 'YES' when he sees what's inside.

'A Spiderman cap! Look, Mum!'

'So great!' Sarah replies. 'Let's see how it looks!'

She adjusts the headband first before Alfie parades around wearing the cap along with the biggest smile I've ever seen.

'Thanks, Nick!' he says, grabbing on to my waist. 'I love Spiderman!'

'Glad you like it, bud! Looks good on you. Let's go and see what the cows think.'

We head into the farm and I hope my nostrils will quickly acclimatise to the smell of manure as it hits me in the face. I smile as I see Alfie wrinkle his nose.

'Job going well?' Sarah asks. 'Matt says they're working you pretty hard.'

Not really, Sarah, it's just easier to say that than admit that I'm distancing myself from all of you.

'Yeah,' I reply. 'No rest for the wicked. It's interesting though, so I'm not complaining. Lots to—'

'PIGS!' Alfie exclaims. 'Mum, can we see the pigs?'

He grabs her hand and begins pulling her towards the

first of the many barns we'll visit today, while Matt and I follow behind.

'He was so excited on the car ride up,' Matt tells me, grinning broadly and carefully stepping over anything that resembles a cow pat. 'Sarah was a bit quiet though. Don't think traipsing through a farm in this heat is quite her thing.'

'Probably not,' I reply, knowing that it likely has more to do with having to see me again after all these weeks of silence rather than the weather. 'Alfie's bound to have enough fun for all of us anyway.'

A crowd around the piglets has already formed, while the larger pigs get some respite from the *ahhing* and *awwwing* which emanates from excited visitors. Sarah manages to squeeze Alfie in near the front of the pen where he points delightedly at the cute little porkers as they snuffle around beside their mother, who lies there looking entirely unimpressed. I chuckle quietly as I see a young dad pull his child's hand away from a curious pig's mouth, mumbling something about not wanting to have to explain to his wife why the kid is missing some fingers.

Matt shuffles around each pen, admiring the snorting beasts, while Sarah glues herself to Alfie, ensuring he doesn't vault over the side to get a better look at the one he keeps eagerly referring to as *Wilbur*. I hang back, feeling a little out of place. I'm hesitant to make things any more uncomfortable than they already are. Even through the stench of pig shit, the atmosphere between Sarah and me still reeks with what's been left unsaid between us.

'Can we see the rabbits now?' Alfie asks, his attention span shortening by the second. Sarah agrees, taking him by the hand as he drags her back out of the barn, while I wait for Matt, who is currently petting a rather large brown hog.

'They're cuter than they smell,' he muses as we follow Sarah and Alfie towards the petting barn. 'Almost makes me sorry to eat them.'

'No more bacon rolls then?'

He grins. 'Almost, mate . . . I said almost.'

Thankfully the brightly decorated petting area is far easier on the olfactory organs, where we find bunnies, guinea pigs, mice, rats, miniature ponies and a large tortoise named Ken. Every area has a chipper member of staff making sure the younger kids don't try to lick the smaller pets, while others hand out food that we can use to bond with the animals. We start with Ken, who plods leisurely towards his lunch, but, as we discover, watching a tortoise eat a strawberry painfully slowly gets boring rather quickly.

Alfie heads for the rabbits next, plonking himself down beside a girl holding a large, fluffy grey bunny, patiently waiting his turn. He's so mesmerised by the animal, it almost makes my heart burst.

'He always wanted a house rabbit,' Sarah mentions as

she waves over at him, 'or a dog . . . in fact, any kind of pet . . .'

She looks at her feet for a moment and sighs. 'A kid should have a pet. One day, when I can afford a place of our own . . .'

Matt wraps his arm around her waist and quickly hugs her, a hug which I can tell implies *you're doing your best, you'll get there.* Sarah smiles and focuses on Alfie who is now happily in charge of Thumper.

As I look around, I see that the barn is jammed full of families featuring all generations: grannies pushing buggies, grandads pacing with their hands behind their back, mums and dads chasing around older kids who have no intention of resting until bedtime. It looks like a lot of work. Fuck, it looks wonderful. Maybe if things had gone another way, it would be me chasing Alfie while—

'Check out those rats,' Matt says, his voice snapping me back to reality.

'Sorry, what?'

He gestures to his right and shudders. 'The rats. Not my favourite.'

I turn to see a member of staff holding two brown and white rats; kids stare up in awe as the rodents scramble over his hands and up on to his polo shirt. No one appears to be in any rush to hold them, however.

'Oh, hell no,' I say, taking a step back. 'When I was younger, our high-rise had a rat problem. They were gross.

By the time I moved out, pretty much everyone in that block of flats had invested in a cat.'

'Those ones are quite sweet though,' Sarah remarks. 'They're not overly *ratty*. You know, like the street rats that hunt in gangs and carry switchblades.'

'Would you like to hold one?'

Sarah takes a step back as the staff member beckons us closer, obviously eager to show off his rats. His name badge informs us that his name is Dean, but his glasses and middle-parting scream Sheldon.

I frown. 'Erm, no . . . I'm good.'

Dean laughs. 'They're very well socialised, they won't bite.'

Sarah turns to look at Matt, who is already retreating.

'I would, but I really need the loo. Back in a sec!'

She scowls as he scuttles off towards the toilets, putting as much distance between himself and the rats as possible. 'Um . . . well, I need to keep an eye on Alfie, so perhaps another time . . .'

She turns to see Alfie, now finished with the bunny, bounding up behind us.

'Is this Alfie?' Dean asks. 'I was just asking your mum if she wanted to hold one of our lovely ratties!'

Alfie beams. 'That's so cool! I've seen *Ratatouille* four times, haven't I, Mum? Can I hold one too?'

Sarah nods in defeat. Alfie just called her cool. There is no way she can decline. I can still say no, though. After playing Santa, my cool rating is at a minus anyway. For the first time today, Sarah and I throw each other a look of anxious solidarity as we walk slowly over towards Dean and his pet vermin.

Alfie dives right in, allowing the little rodents to sniff and explore him, while Sarah and I stand there with forced smiles, hoping that Dean will suddenly announce that visiting hours are now over. Sadly, it isn't to be.

'Nick, you hold one too!' Alfie insists. 'Come on!'

Sarah, considerably braver than me, bends down and starts by gently stroking Alfie's rat as he holds it out towards her. I manage to hold the smaller rat for three seconds before it senses my aversion and decides to go back to Dean on its own. I feel quite offended.

'Mum! I think it likes you!' Alfie says as he watches the rat rise up and sniff Sarah's slightly tense face, his little whiskers tickling her nose.

'His name is Byron,' Dean informs Alfie, 'and I think you're right.'

Sarah grins. 'He's softer than I thought ... actually rather ... woooahh!'

Quick as a flash Byron leaps from Alfie's hands and disappears down Sarah's top towards her waistband, his little body moving swiftly under the fabric.

'Don't panic,' Dean insists, his voice breaking slightly. 'Nothing to worry about.'

Alfie, finding this hilarious, gives everyone a play by

play of where the rat is going next. 'Hahaha, is he in your pants now? I think I can see his ear.'

Sarah yelps as we see the shape of Byron under her dress, lingering at her hips before heading north again. Her now crimson face pleads with Dean to make this stop.

'Nothing to worry about,' Dean repeats, reaching into his little food bag. 'Byron is just playing. They love tunnelling and warmth, he's very happy in there.'

Dean, now sweating a little, waves a peanut butter treat near the opening to Sarah's dress but in his clumsy rush to help, drops it down her cleavage.

'Are you KIDDING ME? You've just given him a snack! He has no reason to leave now!'

Dean scrambles in his bag to find another, apologising profusely. 'I – I'm so sorry, I'll just try—'

'Can we remove Byron from my nipple area,' she growls quietly at Dean. 'I'd like to walk out of here with two.'

Dean scrunches up his face in mortification. 'Um, ideally someone would reach *down there* and retrieve him, but I don't think it's appropriate that—'

Sarah shoots a look towards the bathrooms where Matt is obviously hiding out, before her eyes turn to mine and begin silently pleading.

'Me?' I ask, before shaking my head in dismay. 'No! I mean, I can't just go rummaging around in there! I'm sure Matt will be back—'

'Oh, come on!' she implores. 'I would do it for you!'

'Can't you just . . . shake it out of there?' I reply, awkwardly pointing towards her chest. 'Dean, dude. Don't you have a manager or a mousetrap or *something*?'

'I'll do it!' Alfie offers, reaching up towards Sarah, who now looks like she's about to burst into tears. *Fuck.* Between Sarah's wobbly bottom lip and the thought of Alfie getting accidentally nipped by Byron, there really is no other choice. I'm going to have to man up and step in.

'It's cool, I'll do it, buddy,' I tell Alfie. 'I have bigger hands . . . if that's alright with your mum?'

Sarah nods gratefully.

'Right, Dean, tell me what I need to do.'

'OK, yes . . . so, madam, if you can just stretch the top of your dress as far as it will go and you sir, just reach in and scoop Byron under his front legs and lift. Don't lift from his tail.'

As Sarah stretches her dress, I move in closer, trying my very best to ignore her white lace bra and concentrate on the furry stowaway, but my best isn't good enough and she knows it. We both start to blush.

Goddammit, Nick, they're just breasts! This isn't the time. Focus!

Spotting a cosy-looking Byron, I slowly reach in, my hand grazing her skin as I grab him gently. She shivers and gives a barely audible gasp, but it's loud enough to make me wonder whether it's from my touch or just from simple, plain old fear.

As I lift Byron out, Alfie gives a little cheer, just as Matt pushes his way past a crowd of amused onlookers.

'What is going on?' he asks, watching me hold up Byron. 'What did I miss?'

'I'll explain later,' Sarah replies as I hand the rat to a very relieved Dean. 'Jesus, that woman is filming, can we just get out of here? I'm mortified!'

Dean mumbles another apology as we leave, obviously as equally traumatised as Sarah, while Alfie immediately recounts the story to Matt.

'That was AMAZING!' Alfie says, skipping alongside his mum as we hastily leave the petting tent.

'Amazing, huh?' she replies, brushing down her dress. 'I'm not so sure, honey.'

Matt laughs. 'I have to agree. Nick lifted that little rat up like he was lifting Simba in The Lion King.'

Alfie gives a little jump. 'BEST BIRTHDAY EVER!'

Sarah smiles in delight and kisses his cheek. 'Well, that's all that matters! Shall we go and see the ponies? I think I can just about handle some ponies.'

By 3pm, we've visited alpacas, cows, ponies, sheep, had a ride on a tractor train around the farm and fed some particularly cute goats. My trainers look like they'll have to be binned but, so far, it's been a very successful day. With the exception of the rat ordeal, Sarah and I have managed to avoid each other for most of it, with Matt and Alfie proving to be ideal buffers.

We head to the café where Sarah has arranged for a birthday cake to be kept behind the counter. We let Alfie play in the kids' area first, while we all grab some much-needed caffeine.

'Anyone want any food?' Matt asks, glancing over at the menu board. 'I think they have sandwiches.'

Sarah shakes her head. 'I'm good, just a latte, thanks.'

'Can I have a Coke, mate?' I ask. 'I'm too warm for coffee. I might combust.'

Matt goes to get our drinks, leaving Sarah and I alone for the first time today. You could cut the tension with a knife.

'So . . .' I say, trying to break the silence. 'Those rats, eh? Quick little blighters.'

'Ugh,' she replies, 'I can still feel it on me.' She shudders. 'But at least it made Alfie smile. I appreciate you stepping up.' She glances at me briefly before her eyes shift back towards the table.

'Don't mention it. Yeah, I think Alfie's having a blast,' I reply, grateful we're talking, however awkwardly. 'Can't believe how much he's grown since I saw him last . . . and everything else? Work good?'

'Great,' she replies, smiling weakly. 'Really great, couldn't be better.'

'Excellent . . .'

She smooths out her skirt as a hush creeps over us

again. I don't think we've ever been together and spoken so little. As she peers over my shoulder to check on Alfie, I notice her face is ever so slightly sun-kissed, a faint dusting of freckles sweeping across her nose, and hard as I try, I can't help but let my gaze linger a little too long. She catches me looking at her and frowns.

'Nick . . . please don't.'

'I'm not . . . I mean, I wasn't . . .'

'It's not fair. We're past all that now.'

'Honestly, I didn't mean . . . look, I just miss you, OK?'

She sighs – it's clearly not OK – and she rises to her feet. 'I'm going to help Matt with the drinks and check what's happening with the cake. Can you keep an eye on Alfie?'

I nod as she walks over to Matt who's nearing the front of the queue. Turning towards Alfie, I quietly chastise myself for being an idiot. She didn't need to know that I miss her; I suppose I lost the right to say that sort of thing to her after the party. Fuck, I feel even worse now.

After a few minutes, I see Matt coming back with the drinks while Sarah brings across a huge birthday cake, complete with five candles. She looks stressed. This is meant to be Alfie's day and I feel like I'm ruining it. I offer to venture into the soft play area and retrieve him, while they light the candles.

'Happy birthday to you, happy birthday to you! Happy birthday, dear Alfie. Happy birthday to you!'

Alfie cannot hide his delight as the entire café joins in to wish him a happy birthday, cheering when he manages to blow out his candles in one fell swoop. Sarah cuts the cake and hands him a piece first before serving the rest of us. My appetite is now at zero, but I take the cake and pick at it while I drink my Coke, reassuring myself that the farm will be closing in an hour and we can all go our separate ways. I'm ready for this to be over.

As the farm starts to empty, we pay one last visit to see the ponies before walking back to Matt's car, all thoroughly exhausted. Matt picks up Alfie and carries him over his shoulder.

'We can drop you off,' Matt says to me, as Alfie rubs his eyes. 'Jump in.'

'No, it's cool,' I reply. 'Your drive home is long enough. I'll catch a cab.'

I lean in and give Alfie a cuddle. 'Happy birthday, buddy; I'll see you soon.'

'Promise?'

'Of course. I'll be back in London before you know it.'

'I'll talk to you tomorrow, mate,' Matt says, unlocking the car. 'Really good to see you.'

'Yep,' I reply. 'Speak soon.'

'Bye, Nick,' Sarah says, while Matt gets Alfie settled into the car. 'Take care of yourself.'

'You too.'

She hesitates before leaning in to hug me.

I hold her tightly, just a fraction too long. She pulls back and slides into the car. Our eyes lock briefly through the glass, and I see them beginning to well up before she looks away.

CHAPTER THIRTY-SIX

Four Months Later

I'll be out of the office from December 22nd to January 3rd and will not be checking email. For urgent enquiries, please contact josephdalton@HLAoxford.co.uk.

Merry Christmas!

Nick Harris

I power down my laptop and slip it into my bag, eager to get going and start my holidays. Even though I no longer live with Matt, his parents have insisted I join them all for Christmas dinner as usual. Spending Christmas alone in Oxford is apparently not an option. I'm not complaining though. A couple of days catching up with Matt in London, followed by a feast in Surrey before I return home sounds like a perfect Christmas.

As I slide out my chair, I hear a small gruff from under my desk.

'Come on, boy,' I tell Spot, the three-legged spaniel who's now sniffing my foot, 'time to go.' I stand up and grab my suitcase. 'I'm off, everyone. Have a brilliant Christmas!'

'You too, Nick,' yells Briony, her flashing reindeer antlers bobbing frantically on her head. 'I've left a bag of dog treats for Spot by the door!'

Compared to every other office I've worked in, this place is a breath of fresh air. I love it here. There's no pretention, no bitching, no competitive bullshit and everyone's role is important and valued, regardless of status. For the first time in maybe forever, I leave work feeling like I've made a difference. I mean, playing Santa gave me a warm fuzzy feeling sometimes, but I technically wasn't responsible for the gifts under the tree. They also let me bring my dog to work here, which is only fair considering they emotionally manipulated me into adopting him after his owner passed away. I let Yvette in accounting rub Spot's belly while I grab my coat and the little festive pack of chicken-flavoured treats from Briony that he will devour later, hearing jolly Christmas wishes from the rest of the staff as I leave.

With forty minutes before the 2pm train departs for London, I take Spot for a quick walk and let him poo – the only part of being a dog owner that I'm not entirely enamoured with. The rest is pretty sweet. It turns out I do like dogs after all. Suck it, Debbie, I would have been a total asset to your stupid dog grooming business.

Living alone for the first time ever has certainly been an eye-opener. My quest to become an independent man has highlighted the fact that I'm not actually that great at being alone, but Spot has made it less solitary. I've only had him for four months, but he's been a brilliant roommate. He's also an excellent woman magnet, wagging his tail profusely at any female who stops to say hello to his dumb little face.

Slowly but surely, I've made a few friends. Most Fridays the office gang go for drinks at one of the nearby pubs. Plus my supervisor Joe and his wife Clare have basically adopted me, and I have a standing invite to their monthly dinner parties, where they'll try and pair me off with a variety of oblivious singletons. So far, I have met Sheila, the bank manager; Deborah, the actress; Amber, the insurance underwriter; Imogen, the artisan baker; Charlie, the police officer; and Maggie, the History of Feminism professor. I've managed to ward off their advances with my dignity mostly intact. My head just isn't in the right place for dating at the minute. It might be months since I last saw Sarah, but my heart still aches a little every time I think about her.

The train ride to Euston is quick and Spot is incredibly well behaved, sitting at my feet and happily allowing everyone to fuss over him and his three legs.

Matt picks us up at the station in his new company car. Promotion certainly has its perks. Spot bounds towards him, pulling me behind.

'Hello, boy!' he says, as Spot excitedly jumps up to greet him. 'You're looking well-fed.'

'Don't fat-shame my dog,' I respond, laughing and leaning in for a hug. 'How are you, mate? Feels like ages since I've seen you.'

Matt opens the door and lets Spot jump into the back seat. 'I'm good,' he replies. 'When did we last see you? August?'

I nod. 'Alfie's birthday weekend.'

I've only seen Alfie and Sarah the once since I moved, at the farm, and we haven't spoken since. I still feel like a rat, reneging on my promise to visit Alfie all the time, but it's for the best. This way I can sleep at night. We get into the car and Matt starts the engine.

'Sorry I couldn't make it for your birthday,' I say as we head towards London Bridge. 'It's chaotic being the new kid and all that.'

'Not a problem,' he insists. 'You didn't miss much. It was just the usual gang. Glad you're here now. Job going well? And how's the flat?'

'Really well,' I reply, 'and the flat is great. Decent-sized bedroom, little garden, private parking for when I eventually get a car. I'm happy. Really happy.'

'Glad to hear it. I have news as well.'

'Really? Like what?' I ask, my mind already jumping to a million conclusions. I bet he and Sarah are getting married. Fuck, maybe she's pregnant. I glance at Matt, but he is concentrating on the traffic and his face gives away nothing.

'Let's grab some beers at the supermarket first. I'll tell all when we get back to mine. It's quite the saga.' He grins sheepishly.

We pull into Tesco and leave Spot in the car with a window cracked while we nip inside, heading straight for the booze aisle. I grab some cans of Stella while Matt lifts a bottle of rosé wine and some frozen strawberry daiquiri mix.

'Is Sarah coming over?' I ask, watching him place them in his basket. The familiar feeling of my stomach doing somersaults returns with a vengeance. I wasn't prepared to see her yet. Does she live with him now? How could he not have told me?

Matt screws up his face. 'This isn't for Sarah.' He actually blushes. 'So, that's what I wanted to speak to you about . . . These are for . . . Karen.'

'Karen who?'

'*Karen*, Nick. We're back together. I'm not with Sarah anymore.'

The beer cans fall from my hands and hit the floor with a crash that startles everyone except me. It's impossible to be shocked when you're already reeling.

'But I thought . . . you guys seemed so happy?'

He nods. 'I wanted it to work, believe me; I loved her, I love Alfie, but there was always something missing. I just assumed it was me being, well ... me. I thought, given enough time, it would just click into place. And then Karen turned up on my doorstep three weeks ago.'

Matt selects a bottle of champagne while I just stand there. Stunned.

'She had just gotten back from New York and wanted to see me. Nick, the moment I saw her standing there, I just knew. I knew I'd never find the part that was missing with Sarah. Anyway, I invited her in, and the old connection was still there for her too. No matter how hard I tried, I guess I never stopped loving her, mate, and she feels the same. Anyway, long story short, we ended up in bed. God knows I never meant to cheat on Sarah but—'

My fist connects with his nose before he can finish the sentence and he decks it, immediately snapping me out of my stunned state and into one of panic.

Everyone in the alcohol aisle has frozen, their mouths open in shock.

'Oh, shit, mate, I'm so sorry!' I exclaim, helping him off the floor. 'Shit, shit, shit, I don't know what came over me.'

'What the fuck, Nick?' he shouts, holding his bloody nose. 'Jesus, I didn't cheat on you!'

As security rushes over to eject us from the store, my hand begins to throb like a bitch. Matt's nose is streaming blood on to his T-shirt and I feel like such a prick.

By the time we get to Matt's car, the bleeding has slowed

to a steady trickle, but his nose doesn't look right. Spot barks from the back seat, happy to see us.

'I think you need a doctor, mate,' I say, trying to touch his nose, but he winces and steps back.

'Fuck you,' he says, looking in the wing mirror. 'What the absolute fuck is wrong with you?'

'I'm so sorry,' I repeat. 'I have no idea what I was thinking. It was just instinct. Sorry, fella.'

We climb back into the car and sit in silence for a moment before Matt finally says, 'It's fine. I deserve it, to be fair. I did a crappy thing. Though, for the record, Sarah took the news better than you did.'

'You told her everything?' I ask. How can the mere mention of her name still give me butterflies?

He nods, wiping his face with a clean part of his T-shirt. 'The next morning, I went to hers and confessed all. I tried to explain about Karen, how she wasn't just some random fling, but Sarah cut me off and told me to leave. I felt terrible. Still do. I tried to call back the next day, but she wouldn't pick up. I sent a message to explain everything – she's read it, but I guess she's still pretty mad. Which is fair enough.'

He tentatively touches his nose. 'Maybe I should get this checked. I think it might be broken. Your hand doesn't look too hot either.'

'We can't both sit in Accident and Emergency and leave Spot in the car,' I say, looking at his little face. 'You go and get checked out. I'll wait with him.'

'Karen is at home. She could watch him. She likes dogs. The flat isn't far from A&E.'

'You've moved her in already?'

'No! Relax! She's just staying in the flat while I go home for Christmas. Her place is being painted.'

I reluctantly agree and we drive to Matt's flat, promising a rather concerned-looking Karen that we wouldn't be long. Matt mumbles something about an accident, while I sheepishly try to hide my huge, swollen hand from view.

A&E is relatively quiet and after we give our details, we take a seat across from a woman with a nasty burn on her hand and an elderly man who's coughing so hard his eyes are watering.

'So why didn't you tell me any of this was happening?' I ask. 'I live an hour and a half away, not on the fucking moon. This is pretty fairly bloody massive news, mate.'

Matt sighs. 'I didn't exactly want to broadcast that I was a cheating scumbag. Even to you. You're in Oxford, living like a monk, celibate—'

'I'm not fucking celibate!' I splutter indignantly, though after almost a year, it's starting to feel that way.

'– impoverished and helping the needy, and I'm working a cushy corporate job and cheating on a widowed single mum. I couldn't handle the thought of you judging me when I already felt like a total dickhead. I figured you would find out soon enough anyway – though if I'd known *how* you were gonna take it, then I definitely would have broken the news over the phone. I guess I also thought Sarah might have told you?'

'Why?' I ask.

'You guys were close. I just assumed you still kept in touch.'

'Nah,' I reply, feeling uncomfortable. 'I've just been so busy, you know, and we weren't really that close . . .'

'Hmm,' he responds, touching his nose again. 'My nose might be broken, but I can still smell bullshit.'

'What do you mean?' I ask, my heart pounding in my chest. I try my best not to look alarmed.

'You weren't really that close? That right hook of yours suggests otherwise. You don't throw a punch like that without some feeling behind it.'

I look at Matt and realise it's game over.

'So maybe there were small feelings,' I admit. 'Like . . . more-than-friend type feelings.'

Matt's eyebrows head skywards. 'Seriously? On whose side?'

'Mine . . . maybe hers . . . I don't know. I never really found out. Not properly.'

'Jesus, Nick. How am I the one that got punched in this scenario? If you didn't have a hand the size of a fucking cauliflower you would seriously be getting your ass kicked right now. Why would you set me up with her if you liked her, for God's sake?' Matt is looking at me incredulously and his voice has gone up an octave.

The woman with the burn is now listening intently, her mouth slightly open.

'Well, I didn't know I was going to fall in love with her, did I?' I mumble, aware of burn lady's stare.

Jesus, Matt's eyebrows are nearly in his hairline now. His jaw is working overtime, his teeth clenching and unclenching as he breathes out. I think he might yet decide to knock me out.

'Wait. Let me get this straight: you were in love with my girlfriend? Are you fucking kidding?'

'I'm sorry,' I reply. 'I didn't mean for it to happen.'

He is silent for a moment, absorbing the news.

'I have a question,' he finally asks. 'That night at your leaving party. When I walked into the bedroom and Sarah was crying, was that . . . did you—'

'Nothing happened,' I quickly interject. 'We were just talking. She asked if we were just friends. You and Alfie came in before I could really say anything, but I promise, Matt, I would never have done anything to ruin our friendship, or your relationship. I swear.'

'Matt Buckley?'

Matt stands, shakes his head at me, then follows the nurse to the treatment area, while I wait with Miss Nosy Burn, who's now feigning interest in her magazine again. This whole day feels surreal. I punched my best friend, told him I had feelings for his girlfriend and have potentially ruined my relationship with him forever.

Before I have time to contemplate this further, a second nurse calls my name and I take my rapidly swelling hand through the double doors.

Forty-five minutes later, we're back in the car. Thankfully Matt only has swelling and bruising, whereas I have a hand in a plaster cast and a prescription for heavy-duty painkillers. Matt finds this amusing.

'Sorry, I'm not laughing *at you*, it's just that you ended up worse off than me and I'm the one who got punched. My nose broke your hand. You are a ridiculous person, Nick Harris.'

'I still feel shit about it . . .' I say, attempting to open a bottle of water with my left hand.

'Well, don't,' he replies, still chuckling. 'You're suffering enough.'

He starts the car and texts Karen to let her know we're on our way back.

'So, I have another question,' Matt says as he opens my bottle for me, taking a swig. I feel my pulse start to race again. What else does he want to know?

'OK . . .'

'Why the hell is your dog called Spot?'

I start to laugh. 'No idea. His previous owner named him. It's what he answers to.'

Matt chuckles. 'Fair enough. It's just been bugging me.'

As we turn into Matt's street, he pulls up at the kerb and turns off the engine.

'I do have one more actual question,' he says, checking his eye in the mirror. 'Your feelings for Sarah. When did they start?'

I pause for a second and think. 'Honestly? Your birthday party. God, I know how that sounds, but you wanted the truth.'

'I guess there's only one thing left to do,' he says, unbuckling his seatbelt.

Oh God, he's going to punch me back. I pre-emptively close my eyes and brace for impact.

'You need to go and tell her.'

I open one eye cautiously. 'Tell her what?'

'Tell her that you love her. Idiot.'

CHAPTER THIRTY-SEVEN

Sarah's flat is a twenty-minute drive from Matt's, however, when I try and fail to summon an Uber with my left hand, Matt rolls his eyes and tells me to put my phone away.

'Wait here.' He nips inside his flat first and returns with Spot in tow.

'Karen said he missed you,' Matt informs me, as we reverse out of the parking space. 'I got a text when we came out of A&E not so politely requesting that we pick him up pronto. She isn't as keen on dogs as I first thought. I think he shat in the hall.'

Spot cocks his head to one side like he's heard every word, while I fasten my seatbelt again, my heart racing at the sheer madness of what I'm about to do.

'What if she doesn't want to see me,' I say, running through a million eventualities in my head. 'What if I totally misread the signals and she never liked me? What if she's not in?'

'Calm it, dude. She'll be packing for her trip to her

parents' house,' he informs me. 'She doesn't leave until tomorrow. Stop worrying.'

I am worrying though. What if she's totally over any feelings she might have had for me? What if I ruined everything forever by not telling her how I felt the night before I left for Oxford? What if she blames me for Matt breaking her heart? 'She might have already met someone else. What if—

'We're here.'

Taking a deep breath, I steel myself to exit the car.

'Nick?'

'Yes?' I turn to look at Matt.

'Get out of the fucking car already.' Matt grins at me.

I slide out of the car awkwardly and walk up the icy path towards her front door, almost falling on my arse at one point. I take a deep breath and knock.

I knock again.

'Sarah?' I yell. 'It's me, Nick. I need to talk to you.'

'She's gone away for Christmas, love.'

Startled, I look up and see an elderly woman leaning out of the window above. It must be Mrs Grainger.

'Oh. When did she leave?'

'About fifteen minutes ago. You just missed her.'

God bless intrusive neighbours. I thank her and run back to the car.

'She left about fifteen minutes ago. I need to get to the station.'

'Which one?' he asks. 'There are twelve major stations in London.'

'I'm sure she once said that her parents live in Kemble ...'

We both start quickly googling, though Matt is decidedly faster with two working hands.

'Paddington!' he declares. 'Trains are every hour. Next one is in forty minutes. If we hurry, we'll make it.'

Matt breaks at least three rules of the highway code en route, but he's clearly determined to get me to the station, leaving me to buy an e-ticket to get through the barriers.

As we reach the drop-off point, Matt wishes me good luck as I sprint from the car, tucking Spot under my fully functional arm. I still have five minutes to spare but I need to find the right platform. By the time I get to the live departure boards, I'm completely red-faced and out of breath. Not the look I was going for.

My eyes scan the board until I see that the train is platform five, but when I get there, the platform is nearly empty and Sarah and Alfie are nowhere to be seen. They must already be inside.

With less than two minutes to spare, I jump on board and set Spot down. I start racing through the carriages, eyeballing everyone I pass while Spot happily pads behind me like this is just another normal doggie day for him.

When I reach the second-to-last carriage, I see them. Sarah is at a little table facing Alfie, whose legs I can see kicking at the side of his seat. She looks amazing, even better than in my head, even though she is wearing a giant jumper and tracksuit bottoms.

I'm almost right beside her before she looks up and realises it's me. She looks like she's seen a ghost. Her mouth literally drops open.

'Nick? What are you doing here?'

'I spoke to Matt,' I pant. 'I had to see you.'

The train conductor starts announcing departure.

'So, Matt sent you to speak for him? Why didn't he . . . wait, is that your dog?'

'What?' I spin to see Spot trying to hump the leg of a disgruntled man two rows behind me. I quickly pull Spot away, mouthing my apologies. 'Oh yes, this is—'

Suddenly the train begins to move, then abruptly jolts, making me fly forward. I knock my hand against the table, howling in pain, and making the rest of the carriage turn in my direction.

'Shit, sit down,' she says, moving her bags to her feet. 'What the hell did you do to your hand?'

'Mum, I think he likes me.'

We both look at Alfie who's giggling while Spot licks his face, having jumped on to the seat next to Alfie.

'Don't let him lick your mouth, sweetie . . . seriously, Nick, what are you doing here?'

I place my stinging hand on the table and take a deep breath.

'I'm not here to speak for Matt,' I reply. 'Although it's my fault you got involved with him in the first place. And I can't believe he did that to you. I'm so sorry, Sarah. God, the last thing I wanted was for you to get hurt. If I'd known that he was still in love with Karen—'

'It isn't your fault, Nick,' she interjects, lowering her voice in the hope that I'll also take the hint and follow suit. Alfie isn't paying attention to us, but it seems at least half a carriage of passengers are.

'Look, I'm fine,' she continues. 'Yes, I was angry with Matt . . . well, furious is probably more fitting . . . but it's been nearly a month since it happened. Besides, he sent me a long text last week, properly explaining everything. I'm not sure anyone knew just how relentlessly heart-broken he was when she left. He kept it hidden well. But I know what it's like to be in love like that . . .'

Her voice wobbles and trails off as she focuses on Alfie. I can tell she's trying to hold it together.

'Look, Matt got the chance to get that love back. I'm certainly not going to hold that against him or you. Besides, dating Matt got me back out there. He made it less scary.'

'Wow,' I reply. 'You're taking this very well. In university, Matt cheated on someone and she threw his laptop out of the window.'

She laughs. 'Maybe ten years ago I would have been the same. Listen, I appreciate you trying to do the right thing, or whatever this is, but—'

'No, Sarah, I'm here because I wanted to tell you that—'

'To be honest, Matt actually did me a favour.'

I stop, confused. 'He did?'

She nods. 'Part of me was relieved when he broke it off. I was also trying to bury feelings for someone else. It's no wonder we didn't fully click. Neither of us were honest. We were doomed from the start. But I guess this frees me up to pursue that now.'

I feel my heart sink. God, I feel so foolish. Here I am, jumping on to trains to tell Sarah I love her, and she's been in love with someone else the whole time. We are now well out of the station – and it's an hour until the first stop. Fucking brilliant.

'You had something to tell me?' she asks.

I shake my head. I'm such an idiot. I don't even know how to hide my disappointment right now. I'm not even sure it matters.

'Forget it,' I mumble, 'I didn't realise you were … I mean, I'm happy for you. And him. I hope you get—'

My words fall away as she leans forward and kisses me, her hair falling against my face.

'There is no *him*, stupid,' she informs me as she pulls her mouth away. She looks into my eyes. 'It's you. It has always been you, Nick.'

'Then why—' I break away, leaning against the back of the seat, my lips still tingling from her kiss.

'I couldn't come between you and Matt. He's your

family. And I didn't know if you liked me back. That night in your room . . .'

I smile. All this time we've both been trying to spare Matt's feelings when his heart was firmly elsewhere. I take a pause, trying to process everything, but all I can think about is that kiss.

'Please. Say something,' she implores. 'You're leaving me hanging here. Again.'

'Well, I came here to tell you that I'm completely, totally, madly in love with you,' I say, 'but you kind of stole my thunder.'

She gives a little shriek and pounces on me, kissing me again like her life depends on it. The woman three seats down gives a gasp, mumbling that this is neither the time, nor the place. The rest of the carriage begins to clap and there are whistles from the less uptight passengers.

'Mum?'

We turn to see Alfie sitting there looking confused. God, I almost forgot he was there. This must be so weird for him. I unwrap from Sarah and she pulls Alfie in for a huge hug.

'Sorry, sweetie, Nick and I were just . . . um . . . sorting things out.'

'I know what kissing is, Mum.'

'Right . . . of course you do,' Sarah replies, blushing. 'Silly me.'

He pauses for a moment. 'So . . . does this mean that

Nick is coming back now? He didn't come to see us for ages.'

Alfie looks up at me with those giant brown eyes and I'm reminded of the first time I saw him. I feel guilt twist in my stomach for letting him down.

'I'm sorry, Alfie. You're right – I should have come to see you, buddy, but I'm not going anywhere now. I'll be sticking around if that's OK with you?' I smile at him and then look up at Sarah who is beaming at him.

'Can I ask something?'

'Anything! I know this must be confusing and—'

'Why does Spot only have three legs?'

I laugh out loud because Alfie doesn't appear to be remotely weirded out by any of this. 'You know, I think he was born that way. Some dogs are just born cooler . . . you know?' Spot was actually hit by a car in a rather awful accident that left his leg pulverised, but that seems a little grim, so I decide to keep that detail to myself.

Sarah spots the food trolley coming down the carriage. 'Alfie, I'll give you money for a sandwich. You can share it with Spot, yeah?'

Alfie agrees and takes Spot by the lead, proudly walking him the fifteen steps to the trolley. Sarah places her hand on my knee.

'That day at the coffee shop . . . why didn't you just ask me out? When you asked for my number . . . I thought I was giving it to you.'

I glance over towards Alfie and make sure he's not within listening distance.

'So, long story short, when Alfie came to see me as Santa, his Christmas wish was for you to be happy again.'

'No way?' Sarah's eyes begin to well up and soon tears are spilling down her cheeks.

I nod. 'And he made me promise to make his wish come true. And I really wanted to. I thought maybe Matt might bring a little happiness into your life – he's so dependable and together and loy—' I think better of my final adjective – 'a grown-up. Whereas I was a total mess, which was the last thing you needed.'

She leans in again. 'You might not have been what I needed, but fuck knows, you were what I wanted, Nick.'

'That's kinda hot,' I inform her, grinning.

'Uh-huh.' She leans in and kisses me again, slower this time.

Alfie brings back a chicken sandwich which he happily shares with a grateful Spot. I think Alfie might have found a new best friend.

'Mum, is Nick coming to stay at Granny's for Christmas?'

She glances at me and bites her lip. 'I'm sure we could make room for a couple of nights.'

I smile and take out my phone.

Keep those beers on ice, mate. I'll be back for Christmas.

CHAPTER THIRTY-EIGHT

Meeting a girl's parents is always a nerve-wracking experience, but turning up at their door uninvited is truly terrifying.

'Relax,' Sarah says as we approach their house, 'I've already texted them. They're happy to have you.'

'But they've never met me,' I reply, frowning. 'What if they hate me? What if they hate my dog?'

Sarah hands the taxi driver a tenner and tells him to keep the change. 'Well, put it this way: if they do hate you, my mum's seventy and my dad's in a wheelchair. You can easily outrun them.'

I laugh in surprise while Sarah exits the taxi, collecting her bags from the boot of the car. Shit. I don't even have a toothbrush; this is a terrible idea.

Sarah's childhood home is exactly as I expected – utterly charming. A quaint-looking, brightly lit, cream-brick bungalow with blue-trimmed windows and a neatly tended garden. The whole village reminds me of a leafy pre-watershed BBC drama where the local midwife rides a bike, the vicar's wife runs the village shop and no one's milk gets nicked from their doorstep.

Alfie and Spot run ahead, making their presence known by loudly yelling and barking the entire length of the wheelchair-adapted path, something I'm sure the neighbours appreciate at 9pm. As the door opens, I see a tall, thin woman in a long tie-dye dress waving us in.

'Oh, and my parents are total hippies,' Sarah whispers. 'I hope you like the smell of patchouli.'

'Sweetheart!' Sarah's mum says excitedly. 'Come in . . . oh my, who's this handsome chap?'

'Spot,' Alfie informs her. 'He has three legs.'

'One more than me,' she replies as Alfie runs inside. 'And who do we have here?'

'Hey, Mum,' Sarah says, hugging her tightly. 'So, this *other* handsome fella is Nick.'

'Linda,' she says, holding out her hand. 'We've heard so much about you.'

They have? I clumsily shake her hand with my left, while she lifts her glasses to peer at my blood-speckled T-shirt and plaster cast. 'Tell me, did my daughter do that?'

'Mum!' Sarah exclaims. 'Just let us in, it's freezing!'

We step inside a porch and then directly into the living room, where Alfie and Spot are sitting with Sarah's dad. Where Matt's parents' living room wouldn't look out of place in an interior design magazine, this is far more bohemian and homely. There are family pictures every-where, colourful throws over the couches, a Christmas tree groaning under the weight of the mismatched dec-orations, and a large wooden coffee table covered with candles in all shapes and sizes.

'There's my girl,' Sarah's dad says, his face lighting up. 'Seems like we have quite the full house this year.'

'Hi, Dad,' she chirps in return. 'This is Nick – Nick, my dad, Stephen.'

'Pleased to meet you,' I say, making my way across the room to shake his hand. 'I'm sorry if I'm imposing. This was all very unexpected ...'

I feel my cheeks flush slightly as my mind shoots back to Sarah's mouth on mine. Everything about this day has been unexpected.

'Nonsense,' he replies. 'It's about time we put a face to the name. Any friend of Sarah's ...'

'... obviously needs their head checked,' say both Sarah and her mum in unison. I chuckle as Stephen winks at them both before gesturing to Sarah to give him a hug. She obliges, joking that he needs a shave before quietly checking on how he's been doing and if he needs any-thing. Their bond is immediately unmistakable and she's as gentle with him as she is with Alfie.

I help Sarah take the bags upstairs, where she dumps hers in a pretty pink room before showing me to the spare room.

'Mum and Dad had an extension built round the side, so they sleep there. The upstairs is all ours.'

She flicks on the light and I'm instantly greeted by a giant stuffed panda perched at the end of the single bed. Who knew they made *Duck Tales* duvet covers?

'And this is your room. Obviously, Alfie would normally sleep in here,' she says, turning on a little star-shaped lamp, 'but ... well, I wouldn't want to just jump into bed ... well, actually, I would but ... oh God, I'm not good at this, am I?'

I grin. 'Listen, it's your parents' house, I get it. It's not a problem. Besides, I've slept in weirder places and I once had *Fraggle Rock* bedcovers ... why are you staring at me like that?'

She kicks the door closed with her foot and kisses me hard, while my functioning hand reaches behind and grasps her hair.

'When we get back to London,' she whispers, 'I swear—'

'NICK, CAN SPOT HAVE SOME OF MY BANANA?'

I pull away and rest my forehead on Sarah's, quietly laughing while Alfie's little voice echoes up the stairs. 'Yes, buddy, just not too much. I'll be down in a second.'

'Sorry,' she says, sighing. 'Maybe not the best timing but ...'

'Bit of a recurring theme for us, eh?' I reply, kissing her forehead. She smirks and attempts to flatten the patch of hair I've managed to mess up during our three-second tryst. I take a deep breath to calm my galloping pulse and hope that the rest of my body follows suit.

We get back downstairs where Alfie is now sitting crossed-legged in front of the television, happily munching on his passion-killing banana. Spot pads over to me and gruffs, indicating that it is well past his dinner time. Along with clothes and toiletries, yet another thing I didn't consider when agreeing to spend the next couple of days with Sarah. I'm killing this.

'Is there a shop nearby?' I ask Sarah. 'He's hungry, I'll need to get him some food.'

'Not one that's open,' Sarah replies; 'nearest supermarket is a few miles away. We could—'

'We'll be eating in twenty minutes,' Linda interjects, 'and I've never met a dog who doesn't like chicken. He'll be fine. Sarah, you can take the car to the supermarket tomorrow and get what you need.'

Agreeing to wait until morning, we all sit down to eat the slightly strange but nonetheless delicious buffet Linda lays out for us. A large rotisserie chicken, cold potato salad, a nut roast with a salsa sauce, sweet potatoes, a bowl filled with rice and black-eyed beans, full-sized sausages wrapped in bacon, and a sweet curry sauce which looks like vomit but tastes surprisingly good.

'We've missed having a dog around here,' Stephen begins, placing some chicken and rice in a bowl for Alfie.

'We had a German Shepherd years ago ... remember Lennon, Sarah. Used to sleep beside your bed.'

Sarah nods. 'I remember he ate every single left slipper I ever owned.'

Alfie laughs, his chin covered in curry sauce.

'I thought about getting another, but with me in this thing now, it would be too much for Linda to deal with.'

'Nonsense,' Linda replies, 'you have limited mobility, not quadriplegia. We could get one of those tiny dogs. I could carry it in my shoulder bag and give it a stupid haircut. Ooh, that might be fun!'

I laugh and take another bite of my sweet potato. Despite my initial reservations, I'm warming to this family quickly. They're utterly mad.

The next morning, Linda offers to walk Spot while Sarah, Alfie and I take a drive to nearby market town Cirencester to get supplies. I only intend on staying one more night, but I need a change of clothes given that I'm forced to wear one of Stephen's brown wool jumpers. My blood-spattered T-shirt has been assessed by Linda, deemed unsalvageable and binned.

'We've missed the Christmas market,' Sarah informs me as she parks the car, 'but the farmers' market should be on and maybe some craft stalls?'

'I thought we were going to Tesco or Waitrose or something?'

'We will,' she replies, helping Alfie straighten his winter hat, 'but I thought Alfie might like to see the Christmas lights. Maybe grab a bite to eat?'

'You mean this trip isn't all about me?' I grin, feeling a tad foolish. 'That sounds fun, actually.'

We walk through the car park towards Market Place, where the buildings line the streets in a terribly civilised, uniform manner and every shop appears to have a home above it. No seven-hundred-foot-tall department stores towering overhead or scaffolding from the next office block in construction – just clean, pretty buildings, lining clean, pretty streets, currently dusted with a fine layer of powdery-looking snow.

Turning into Market Place, I understand why Sarah wanted to bring us here. The festive decorations alone are well worth the visit, even during the day. Huge strings of lights hang overhead while the remarkable Christmas tree stands in front of the charming parish church, with the festive stalls nearby already bustling with customers.

'So, are we on a date?' I ask Sarah, while Alfie investigates the brass band playing 'Jingle Bells'. 'It kind of feels like a date.'

She links her arm in mine and sighs. 'I don't tend to date men who dress like my dad ... *Alfie, don't touch the nice man's trombone!*'

I laugh as she runs to retrieve Alfie, thinking that Matt

was wrong about ice skating being the perfect romantic date, because this is about as perfect as it gets.

'Let's get a hot drink,' Sarah suggests, pulling Alfie back by the sleeve. 'Maybe some food?'

'Sounds good,' I reply. 'I'm pretty sure I smell doughnuts. Alfie, what do you think?'

Alfie, known for his tendency to run wildly towards the mere mention of a food stall, gets in between Sarah and me, taking both of our hands. I don't even care that he's holding my cast, it's adorable. As Sarah and I glance at each other and smile, it happens; my heart finally bursts.

CHAPTER THIRTY-NINE

A heavy overnight snowfall means that my initial plan to return to London to spend Christmas with Matt and his family isn't going to happen. I can't say I'm entirely disappointed. Despite the fact I'm now dressed head-to-toe in the supermarket's basic joggers and jumpers range, I'm having a bloody ball. Between sightseeing, finding new places for Spot to explore and rampant over-the-clothes touching when Alfie's not around, I'm in no hurry to tear myself away.

'But you have to come back, mate,' Matt insists, his face freezing as our video call connection drops out for a second. 'It's Christmas Eve. Mum's bought you some driving gloves.'

'Don't make me feel bad,' I reply, wondering why his mum suddenly thinks I own a car. 'You know I feel shit as it is, but they've cancelled all the trains. Anyway, isn't Karen going with you?'

'Nah, she's seeing her own family,' he replies before

his face wrinkles with unease. 'Um, I haven't exactly told them we're back together yet . . .'

'Wow!' I laugh as the screen freezes again. He looks like a puzzled baby. 'That'll be an interesting conversation.'

He laughs. 'Not as interesting as the one where I tell them you're blowing them off to spend Christmas with my ex-girlfriend . . .'

'True.'

' . . . or the one where I explain why I have a black eye.'

Now I'm wrinkling up. 'Shit. God, I'm so sorry . . . is it still sore?'

He shakes his head. 'Only when I need to look at something. How's the hand?'

I hold up the cast, which now has Alfie's signature and three superhero stickers attached to it. 'Smarts like a bitch,' I reply, 'but the painkillers help.'

He nods and stay silent for a moment. Why does he look concerned? Fuck, is he reliving the punch? Am I going to be apologising for this for the next fifty years?

'Um . . . how is Sarah?' he finally asks. 'Does she hate me?'

I smile with relief. 'She's good, mate, and no, she doesn't hate you.'

'OK, good. Great. Great news.' I'm sure the look of relief on his face is visible but the camera has frozen again.

'She does think you're a bit of a prick maybe, but that'll pass.'

He laughs loudly. 'That's fair enough. Just make sure she knows I'm sorry, yeah?'

'I will . . . Wish your parents a merry Christmas from me, will you? I'll send them some Christmassy flowers or something.'

'Nice idea,' he replies. 'Damn, you were always the more thoughtful son. I'll speak to you lat—'

The connection finally drops as Sarah's parents' terrible Wi-Fi flatlines. I swear, somewhere in this house is a dial-up modem from 1998.

I head downstairs to the living room where everyone is snuggled up watching *Elf*. Alfie, lying on the floor, scoops handfuls of popcorn from a bowl in front of him, kicking his legs as he laughs in delight.

'We've just opened the mulled wine, Nick,' Stephen announces. 'Linda, grab him a glass, honey.'

'Sounds lovely, thank you,' I reply, sitting down beside Sarah, who is engulfed in a giant, fluffy green blanket, also nursing a bowl of popcorn. She lifts a section and places it over my legs. 'Dad made apple and goat's cheese crostini,' she informs me, pointing to the table. 'So good.'

'Crostini? That's impressive!' I reply, placing one on a napkin. 'I can barely make toast.'

'It's nothing,' Stephen says dismissively. 'Slice a baguette, drizzle both sides in olive oil, grill them for a few minutes, then chuck stuff on top. Wait 'til you taste the devilled eggs I made with sriracha mayo. They have quite the kick.'

Linda hands me a large goblet of mulled wine. 'He's excellent in the kitchen. When we first met, he used to make the best hash brownies from scratch. We were pretty much high for the first year of our marriage . . . God, those were good days.'

'MUM!' Sarah exclaims, laughing. 'Small ears are listening.'

Stephen laughs. 'It's true, honey. Before you know it, he'll be El Chapo. We're like gateway grandparents.'

We laugh as Sarah throws a piece of popcorn at her dad. I feel quite honoured to be part of this, to meet the people who raised the woman I'm so fucking crazy about.

I clear my throat. 'It's corny, but I just wanted to say thank you for allowing me to spend Christmas with you. I'm not sure many would have been so understanding if their only daughter arrived home with some guy in a bloodied T-shirt, sporting a broken hand, but—'

'He deserved it,' Stephen announces, his eyes still fixed on the television.

I glance at Sarah, who purses her lips, letting me know she spilled the beans.

'Well, I'm not proud of—'

'And looking after my grandson with such patience and kindness to the point where he talks about you incessantly is more than enough reason to welcome you into our home,' he continues. 'The two most important people in our lives think the world of you and that's good enough for us. Now drink your wine before my darling wife starts to cry.'

I hear a loud sniff from Linda as Sarah leans over and gently takes her mum's hand.

'I'm fine,' she insists, 'I'm just thinking about . . .'

Sarah grins. 'You're thinking about those brownies, aren't you, Mum?'

I splutter into my wine as we all erupt into laughter.

'I'm trying to watch the *Elf*!' Alfie yelps, but we're too far gone.

With an overly excited Alfie finally asleep, everyone mucks in to finish wrapping and arranging his presents under the tree. Thanks to the market stalls, I'm able to add three of my own: a gift basket filled with home-made chutneys, pickles and jams for Sarah's parents, a new Frisbee for Alfie, to replace the one that Spot destroyed on the first day, and a silver family tree which has twelve little locket-shaped frames hanging from its branches. This was the trickiest to buy and I had to rush across the street to purchase it while Sarah took Alfie to the bathroom. Unbeknownst to Sarah, Linda has provided me with baby pictures of her, Stephen, Sarah and Alfie to start her collection. I think she'll love it.

By 11.30pm, we're all worn out, except for Spot who stands by the porch door, whining indignantly.

'I think someone needs the loo,' Stephen says, grinning. 'You can just let him out in the garden.'

'Or we could take him for a walk?' Sarah suggests. 'I could use the fresh air.'

'Fresh air? It's sub-zero!' Before I can go on to explain how bloody exhausted I am after all that mulled wine, she throws me a look which says *alone time, idiot*.

'But yeah,' I reply, getting to my feet. 'It'll tire him out. You wanna go for a walk, Spot?'

I see Linda and Stephen glance at each other. With a combined age of one-hundred- and-forty-three, it's safe to say they're not buying this.

Spot grabs his leash from the door hook and circles around in excitement.

'Take one of my fleeces,' Stephen says, 'and watch the pavement. The gritters sometimes neglect our little street.'

We wrap up and step outside, watching Spot slide his way down the wheelchair ramp, leash still hanging from his mouth. I laugh softly as Sarah closes the door behind her.

'Something funny?'

'You mean apart from my dog being a dumbass?'

We walk over the garden grass and then on to the road, which is infinitely less icy, but the falling snow will soon put paid to that. Spot allows me to hook him up before zipping as far in front as the leash will allow.

'I was thinking about last Christmas Eve, actually,' I say

as we stroll down the middle of the silent street, a small but growing flutter of snow landing across our path as we walk. 'You were here with your awesome family, and I was alone and on my arse in the middle of the street after failing to navigate ice, once again.'

'Aw, don't! That hurts my heart!'

Sarah links into my arm, being careful not to cause my hand any further injury. 'But here we are now . . . arm in arm . . . completely alone . . . potential targets for anyone feeling a bit murdery . . .'

'Wow, that's dark.'

She laughs. 'I know. I've been listening to way too many true crime podcasts.'

'It's a fair point though,' I reply, looking down at my hand. 'With a three-legged dog and me in a cast, you're pretty much on your own.'

We continue down the street, turning into a small grassy area, where Spot does his business before completing a few evening victory laps. I can tell he's as happy as I am.

'So, I was thinking that, maybe when I get back—'

'Shh.'

'I mean, I know it's probably too soon, but maybe you could come up to Oxford and—'

She places her finger over my lips. 'Shh. Listen . . .'

In the distance I hear the church bells strike midnight, followed by faint festive declarations from nearby homes. Sarah turns and wraps her arms around my neck.

'Merry Christmas, Nick.'

'Is it weird that the *shh* thing turns me on?'

'Focus, Nick.'

I grin. 'Sorry. Merry Christmas, Sarah.'

And under a flurry of powdery snow, we kiss like it's the first time, and I never want this moment to end.

EPILOGUE

'Do you think this would look nice in the living room?'

Sarah picks up a large red cushion and inspects it more closely. Ever since we bought the flat in Oxford, she's been a home furnishing machine.

'Um, probably,' I reply, doing my best to sound interested. 'Get it if you like it.'

She smiles. 'I knew you'd say that. Honey, we may have been together for two years, but living together is entirely different.'

'I know.'

'And sometimes having to look at cushions or other items that you dislike day in, day out can cause unnecessary tension in a relationship.'

'You're alluding to my tapestry, aren't you?'

'It's not a tapestry, it's an old, frayed tea towel-looking monstrosity and I hate it.'

We continue walking around the market, killing time before I meet with Matt. London is unusually mild for

December, but still cold enough for Sarah to wear her white bobble hat. God, she looks cute as hell in that hat. We have the whole weekend to ourselves and I intend to spend at least sixty per cent of that naked.

'OK, I'll make a deal with you,' I say. 'I'll get rid of the *tapestry*, if you get rid of that creepy picture.'

'What picture?'

'The one in the hall.'

'Miss Fox? I love that sketch. It's—'

'It's a fox in a Victorian nightdress, holding a duck! It's weird, and frankly, a little disturbing!'

She thinks for a moment and finally agrees to put it in the loft if I'll surrender the tapestry.

'But if she escapes the frame and haunts the loft out of spite, it's your fault.'

I'm not sure she's kidding.

'Oh, Alfie texted me from Mum's phone. He says Spot's having a great time and says good luck!'

'Aww, that's sweet,' I reply, smiling and taking Sarah's hand, hoping she doesn't think too hard about the good luck part of the message. I can tell she's missing Alfie but having him stay with his grandparents for a few days has given us a much-needed rest.

She shrugs. 'Not sure why you need luck, but I guess seven-year-olds rarely make sense at the best of times. Listen, after we've done our visiting rounds, can we just go back to the hotel and chill?'

'Room service and trash TV?'

'I love it when you talk dirty.'

We take the bus to Southview Shopping Centre, a place I haven't stepped foot in since I hung up my red suit three Christmases ago. I've arranged to meet Matt in the bar next door, allowing Sarah to grab some last-minute gifts for Alfie while he's busy being spoiled by his grandparents.

'OK, it's half four now,' Sarah informs me. 'I don't have much to get, so just text me when you're done, and I'll meet you.'

I agree, kissing her lightly on the mouth before heading out into the snow.

Matt and I haven't seen each other in months, but we greet each other like it's been much longer. He looks good. Marriage obviously agrees with him.

'Two spiced rum and Cokes, please,' I say, as we sit at the bar. 'No ice in mine.'

'God, it's good to see you, mate,' Matt says. 'How's life? Did the move go well?'

I nod. 'As well as moving to a new flat can go, but yeah, we're getting there. Still unpacking. Sarah's so much closer to her parents, which is great, and Alfie really likes his new school.'

Matt looks delighted. 'And how is Sarah's new job? Is she enjoying teaching?'

When she and Alfie moved up to Oxford, Sarah got a job teaching art at the local college. It's perfect for her: she loves the students and it gives her time in the afternoons to work on her own stuff.

'Jesus, what a turnaround. Can you believe that three years ago, you were dragging your arse down here every day to play Santa?' Matt shakes his head.

'I know. But it made me the man I am today, even if it sparked a mild addiction to selection boxes. And you? I haven't seen you since you got back from your honeymoon. How's it all going?'

'Yeah, everything's great. Though Karen's getting fat.'

I nearly choke on my rum. 'Jesus, Matt, you can't say that about . . .'

I stop chastising him when I realise what's going on. I could toast bread on the glow coming from his proud, grinning face as he hands me a sonogram.

'No! Aww, mate, congrats!!'

'Fourteen weeks. I'm so stoked, it's unreal.'

'Bloody hell. I'm so pleased for you!'

As we cheers, I knock back the rest of my rum and ask for another.

'Slow down there, Oliver Reed, it's only half four.'

'I know,' I reply. 'Dutch courage.'

I reach into my jacket and pull out a small silver box, handing it to Matt. He opens it and stares inside.

'What do you think?'

'I mean . . . I like you and everything but, mate, I'm already spoken for.'

'Fuck off, I'm nervous as hell. Do you think she'll like it? It was my mum's.'

He closes the box and hands it back. 'Nick, I think she'll love it. Why are you nervous? She adores you!'

'I don't know,' I admit. 'She's got a lot going on just now. New house, new job . . .'

He frowns. 'Is it because she's been married before?'

Damn, he does know me well. I can't help worrying that Sarah won't want to get married again. Maybe that was it for her? I've always been hesitant to bring it up and she never has.

'I don't want her to feel like I think what we have isn't enough,' I respond. 'Like maybe Alfie's dad was the one true love of her life and she'd think I was trying to replace him?'

'I think you think too much. Look, she just got a fixed-rate mortgage with you. That's way more binding than marriage. She loves you. Alfie loves you.'

'I asked his permission, you know. He's so excited, even wished me good luck.'

'See, there's nothing stopping you! What are you waiting for?'

I slip the ring back in my pocket, down my second drink and slide off the bar stool.

'You're right. What *am* I waiting for?'

'What, *now*?' Matt splutters as I march myself towards the pub door. 'You're doing it now?'

'We'll be back in fifteen! Get another round in!'

I hurry out and back into the shopping centre, my eyes darting around as I look for Sarah and her bobble hat. My heart is racing. This has the potential to either be the best or worst day of my life. Adrenaline pumping, I weave in and out of shoppers, checking stores, before finally ending up at her old coffee shop at the end of the mall. I see her through the window, sitting at a table with two of her old colleagues.

'Nick? Is that you?'

Startled, I whip around in the direction of that familiar voice and see Izzy, in full elf costume, hands on hips and frowning at me like she's just caught me shoplifting.

'Hey! Izzy. Long time.'

'I thought it was you. It's very nice to see you.'

'You sure? You look mad at me.'

'I am sure.'

'Still spreading Christmas cheer, I see,' I say, gesturing to her outfit.

She nods. 'But this Santa is no good. Always with the nose blowing. You were better . . . Why you keep staring at the window?'

'Sarah is in there, I'm just—'

She peers in. 'Oh, *this one* again with the little boy! Sorry, but she doesn't work here anymore.'

'Oh, I know, she's just—'

Izzy starts to laugh. I'm not sure I've seen Izzy laugh

before. 'First time you come here, you stare at her like a *cachorro*, wagging your tail when she talk with you. Now you come back and . . .'

As Izzy continues to ramble, my mind flashes back to the time Sarah first ran into the grotto to find Alfie. How she looked at me and took my breath away. When I see her emerge from Belle Blend, I know exactly what I need to do.

'Izzy,' I say, interrupting her flow, 'how do you say "good luck" in Spanish?'

'*Buena suerte.*'

'Thanks!'

She tilts her head in confusion as I rush over to Sarah and take her by the hand, leading her towards the grotto.

'Come on!'

'What? Why? Nick, I don't think you're allowed to just—'

'Please,' I say. 'Just trust me.'

We both slip under the rope and I instruct Sarah to sit on the throne.

She places her bags on the floor and takes a seat, looking around her nervously. I see the security guard at the door stop to stare at us. I don't recognise him. I wonder what happened to Charles and his stupid beard.

'You're sitting in the same place I was when I first met you,' I begin. 'Three years ago, almost to the day.'

Her face lights up and she laughs. 'Oh my God, you're

right! I must have looked a right state, I was so flustered from racing around, looking for Alfie.'

I shake my head. 'I thought you looked beautiful. There's not a day that goes by that I don't think about how beautiful you are.'

'Aww, honey, that's so sweet of . . . um, Nick, that security guy is heading over here, we should probably move.'

I glance over my shoulder to see him marching towards us. Fuck. I need to be quick.

'Sarah, I love you . . . in fact, those words don't even come close to how I feel about you,' I say, reaching into my pocket. 'I'm not even sure there are words—'

'Sir, the grotto is closed, you can't be in here.'

As I get down on one knee, I hear Sarah gasp.

'Just know that meeting you changed my life and—'

'David, you take one more step and I kick you to death with my pointy shoes, *tú hijo de puta*! You want to ruin the magical moment my friend is having? Shame on you!'

To my right I see a tiny Izzy squaring up to the six-foot-two security man standing outside the grotto. He physically recoils as she continues to block his path.

Taking the ring box from my pocket, I open it in front of Sarah, who's laughing and crying at the same time.

'Oh, Nick, it's beautiful.'

'Sarah O'Brien. Will you marry—'

'YES!' she squeals, before I can even finish the question. 'Fuck yes, I'll marry you!'

I slip the ring on to her finger, seconds before she launches herself from the throne, sending us both tumbling, along with that damn penguin who still can't stay upright to save his life.

And there, on the grotto floor, I kiss my future wife while a Spanish elf, still arguing loudly with a security guard, drowns out the Michael Bublé coming from the shopping centre sound system.

God, I love Christmas.

ACKNOWLEDGEMENTS

I want to thank the following people, like they do in the Oscars, only with far more emotion and face fanning.

Firstly, my editor Rachel Neely, because without you there would be no book. A million thanks for choosing me to write your wonderful story!

Next a big shout out to the staff at Quercus who are always a pleasure to work with, as well as everyone at Susanna Lea Associates, especially my genius agent Kerry Glencorse. Thank you for continuing to champion me, even though I swear too much.

Also, a huge thank you to all my amazing friends and family who have kept me sane during lockdown. I will hug you all an unreasonable amount as soon as we're allowed within six feet of each other.

Finally, the biggest thank you of all goes to my beautiful daughter Olivia. You are so, so loved.

Loved *All I Want for Christmas*?
Read on to discover more heart-warming and
hilarious books from Joanna Bolouri . . .

The List

One list, ten wishes, and absolutely no chance of *actually* falling in love . . .

Reluctantly single Phoebe Henderson has spent twelve months trying to get over her cheating ex, but no amount of wine or extensive relationship analysis with best friend Lucy has seemed to help.

Facing a new year with no new love, Phoebe concocts a different kind of resolution: The List. Ten things she's always wanted to do in bed but has never had the chance (or the courage) to try. One year of no-strings-attached adventure. What could possibly go wrong?

'Sexy, smart and scandalous'
Victoria Fox

Available now in paperback, eBook and audio.

Quercus

I
Followed
the
Rules

*My friends think I'm insane, I'm stalking men
all over town, and I'm on a deadline.*

High-flying journalist Cat Buchanan has been single
for six years. So she's sceptical when assigned to write
a story on *The Rules of Engagement*, a book which
promises to teach women how to find the man
of their dreams in ten easy steps.

As far as Cat's concerned, the book belongs in 1892, but
she's promised to follow it to the letter. After all, what does
she have to lose by playing love at its own game?

**'If you hear someone snorting beside the pool
this summer, they'll be reading this'**
Grazia

Available now in paperback, eBook and audio.

Quercus

The Most Wonderful Time of the Year

A laugh-out-loud romantic comedy of family politics, fake boyfriends and festive mayhem.

Emily has it all: a good job, awesome friends, a great boyfriend, and a wonderful flat exactly 411 miles away from her nightmarish family.

But when her boyfriend Robert dumps her days before Christmas, Emily's devastated. Knowing there's no way she can face her family alone, Emily enlists the help of her party-boy neighbour Evan. All he needs to do is pretend to be Robert.

The only trouble is Evan's not exactly boyfriend material. He likes flirting, loud music, and louder sex. Can Emily handle Evan and her family, or is she heading straight for disaster?

'Hilarious'
Isabelle Broom

Available now in paperback and eBook.

Quercus